JOANNE TRACEY

THE LITTLE Cafe by the LAKE

A BEACH ROAD CAFE NOVEL

First published in Australia in 2021

by Joanne Tracey

https://joannetracey.com

Copyright © Joanne Tracey 2021

Print ISBN 978-0-6450735-3-9

Kindle ISBN 978-0-6450735-4-6

Epub ISBN 978-0-6450735-2-2

Cover design by Louise West of Book Coverology

 A catalogue record for this book is available from the National Library of Australia

For Grant and Sarah...

Always

GLOSSARY

Because I wrote this book using Australian/New Zealand spelling and grammar, it may contain some words and phrases which are new to you. A few of these are below:

All Blacks – the New Zealand rugby team

Autumn – fall (season)

Bach – holiday house, pronounced as "batch"

Barbie – barbecue

Biscuits – similar to American cookies

Bro – a term of endearment – usually used between male friends

Cheese roll – not what you'd think. A snack most commonly found in the south of the South Island, a cheese roll is almost like a Welsh Rarebit turned inside out and rolled up into a tube before cooking.

Chilly bin – an esky (Australian) or portable (usually hard-sided) container that keeps food and drinks cold.

Chips – this is where it gets confusing depending on who you're talking to. Chips are hot chips (but not French fries) like the ones you get in a fish and chips shop. Chippies are crisps or sometimes even potato chips. French fries are skinny hot chips sold at McDonald's.

Chook – chicken

Dairy – a corner store that sells convenience items as well as (usually) pies and sandwiches.

Eh – pronounced 'ay'. A common way to end a sentence and is usually said with an upward inflection as if asking for affirmation. 'It's nice weather, eh?'

Good as gold – an affirmative answer.

Hooly Dooly – an Australian phrase expressing surprise or amazement.

Jandals – flip-flops or thongs (the kind you wear on your feet)

Kumera – Sweet Potato

Munted – broken, ruined. It can also refer to someone being intoxicated.

Ruck – a rugby term for a loose scrum

Scone – similar to American biscuits

Section – block of land, the land on which a house is built

Snag – sausage

Stoked – happy, chuffed

Sweet (or sweet as) – good, great as in 'that's great'

Track – a hiking (tramping) trail.

Tramp – to hike

Yeah … nah – I hear what you're saying, but no, that's not going to happen

CHAPTER ONE

'What if I ask nicely?' Jess rested her bum against the stainless-steel bench in the mezzanine kitchen of her café, Beach Road.

'No, Jess, I'm still not doing it.' Dan didn't take his eyes from the poached egg he was carefully placing on top of the bacon that sat on a potato rosti. The craggy potato had been cooked to perfection with the crunchy bits golden against the white serving plate. After drizzling some hollandaise over the egg and checking the leafy garnish, he gave the plate a quick wipe with a clean cloth and pushed it to the front of the bench.

Holly, Dan's sous chef, sneaked past him and placed a generous bowl of granola and yoghurt on the bench, adding some pansies and nasturtium flowers, before pressing the buzzer that would have Marty or Paula bounding up the stairs to collect the order.

'It would take you hardly any time at all,' Jess continued, trying to catch Dan's eye. 'A piece of kumera, maybe some pumpkin?'

Dan looked up briefly from plating up the next

order, his eyebrows raised. 'It hardly seems worth the effort.' Flicking his attention back to the hob, he flipped some mushrooms in the pan. 'Holl, how are you going with that smashed avo?'

'Coming right up,' she replied, pushing across the plate. 'French toast will be three minutes.'

'Thanks,' he said. 'We have another two bennies, a hotcake, three smashed avocado specials, two pea fritters, a veggie stack and a scrambled egg with a side of bacon.'

'On it.'

Jess remained leaning against the bench, watching as they worked together, a smile of satisfaction curling her lips. One of her brother Richie's closest friends, Dan, had become *her* closest friend in the time they'd worked together at Beach Road. Like Richie, Dan had gone travelling after completing his apprenticeship and hospitality qualifications. Unlike Richie, though, he'd come home to New Zealand within a few years – the rush of London kitchens quickly losing their appeal – and arrived back in Queenstown just in time to take on the job as head chef at Beach Road Café on the shores of Lake Wakatipu.

It was Dan who'd helped her through those first couple of years as she slowly built the business and Dan who had helped bring her vision of how Beach Road *could* be to life. Now, four years later, the café was unrecognisable. Jess had replaced the pine furniture with one long communal table with bench seating and a scattering of smaller timber tables with an assortment of mismatched chairs. Outside, on the lakefront, she'd opted for outdoor furniture, with patio umbrellas to provide shade during the sunniest part of the day and outside heaters and tartan blankets for chillier days.

Instead of plastic-wrapped sandwiches and ordinary coffee, from seven each morning to three in the afternoon, an all-day breakfast menu was available with an ever-changing board of seasonal specials, all ingredients sourced locally where possible. The kitchen also prepared a daily selection of pre-made rolls and wraps and soup in the winter months. A local baker supplied them daily with a range of savoury tarts, pies, sausage rolls and pasties. A few days a week, Richie's partner Maxine (everyone called her Max) came in and baked up a storm in the kitchen to stack the boards and cabinet with cakes, scones, slices and biscuits.

As a result, Beach Road was now a destination café, with Dan and Holly's plates (and Max's bakes) appearing regularly on Instagram feeds.

'What are you thinking?' Dan asked with a grin. He straightened and rolled his shoulders, pushing his spiky blonde hair back from his forehead with the back of his hand. 'I always worry when you're quiet.'

Jess chuckled, pushed away from the bench and sat on the stool directly opposite Dan. 'I was just thinking how far we've come and how I couldn't have done it without you.'

'I'm still not cooking perfectly good vegetables for you to play games with,' he said, the dimple in his left cheek showing his amusement.

'But it'll be fun,' she coaxed. Dan raised a shoulder once to show his care factor was close to zero on this one.

'What's this about?' asked Holly, joining them at the bench.

'The game, of course,' said Jess. 'It's a blindfolded taste test for the baby shower this afternoon. I'll put it into little jars, get a heap of spoons and the guests have to pick the mush correctly.'

'Between kumera and pumpkin? Not much of a taste test,' said Dan, pressing the buzzer for service.

'Well, I don't know what babies eat,' said Jess. 'Holl, what do babies eat?'

Holly flashed a quick grin in Jess's direction as she expertly spooned avocado onto toasted sourdough, made sure the micro herb garnishes were all in place and pushed the plates forward. 'How would I know?'

'Your sister's got a couple of kids, hasn't she?' asked Jess.

'Yes, but I've never paid a lot of attention to what they eat. Why don't you google it?'

'Great idea,' said Dan. 'That might keep her quiet for a little while,' he added under his breath.

'I heard that,' said Jess, already busy on her phone.

'And, for your information, I'm capable of talking and googling at the same time. It's called multitasking. Here you go.' She held up her phone triumphantly. 'Babies also like mashed avocado, mashed banana, mashed stewed apples or pear, and porridge made with breastmilk. Where would I get breastmilk from? I could probably use formula, I suppose,' she mused.

'You'd buy a whole tin of the stuff just to make some porridge with?' Dan stopped what he was doing and looked at her, his nose scrunched. 'You can't make people taste that.'

'Okay, maybe not the porridge, but we could do the rest. Come on; it would be fun to watch.'

'But I won't be watching it because I'll be at Tom's winery drinking with the boys – which is why I'm not mashing anything for you. It's a busy morning, we're closing early, and I want to get out of here on time. If you'd thought of this before today, I might've been able to help, but now it's a no.'

Realising Dan wasn't going to budge, Jess turned her attention to Holly. 'What about you, Holl? Surely *you'd* help me?' Jess coaxed.

'Sorry, Jess. I'm with Dan.' Holly's cheeks flushed with colour, and she concentrated harder than she needed to on spooning berry-swirled yoghurt onto the raspberry-topped French toast.

'Why don't you do it yourself? Even you're capable of microwaving some vegetables and mashing some fruits,' said Dan.

'Because I'm taking Max out for a spa morning – god knows when the last time was she saw her toes, let alone could paint them.'

'Well, get Nathan to do it then,' suggested Dan. 'I take it he's here this weekend?'

'He sure is.' Jess couldn't hide the smile that burst out whenever her boyfriend came up from Stewart Island to spend time with her. 'But he can't do it either. After breakfast, he's off to the lake house to help Richie. Secret men's business or something.'

Jess didn't know whether Dan's shrug was to say he didn't know what the secret men's business was about or to show he didn't much care what Nathan was up to, but figured it was more likely to be the former than the latter.

'I don't think we need the taste test,' said Holly. 'You've organised plenty of games, and your mother and Nathan's mother have been baking up a storm. You have a competition to guess the size of Max's tummy, little string bracelets for every time someone mentions the word baby, and that's before we paint the bibs and singlets. We won't have time for another game.'

Jess didn't miss the complicit look that Holly and Dan exchanged, and even though she was being gently manipulated, she nodded slowly. The blindfolded taste test had seemed like a great idea when she thought about it in the shower this morning, but Holly was right, it *might* be overkill. 'Okay, you win.' she said. 'I'll be off then. Holl, have you finished icing the cookies? I'll take them over to Mum's when I pick up Max.'

'I sure have. I did them yesterday afternoon. They're in a tin in the pantry.'

The tin was on the shelf directly in front of her as she walked in. Lifting the lid, she exclaimed, 'These are fabulous – you're so clever!' Inside, butter cookies were cut into the shape of teddy bears, bibs, baby playsuits, prams, rattles, and bottles. She'd iced them mostly in white with alternating pink and blue detail.

Impulsively, she rushed across the kitchen and kissed Holly's blushed cheek. 'Thank you.'

She opened the lid again so Dan could peer inside. 'Good job, Holl,' he said before switching his attention back to his pans and the line of orders, in the process missing Holly's beaming smile of pride.

Jess closed the lid of the biscuit tin. 'Okay you two, I'll get out of your hair—'

'At last,' Dan said in a dramatic stage-whisper.

'And get over to Mum's to pick up Max. I'll see you later, Holl.'

'You sure will,' said Holly.

'And you make sure my brother and my boyfriend behave themselves this afternoon,' Jess said to Dan, grinning at the mock salute he gave her.

She got halfway down the stairs before remembering her other reason for being there, whirled around, and headed back up. As she would've opened her mouth, Dan said, 'Breakfast?'

'Yes, please. There's nothing in the fridge at home except—'

He waved away her excuses with a grin, knowing she and Nathan always ended up having breakfast here at least once on the weekend.

'The usual for Nathan?'

'Please. You know he can't go past your eggs bennie. What's on the specials today?'

'Holly's smashed avo with crispy fried eggplant, some fried leek and a poached egg. You'll have to give it a go – the eggplant's like a hash brown on the outside and soft and smoky inside. It's inspired.'

Jess grinned as Holly's cheeks coloured again at the praise from Dan. 'How can I resist a review like that? You two really do make the perfect team,' she said, somehow keeping her expression deadpan as Holly's cheeks went from pale pink to almost fluorescent.

'Are you on track next week?' asked Dan.

'I'm in on Monday and Tuesday, but then on track – the last back-to-back for the season. Routeburn from Wednesday and then Milford from Saturday morning.'

'You'll be glad the season's done,' said Holly. 'I don't know how you manage to juggle it all – the guiding and the café.'

'I'm lucky I have a good team here,' said Jess. 'I couldn't do it without you guys. Anyway, I'll be back on deck on Thursday.'

'No problems,' said Dan. 'See you then.'

Jess raised her hand to give them a wave and headed back downstairs.

Nathan had secured them a seat in the corner near the front door. The seats outside overlooking the lake were always the first to be filled when the sun was shining – as it was today. Jess paused for a second and admired him as he sat reading a newspaper, concentration on his face, his broad shoulders filling out the khaki t-shirt – the one she loved because it brought out the golden tints in his hazel eyes – his tanned arms and the way the light streaming in through the window hit the sun-bleached tips of his brown hair. Having met on the Milford Track late last year, they'd only been together a few months, but Jess didn't think she'd ever get tired of looking at him like this.

She kissed as close to his lips as she could manage from this angle and slid into her chair. 'Sorry,' she said. 'That took longer than I expected, but I've decided not to worry about the blindfolded taste test. Holl's finished the cookies, though, and they look amazing.'

Nathan looked up from the newspaper he was reading. 'Let me guess, Dan refused to mash vegetables for you.'

Jess returned his grin, not at all embarrassed at being caught out. 'Something like that.' She drained her coffee cup, screwing her nose up. 'I must've been up there for ages – my coffee's gone cold. I'm so sorry.'

'It's okay,' he said. 'I've been catching up on the news.' He folded the paper and laid it on the seat beside him. 'To be honest, it's something I get used to – and before you bristle, it's all good, I get it.'

Jess searched his stubbled face for something more, and upon finding nothing, sprang up from her seat. 'I'll get some more coffees underway,' she said, giving a slight frown when Nathan opened his paper again without saying a word.

When Dayna saw her approach, she said, 'Another two coffees?'

'Yes, please.' Jess examined the contents of the savoury window, her brow furrowed. 'Is it my imagination or have Johnson's pies started to look a little, um—'

'Mainstream?' finished Dayna.

'Yes, that's exactly it! The sausage rolls are too thin and perfect. Something a bit more artisan would be great; keep the basics, but amp up some of the other flavours, maybe? Give them more of a handmade look?'

Dayna nodded, focusing on the glass display cabinet. 'At the moment, they look a bit out of place with everything else. The tarts are okay, but I agree, the pies and sausage rolls are too neat.'

'Okay, I'll have a chat with Dan, see what he thinks, but I'd like to see some local flavours and ingredients being used.'

As she picked up the coffees to take back to Nathan, she noticed a man at the front of the queue. There was something familiar about him, but Jess couldn't put her finger on what, and he was staring at her as if he knew her too.

'Do I know you?' she asked, stopping in front of the man.

'I was wondering the same.' He smiled confidently, and her feeling of recognition grew stronger. 'What's your name?' he asked.

'I'm Jess Fletcher. I own this place.'

His eyes widened in surprise. 'Are you any relation to Cameron Flet cher?'

'Yes, he's my father.'

'That explains it then.' The stranger's grin was wide, and his accent was English. 'Your father and I were friends years ago back in Australia.' He bit his top lip and frowned at the ceiling as if trying to catch hold of a thought or memory. 'Of course! I remember hearing he and Melinda had moved here. What's he doing with himself these days?'

'Well,' said Jess hesitantly. 'He and my brother Richie run Lakeview Landscaping. It's out on the Frankton Road towards the airport – you can't miss it.' She paused and raised a quizzical brow. 'What's your name? I'll tell Dad you were asking about him.'

'No, don't worry about it,' the man said with a shake of his head. 'I'm only passing through, so probably won't have time to drop by.' He took his coffee from Dayna. 'It was nice to meet you, though.'

'Yes, you too,' said Jess, but he'd already turned and headed out the door.

'What was that about?' asked Nathan when she slid into the seat opposite him.

'Nothing – just some guy who said he used to know Dad.' The lanky stranger was still standing out the front of the café, sipping his coffee. 'I thought he reminded me of someone, but he's probably one of those people who always looks like someone you know,' she said.

Before she could think any more about it, Marty was at the table with their breakfast. 'Your usual bennie, with an extra hash brown,' he said, placing a plate in front of Nathan, 'and one smashed avo special for you, Jess.'

'Thanks, Marty,' said Jess. Once they were alone again, she said, 'So what are you and Richie up to this morning that's so secret?'

Nathan put his elbow on the table and rested his chin on the palm of his hand, his eyes crinkling at the sides. 'Well, I could tell you, but …'

His grin was wicked, and Jess's insides dissolved into a molten mass. 'How about we finish this and go back to mine so I can show you just how nicely I can ask?'

'And I can show you how much I'll miss you next

week when you're off counting sharks. Sadly though, both of us need to be places this morning.'

Jess's breath caught in her throat at the intensity in his eyes, the gold flecks almost glowing, his words stroking along her skin in a way his hands would when next they were alone.

The ringing of her phone broke the spell.

'Hey, Mum,' she said and mouthed, 'sorry' to Nathan, who just smiled another of his slow, sexy smiles, dropped his eyes from hers, and gave his full attention to his breakfast. 'What's up?'

'Nothing, darling,' said Milly. 'I was just wondering what time you'll be by this morning.'

Jess took a glance at her watch. 'Is that the time?'

Her mother's soft chuckle came down the line. 'I had a feeling you might've lost track of it.'

'I certainly have. I'm leaving now,' she said, grinning when Nathan reached over to spear the last piece of her eggplant.

'See you soon,' her mother said and rang off.

'I have to go,' Jess said to Nathan, swiping some of the hollandaise he hadn't quite finished mopping up.

'So do I,' he said, watching closely as she sucked the sauce off her finger.

'And you won't tell me what you guys are up to?'

'Nope. I'm sworn to secrecy.'

'Does Mum know?'

'No.'

'What about your mother? Does Kate know?'

'No.'

'Max?'

He rolled his eyes. 'Hardly, it's her surprise. You may as well give it up, Jay. I'm not telling you.'

'Fair enough.' Jess shrugged, stood and slid her phone into the back pocket of her jeans, and swung her bag over her shoulder. 'I'll see you tonight.' She leaned over and kissed his lips, wiping a rogue drop of sauce from the corner of his mouth with her finger.

'I'll look forward to it.'

On the way out, she remembered she hadn't spoken to Dan about the pies. As she would've twirled to head back up the stairs, Nathan said, 'Go! Whatever it is can wait.'

She glanced up the stairs and back at Nathan. Yes, it could wait until Monday. Blowing him a kiss, she left.

CHAPTER TWO

Richie rested his paintbrush on the lid of the tin and nodded in satisfaction. Even though it still smelt of paint, the room looked amazing. He shook the white timber cot he and Nathan had wrestled to put together last weekend. Yes, it was sturdy enough; and thankfully the mobile that his sister Cate had sent over from Sydney – a teddy bear asleep in the crescent of a moon amidst plenty of fluffy white clouds – was hung far enough over the cot not to hit him in the eyes.

The shelves on the wall were straight – as were the six garden-themed prints that had caused him and his father so much grief during the week. Lining them up in the two rows of three Max had wanted had been a nightmare. At one point Fletch had asked, 'do they really need to be level? Why don't we stagger them instead?'

Richie was glad they'd persevered. He tilted his head to one side, squinting, and checked them with the spirit level one more time to be sure.

The wing armchair they'd commissioned had also

given him a few worries when the supplier had phoned to warn him about potential delays in delivery. He hadn't had the heart to tell Max and thankfully it had been delivered on Thursday, so he hadn't needed to. Max had been right – the patchwork blue, soft green and paisley fabric worked well against the light sage walls. He closed his eyes briefly, imagining her sitting in the chair feeding their baby, a lamp on the small round table beside it casting a soft light.

The *pièce de résistance*, though, was the mural he'd spent so many hours creating and then painting. In hindsight, it had been easier to paint than it had been to come up with reasons to stop Max from coming out to the house this week. He'd never been able to lie to her successfully, and there were only so many nights he could plead he was working late – especially when his boss was his father, and *he* had made it home in time for dinner each night. Thankfully, Fletch was in on the secret and had invented a new client who was only available for consultations after hours. Another night, Fletch said he needed Richie to attend the local Chamber of Commerce meeting on his behalf, and on Thursday night, Richie took advantage of Jess dragging Maxi along to a book launch at Kate's bookshop in Arrowtown, Cover To Cover, to get some more painting time in.

Now it was done, and the white lies he and his father had told were worth it.

He stepped into the doorway and, leaning against the doorframe, took it all in – the woodland scene a nod to Max's English heritage and Brookford, the village in The Cotswolds where she'd grown up.

It had amazed Richie at the amount of "stuff" a baby needed. Sure, he'd known about the cot and assumed he or she would also need a pram, a car seat and somewhere to keep their clothes, but until his mother had begun buying things like bouncy seats and change tables, he hadn't realised how much a baby accumulated before they were even born.

Max had bags of clothes stashed away that had been purchased or gifted, and Jess was always coming home with something new that she just happened to see when she was out and about. Given that Jess spent all her time either at Beach Road or on track, she had very little opportunity to randomly be "out and about". The purchases were all part of her campaign to be elected godmother – as if he and Max would consider anyone else for the role.

His mother was just as bad, and Max had shown him only a fraction of what would soon fill the shelves in the wardrobe. He couldn't wait to see it all in there, to complain good-naturedly in the way he was supposed to about the number of bibs, bonnets, booties and tiny singlets. Piglet, as they'd taken to calling the baby, would be here in weeks and Richie couldn't wait. He was even looking forward to the night feeds and being able to watch Max bond and snuggle with the baby he'd never thought would be theirs.

Even though he'd spied the wedding ring on her finger, Richie had fallen in love with Max the minute he laid eyes on her five years ago. She'd cycled into Blossom & Buds, the garden centre he managed in Brookford, with absolutely none of the horticultural qualifications he'd been looking for. Thanks to the hours she'd spent at the local allotment scheme working alongside her grandfather, Horrie, and a cast of local characters, there was, however, little she didn't know about growing vegetables – and even less about creative ways of cooking them. He'd hired her on the spot. They'd quickly become close friends, and despite Max's husband, James, spending much of his time working in London or travelling, Richie had never tried to take advantage of James's absences. He'd convinced himself he was happy being "just friends" and had dated other women from time to time to prove it to himself. Despite his best efforts, no one had come close to Max – and inevitably, it was his friendship with her that ended every (short) relationship he'd had in Brookford.

But when James announced last January that he'd accepted a job in New York, Richie knew it was time to come home to Queenstown and give up on his dream that one day she'd recognise her husband for the two-timer he was and grow to love *him* instead. He would never have thought that just over a year later, he'd be putting the finishing touches on the house by the lake they'd be living in together and looking forward to greeting the baby they'd created. Every night when he held her before they went to sleep and every morning when he kissed her awake and brought her the cup of English breakfast tea without which she was incapable of starting the day, he gave thanks for the circumstances that had bought them together.

Richie smiled as he pictured the look on her face tomorrow when she saw the completed room for the first time.

A hand come to rest on his shoulder. 'You've done a good job, Rick,' said his father, who'd snuck into the room. 'Max will love it.'

'You think?'

Fletch nodded. 'No doubt about it. If you don't believe me, ask Tom and Nathan.' The two men poked their heads around the doorframe.

'Sweet.' Nathan nodded. 'She's going to love this, dude.' A wide grin filled his face. 'But Jess is going to kill me when she finds out I've been keeping it a secret from her!'

'As will Kate,' said Tom. 'I told her we were putting together some flatpack furniture.'

Fletch chuckled. 'Wait until Milly works out I've been covering for Rick.' He slapped Richie on the back. 'She'll be so proud of you.'

Nathan prowled around the room, opening cupboard doors and letting out a low whistle at the stack of nappies on the shelf. 'Man, babies need a lot of shit,' he said. He picked up a basket under the change table, sniffed suspiciously at the talc and held up a tube of cream. 'What do you reckon this is for?'

Fletch chuckled. 'You don't want to know.'

The four men gazed around the room for a few seconds more before Tom said, 'I know it's early, but this calls for a beer.'

'Absolutely,' Fletch said, slapping Tom on the back, 'although just the one – we have to head back and help Milly move furniture about for the party. Rick and Nathan are staying here to finish the last of the jobs.'

'When's the baby actually due?' Tom asked when they all had beers and were settled outside on the garden furniture Nathan, Tom and Fletch had just finished putting together.

'Four weeks,' said Richie.

'Nothing like taking it down to the wire,' said Nathan looking around at the newly finished house.

While Richie hadn't done any landscaping, he was pleased with how the house sat on the section of land, perfectly positioned to catch the expansive views of the lake and the mountains rising behind it. The exterior was a mix of timber, local stone and cladding and would blend into the environment once the garden was complete.

'Tell me about it, but I really wanted for us to be in and settled before the baby comes. It would be nice if Max could relax for a week or so at least.'

Nathan nodded thoughtfully while Tom and Fletch looked at each other and grinned.

'You have no idea what you're in for,' said Tom.

'None at all,' said Fletch. 'But on that note, we'll be off.'

'See you two later at my place,' said Tom. 'While the girls are eating pastel coloured food and playing baby games, we'll light up the barbie and the firepit and open some red wine.'

'Sounds good,' said Richie, standing to shake hands as they moved to leave.

When the two older men had left, Richie and Nathan sat outside for a while longer, both seemingly content to relax for a few precious minutes. On the adjacent section blackbirds scratched about looking for insects. Voices from anglers in a small fishing boat down on the lake drifted up in the breeze.

After a time, Nathan said, 'I can't imagine what it must feel like to know you'll be a father in a few weeks.'

Suddenly unable to answer, Richie couldn't meet Nathan's enquiring eyes, and he hoped the panic that had been simmering close to the surface these last few weeks and was now rising to choke him didn't show on his face.

Nathan lightly punched his arm. 'Hey mate, are you okay?'

'Yeah. It's just…' Richie wasn't sure how to explain the enormity of what he was feeling.

The day Max told him she was pregnant ranked up there with one of the best days of his life – right up there with the first time they kissed, the first time they made love, and the first time she told him she loved him. But when Max told him he would be a father … Richie hadn't been able to stop the emotion from bubbling over or the tears leaking out his eyes. And watching their child grow within her, the way her (much fuller) breasts filled his hands, the smooth roundness of her belly, the soft curve of her hips, the feel of the baby kicking when he laid his cheek against her tummy – he'd loved every minute.

Maybe it hadn't been quite as great for her – she was regularly sick for the first few months and tired easily, and now she complained that turning over in bed was like trying to manoeuvre a large ship – the *Queen Mary*, she said. Despite all of that, she'd bloomed – and was hornier than ever. Insatiable even – not that he was complaining.

'Is Max alright?' Nathan's brow was furrowed with concern.

'Yeah, she's fine. Says she's having problems moving about, but apparently that's normal. She keeps going on about big she is, but I don't think she's ever been more beautiful.' He let out a short chuckle. 'Man, that sounds soppy, but it's the truth. It's just...' he to find the right words. 'It's just I'm beginning to worry about what happens, you know.'

'When the baby comes?' Nathan guessed.

He nodded; his lips pursed. 'I don't know what to do and I don't know how I'll handle seeing her in pain. And then there's what happens when we bring Piglet home. Up until now it's all been a bit of a rush, but now...'

'It's got real?'

Richie nodded. He and Max had gone straight from the bubble of new love to the bubble of early pregnancy. It didn't surprise Richie it had taken so long for reality to seep through.

'You've both been busy, it's no wonder it's only just hitting you now,' said Nathan.

'I know. We've both been flat chat for the last six months. I've been working with Dad trying to learn the business – and trying to convince him to take on more design work.' Richie rolled his eyes to indicate how that was going. 'Max is at Beach Road three days a week and is also keeping your mother supplied with scones and whatever else she bakes for the coffee shop at Cover To Cover. Then there's been the rush to get this place built before Piglet arrived.' He opened his hands and waved them in the direction of the house. 'We've been lucky it was such a fine summer...'

They'd spent every weekend either sourcing furniture and fittings or painting and decorating. The few bits and pieces Max had put into storage before she left England had arrived a month ago, and the house was now all but done. Their bed would go up next; this afternoon, and tomorrow night they'd spend their first night in their new home – right on target.

It was only now when the finish line was so close that the little tendrils of fear curled around his brain. Most of the time, he could pretend it wasn't there, that they'd be okay, but there'd been nights when he held Max in his arms, lying awake, willing the anxiety to go away.

Nathan's voice cut into his musing. 'I reckon I'd be petrified too.'

'You? You dive with sharks – there's not much that's scarier than that.'

'Not yet – I'm scheduled to do my first cage dive next week. But I'll have a cage around me and a clear set of processes, so I know what I'm doing. Babies, from what I've heard, don't come with instruction manuals.'

Richie nodded slowly and fiddled with the label on his beer bottle. 'To be honest, mate, I'm shit scared. It's different for Maxi; she's carrying it, Piglet's part of her, but what if I'm like my father and can't handle it?'

Nathan gave a slight shake of his head, a blank look on his face. 'But Fletch?' Richie could pinpoint the exact moment when the penny dropped. 'That's right; Jess told me Fletch isn't your or Cate's father. Sorry mate, now I've gone and put my foot in it.'

'It's okay. Fletch is the only dad I've known.'

'What happened to your birth father … if you don't mind me asking?'

'It's cool. It's all ancient history. Apparently, he cheated on Mum when she was pregnant with me, and he left when I was still a baby. I haven't seen him since.' He paused before saying, 'I just want to be a good dad, you know?'

'You will be, mate.' Nathan punched his arm lightly. 'Mum once said good fathers are made, not born. She also said when I came along, she had no idea how to be a mother, but I knew how to be a baby, so at least one of us knew what was supposed to happen.'

Richie snorted a laugh and rubbed at the back of his neck.

'I mean it – you *will* be fine. You adore Max and will always treat her right, so you're halfway there, I reckon. Your primary job is to look after her so she can look after the baby – but hey, what do I know?' He contemplated the label on the bottle in his hand. 'I can't imagine being in your situation – Jess is the longest relationship I've ever had – although I'm not sure I should be admitting that to her brother.'

Richie laughed at the sheepish look on Nathan's face. 'She doesn't have such a great track record either. She used to fall for the seasonal guys – the winter snow boys or the summer adventure seekers. The most meaningful relationships were with her café and her hiking boots until you came along.'

Nathan turned away and drained the last of his beer.

'Hey, there's nothing going on with you guys, is there?' asked Richie. 'You're not planning on buggering off back to Queensland and breaking my sister's heart.'

'Somehow, I think the opposite is more likely.'

Nathan grimaced, and Richie wondered what Jess was playing at – not that it was any of his business. The pity was he liked Nathan – he was one of the good guys – and he treated his sister better than anyone else had done in the past. Maybe that was the problem. Richie made a mental note to talk to Max about it – see if she could get anything out of Jess. If he asked Jess what was going on, the discussion would only end one way – and it wasn't a good one.

'Okay,' Richie said, finishing his beer. 'Let's get this bed built and head over to Tom's. I hope someone's remembered to make cheese rolls because I'm starved!'

CHAPTER THREE

'Thanks so much for helping with this.' Milly Fletcher carefully placed small squares of lemon crumble shortbread slice onto a plate. 'I know Max wishes her mother could've been here for her baby shower, so it's important to me it's as perfect as it can be.'

'And that's completely ignoring the fact that this is your first grandchild, and you love Max as if she was your own daughter.' Kate grinned and poured chocolate ganache onto the top of a double-layered chocolate cake.

Milly giggled. 'You're right, of course, on both counts. And nor has it anything to do with the fact that Max brought Rick back home to us. But my original comment stands – I really appreciate you helping.'

'It's no problem at all,' said Kate. 'I love doing things like this. It reminds me of the high tea we put together for Ash before she got married.' She paused, the palette knife she'd been using to smooth the ganache held in the air. 'It seems like another lifetime ago, but it wasn't even twelve months ago.' Sadness flitted across her face, followed by an imperceptible shake of her head and the squaring of her determined jaw.

'You miss her,' said Milly. 'I know how much I missed Cate when she moved to Sydney, I can only imagine you felt the same when you left Ash there.'

There was something about daughters. What was that old saying? Something about how you lost your son when he found a wife, but a daughter was forever. She smiled to herself – she'd been lucky enough to not only regain her son but find another daughter in Max.

Kate nodded, refocusing on the cake. 'I do, but I know she's happy, and we talk or text every day.' She opened her mouth to say something else, then closed it.

'You miss him too,' Milly guessed, quickly touching her friend's arm.

Kate began expertly smoothing the ganache along the side of the cake, but not before the tell-tale glitter of tears formed in her friend's eyes. 'Yes, it's different now to how I used to miss him, though, and sometimes I feel guilty because I forget to miss him all the time.'

'It hasn't even been a year yet, Kate, you'd still be adjusting. I can't imagine what you must have gone through – to fall in love with Neil all over again only to lose him so suddenly.' She smiled gently at her friend. 'Besides,' she added. 'It was beautiful that you and Nathan were able to walk Milford Track in his honour.'

Kate blinked a couple of times. 'Sometimes I feel as though it was Neil guiding me to do that hike. After all, Nathan and Jess met and fell in love, and I did too – with this community. I don't know what I would have been doing if I'd stayed in Sydney – but it certainly wouldn't have involved running my own bookshop.' She let out a short, rueful laugh. 'I know I shouldn't, but sometimes I feel guilty about the way things have worked out too.

'And Tom?' Milly asked. 'Do you feel guilty about Tom?'

Kate shook her head. 'No, although sometimes I feel guilty because I don't feel guilty. Meeting him on the walk was so unexpected. He's a good man – and makes amazing wine. He's had his own things he needs to work through, so we're taking things slowly. It probably sounds weird or as if I'm trying to justify being with another man so soon after Neil passed, but I think Neil would be happy for me. It's all he ever wanted.' She flashed Milly a quick, rueful smile. 'Even during the years we were apart, Neil wanted me to be happy.'

'Are you happy?'

'Yes, I think I am. I know it's early days, but I love my cottage and am pleased with the way Cover To Cover is going. As for Tom and me, well, it's nice, he's nice. I don't know if it's love yet – whatever that means at our ages – but it's good.' A delicate pink flushed Kate's cheeks. 'It's also been great having Nathan here as often as he has been, and now that he's based down at Stewart Island, I get to see even more of him – as does Jess. It must've been hard on them both with him travelling back and forward from Cairns.'

Milly opened the fridge and took out a rolled lolly cake. She began cutting the soft "cake", placing the slices so the pastel bright of the sweets caught the eye. 'I know Jess said something about Nathan working with sharks – what's that about? They get some real monsters off the coast of Stewart Island.'

Kate grimaced. 'I was much happier knowing that the marine animals he was researching in Far North Queensland had far fewer teeth! But yes, it's an ongoing research project around the migration of the great whites that congregate off that coast during the late summer and early autumn – and what makes them so huge. I don't like the idea of him swimming with them – cage or no cage, but he tells me we're not their natural prey, so I don't need to worry. I'll be very glad when he's done with that project, though.'

'It's definitely short term?' Milly felt Kate's eyes on her as she asked the question.

'In other words, is he heading back to Australia afterwards?'

'Was I that transparent?'

Kate stopped what she was doing and offered a gentle smile. 'I'd think the same as you do if it were my daughter. Nathan hasn't said a lot to me, but I know he's serious about Jess, which is why he's taken a leave of absence from his job for a few months to see if they can make it work. He's committed to this project until April and after that?' She shrugged. 'I know he's due back in May. The humpback migration is from June – and he was also talking about a national coral census on the reef – but to be honest, I have no idea what he's thinking. I don't think he *is* thinking too far in advance.'

'Hmmm,' said Milly. 'He's said more to you than my daughter's said to me.'

'You're worried that someone will get hurt?'

Milly covered the plate of lolly cake with cling wrap and put it back into the fridge. 'Let's just say Jess has a habit of falling heavily into short-term relationships with men she knows are going to leave. Not that it seems to worry her – she dusts herself off and does it all over again. This time with Nathan seems different – and I hope she realises it *is* different. Nathan has certainly made some compromises for her, but she can't expect to have it all her own way.' She smiled quickly at Kate. 'Anyway, that's their business, I suppose. Right, what else do we need to do?'

Kate picked up the list they'd made the previous week. 'The chocolate cake is done, there's the lolly cake, the crumble slice, the Louise cake, some scones, and these gorgeous cookies that Holly made – even though I know Jess said we weren't to have any baby-themed food.'

'Jess also said we weren't to arrange any baby-themed games, and she soon forgot about that too,' chuckled Milly. 'But in typical Jess style, once she decided the shower was happening, it became all her idea.' The front door shut. 'And our timing is perfect – here's Jess and Max back from the beautician.' She took off her apron and fluffed her short brown hair. 'Let's get this show on the road.'

Jess leant against the doorframe surveying the mess. Max sat on the lounge surrounded by what seemed like the wrapping from a million presents. What was it about wrapping paper that was so voluminous? With her pixie-short hair, green eyes and massive baby tummy, Max looked like an elf who'd had a very naughty time of it. There was a splotch of paint on the sleeve of the tight white t-shirt she wore under her olive dungarees and a dab of a different colour on the tip of her little upturned nose, and looped loosely around her wrist was the length of string they'd used to measure the size of her belly. Was it possible to be any more pregnant than Max appeared to be?

While not conventionally pretty, Max had always struck Jess as being naturally and effortlessly attractive – if that was such a thing. She rarely wore make-up, and Jess had never seen her wear heels – despite being just a few inches over five feet tall and Richie being a foot taller than that. After going straight from working outdoors in the European summer to a warmer than usual summer here in New Zealand, her perfect English rose skin had lightly tanned, and Max was blooming. As clichéd as it sounded, there was no other word for it.

Jess had fallen under Max's spell the minute she met her. Max made Richie happy and, Jess thought without a trace of envy, if Richie was happy, her parents were happy. And if her parents were happy, so was Jess. That was the thing about Max – people liked her, even though she didn't seem to make any effort in that regard. Milly loved her as if she was one of her own, and, after a misunderstanding at the beginning, Fletch too thought of her as a third daughter. She'd had Dan eating out of her hand within a day, and Holly worshipped Max almost as much as she worshipped Dan. The regulars at Beach Road liked her, and since she'd also been helping Kate out at the bookshop, the regulars there liked her too – and virtually all of them had come along today. The only two people who hadn't taken to Max were Amy, who Max had taken over from at Beach Road, and Jodi, Richie's ex from years ago. The former because Max cooked way better than she did and was more reliable, and the latter because she'd wanted Richie and Richie only had eyes for Max.

Other than Kate and Holly, the guests had left. Kate was moving around the room with a garbage bag, collecting wrapping paper and stray pieces of rubbish. Milly, who had string bracelets all up her arm, had taken control of the cards and had written on each what gift had been bought – knowing Max, she'd probably send a personalised email of thanks to everyone – and Holly was packing away what was left of the food into Tupperware containers and Ziplock bags.

'Alright, you lot,' Jess announced, having had enough of all the baby talk. 'The important people are still here, so I say we ban all talk of babies for the rest of the afternoon and open a bottle of something bubbly; you can bet the boys would be onto beer by now, and there'd be no deep and meaningfuls happening there. And yes, I know you can't drink it, Max, but you can pretend to be okay with that.'

Milly opened her mouth to chastise Jess, but a wide grin spread across Holly's face. 'Christ, yes, I need a drink.'

'I thought you'd never suggest it,' said Kate.

'Oh, go on then,' said Milly. 'Make mine a large glass.'

Jess poured champagne into glasses and found a non-alcoholic sparkling wine for Max. 'Here's to Max and her Piglet,' she said.

'To Max and Piglet,' the others chorused.

From her spot on the lounge, Max beamed. 'It was a lovely party, and thank you for making it happen,' she said, 'but can we please talk about something other than poo and breastfeeding? I'm going to see the contents of Piglet's nappies soon enough that I don't want to imagine it right now.' She used the arm of the chair to lever herself into a standing position. 'I need the loo so often now, but sometimes the effort of getting up to go is just too much. I'd hold on, but Piglet is dancing a jig right on my bladder.'

'Too much information,' cried Holly.

'Just you wait,' said Max with an impish grin. 'It will happen to you one day.'

'I'd have to have sex for that,' said Holly with an exaggerated sigh, 'and let's just say I'm in the middle of a very dry spell.'

Max laughed and disappeared in the direction of the bathroom.

Jess finished her champagne and poured another, leaning across to top up Holly's glass. As she did, a speculative gleam came into her eyes. Now, there was an idea. 'Holly, when are you going to pull your big girl undies on and ask Dan out for a drink. Everyone knows you've been in love with him for as long as you've worked at Beach Road, so I think it's about time you did more than lust wistfully after him.'

'Jess!' chided Milly.

'Does everyone know?' asked Holly, her eyes wide with shock. 'Does Dan know?'

Jess gave a quick nod and caught Max's as she waddled back into the room. 'You know, don't you Max?'

'Don't bring me into it,' warned Max manoeuvring herself back into a comfortable seated position on the lounge, 'but yes, I had noticed. I don't think everyone knows, though.' She smiled reassuringly at Holly.

'Actually,' said Jess, 'I think you'll find that they do; they just haven't said anything. Dan's the only one who doesn't know.'

'Typical,' said Kate. 'Just like a man. Maybe he needs some help.'

'I don't know,' said Max. 'Some things are better left to unfold of their own accord.'

'And we're just the women to point him in the right direction,' said Jess, ignoring the warning in Max's tone.

'It's hopeless,' said Holly. 'I work so close beside him, and he's never looked at me in that way. The girls I see him out with are the opposite to me.'

Jess grudgingly admitted that was true. Rugby-playing Dan, who was over six-feet tall, went for girls almost as tall as himself and definitely as fit as he was – the girls who breezed up and down the ski slopes, who came to town for the bungy jumping and adventure sports and partied all night in short skirts and high heels. Holly, who looked younger than the twenty-two she was, wasn't much taller than Max, and with her round face, guileless blue eyes, dimples in both cheeks, and short blonde wavy hair was soft and pretty and not at her best in the clompy black boots she, Dan and Max wore in the Beach Road kitchen. At least Jess hadn't insisted they wear proper chef's checks and whites rather than the jeans, tees and navy aprons the team wore.

Max leant over and patted Holly's hand. 'You're

gorgeous, Holl. I think it's just that you began as his apprentice, and he probably doesn't want to take advantage of you.'

Jess didn't know whether it was the despairing look on Holly's face, the champagne or just the understanding that unrequited love was a real bitch – not that she'd ever been afflicted, but it made otherwise rational people do stupid things. She decided then and there that Holly and Dan were perfect for each other. Men were easy; they simply needed a bit of a help along every so often.

It was like Nathan – he'd needed a nudge in the right direction, especially now he was here in New Zealand rather than in Far North Queensland. Sure, *officially*, it was just for a few months, but she was sure Nathan would never want to leave. Not only did he no longer need to do all of that back-and-forth travel he'd been doing from Cairns to here, but it was an opportunity for him to study different animals. How many humpback whales and turtles can you count before they get boring? Okay, Stewart Island wasn't exactly a commutable distance from Queenstown, but once he'd caught the ferry to the mainland, it wasn't *that* much of a drive. Besides, how could they decide whether this thing between them would work if they never saw each other? And, Jess shivered at the thought, their coming together after each short absence was sweet indeed. Absence, it seemed, really did make the heart grow fonder.

Short-term relationships had satisfied Jess in the past; she knew where she stood with men who were here for the season, so her heart was never at risk. The café was busy and, particularly in those early few years when she was establishing the business, she had no emotional energy for anything more. With Nathan, though, maybe she could have it all – a successful business and the happy ever after she saw Max and Ritchie enjoying.

It was only now she was part of a pair she realised how much she'd needed that, been craving it. Nathan, quite simply, made her happy, and during the week when he was away, her little townhouse on a hill behind Queenstown felt empty when previously it hadn't.

In fact, Jess was so happy with Nathan that maybe she owed it to Holly and Dan to help them find the same happiness? Max was warning her not to meddle, but it wasn't really meddling if she had their best interests at heart, was it?

CHAPTER FOUR

'I'm too heavy, Richie,' Max protested when he stopped at the threshold of their new home and moved to pick her up.

Richie smiled down at her and lifted her easily into his arms. To him, she was perfect, always. A little heavier to be sure (not that he'd admit as much to her) but perfect. 'See,' he said, 'you're still light as a feather.'

She wrinkled her nose as if to protest, so he kissed it instead.

Richie and Max had designed their house in an L-shape to maximise the views of the lake, with The Remarkables rising behind it. The shorter side of the L, and the centre of the house, was a large open-plan kitchen, dining and living space with an open fire with a stone surround at the end. The kitchen and dining area floor was polished concrete, while the living room was a soft grey carpet that they'd also used in each of the three bedrooms. The high-pitched ceiling gave a feeling of space and light with feature trusses and floor-to-ceiling windows offering that incredible vista and huge sliding doors leading out to the covered deck and barbecue area. The kitchen was massive with a double oven, double hob, a stunning black glass splash-back and a massive island bench.

Max had already filled the cupboards and drawers with everything a kitchen required. All she needed to do was add some cushions and throws to the lounge, and this room was complete. Even so, Richie watched her as she stood in the centre of the room and slowly turned to take it all in.

'It's everything we hoped it would be, isn't it?' she said finally, her eyes glistening.

'It certainly is. Now that I've sketched out some ideas I can't wait to get started on the garden,' said Richie.

'Me neither,' she said. 'A veggie path, some fruit trees and a lawn for the kids to run around on – it'll be my dream garden come to life.'

Richie held her hand and led her down the hall to their bedroom. The last time she'd seen it, the walls had been painted, but the furniture lay in a flatpack in the middle of the floor beside bags of bedding and rolls of wallpaper. With the grass-cloth textured wallpaper hung, the bed constructed and made up, and the full-length curtains opened to capture the lake and the mountains, it felt as though the view outside was part of the room.

'The wallpaper's up,' she said in wonder. 'Nathan?'

'Yes.' Richie nodded. 'He helped me hang it last Sunday, and we put the bed together yesterday.'

'As well as the outdoor furniture?'

'Yep.' Richie's chest puffed out with pride. 'Dad and Tom helped too, but we had a busy morning.'

'I'll say you did.' She reached up on tippy toes and brushed a kiss on his lips. 'Thank you, this is perfect.'

Richie cupped her face and deepened the kiss, the softness of her lips under his sending, as it always did, desire rippling through his body. Reluctantly, he pulled himself away and rested his forehead against hers. 'As much as I'd love to christen this bed right now, we still have Piglet's room to see,' he said, thrilling at her little moan of disappointment.

'And then?'

'Then, my darling Maxi, you can have your wicked way with me.'

Smiling, she skipped – as much as a woman as pregnant as Max could skip – down the hall towards the nursery. Before she could fling open the door, he put his hand over hers on the door handle.

'Shut your eyes,' he said.

She tilted her head to the side and smiled up into his eyes. 'Really?'

'Yes, really.'

She screwed her eyes shut and waited as he turned the handle. 'Keep them shut until I say so,' he warned.

She nodded eagerly. With his heart in his mouth,

he pushed the door open. 'Okay, you can open them now.'

Her eyes remained tightly closed. 'Maxi, you can open your eyes.'

'I'm too excited,' she said.

He stepped in front of her and kissed each eye gently, then her lips. 'Open your eyes,' he said, turning her to face the room.

Richie waited beside her, her hand in his, as she took in the furniture they'd carefully chosen together. Finally, her eyes rested on the oak tree he'd painted, its branches spreading across two walls, leaves drifting down, and birds flying around it, bluebells, rabbits and hedgehogs at its base. When she stilled, Richie's heart skipped a beat. Had he got it wrong? But when she turned to face him, beaming, her eyes bright, tears sliding down her cheeks, he knew he'd got it very right indeed.

'Richie, this is … it's so … how did you?'

'You like it?' he asked, his own eyes welling.

'I love it.' She threw her arms around his neck and brought his head down to hers. 'I love it so much, and I love you.'

Coming up for air, she said, 'That day in the bluebells before you left Brookford, that was when I knew how I felt about you.'

That day was etched in his memory too. They'd been walking the path above Brookford and had lain down in the bluebells together. He'd looked into her eyes and known he'd made the right decision to leave town and give her a chance to live her life with the man she'd married, but she'd looked so lost it was all he could do not to kiss her until she had no room for thinking of anyone but him.

Max traced her fingers over the delicate blooms and said, 'I'm glad you included the bluebells. It's a little part of Brookford.'

'Do you miss it?' he asked, his arms tightening around her.

'No,' she said. 'I have everything I need right here.'

'Yeah,' he murmured, bending his head to kiss her again. 'So do I.'

Jess stretched out under the sheet and watched Nathan stride from the bathroom back to bed. Tall, with long, lean legs and the shoulders and arms of someone who spends a lot of time swimming, clothed, he looked fabulous, but naked (as he was now) he was divine.

'What?' he asked in a tone that showed he knew exactly what was going through her mind but wanted her to say it aloud anyway. Jess was happy to play any games he wanted this morning.

'I was thinking how very nice you are to watch.'

'And?'

'How I wished that you'd hurry up and come back to bed.'

'I thought I might stand here and let you ogle me

some more,' he said, a wolfish grin on his gorgeous face; his hair mussed and his jaw stubbled. She shivered at the thought of how the stubble felt against her soft skin.

'Or you could stand there and watch me start without you,' said Jess, sliding her hand over her stomach, inching it slowly towards the V of her legs. Two could definitely play this game.

Sometime later, Jess lay sprawled beside him in a tangle of sheets and limbs. 'I can't believe that pregnant sex might be better than that,' she said, her breath still coming fast.

Beside her, Nathan lifted his head briefly, confusion written over his face. 'Pregnant ... sex? Is there something you need to tell me?'

Jess detected a smidgeon of fear in his tone. 'No need to panic, lover boy, it's just what Max, Mum and Kate were saying yesterday about how pregnant sex can be amazing and creative – apparently, it's a position thing. Trust me, you don't want to know what my mother was saying – way too much information and an image I can't get out of my head.'

'I don't think I want to know what my mother was saying about it either,' said Nathan with a laugh. 'You know they must've had sex – at least twice in the case of Mum – but anything more than that? No. Thank. You.'

'I agree, which is why I said that it couldn't possibly be better than normal non-pregnant sex, Nathan-sex in other words.'

'Oh god, Jess, please don't tell me you talked to my mother about our sex life,' he groaned.

'I started to, and then I remembered Kate was actually your mother and not my friend – although obviously, she's a friend, she's especially my mother's friend, as well as being your mother – so I said it wasn't that great.'

'You told my mother that sex with me wasn't that great?' He'd propped himself up on his elbows. The look on his face was hard to distinguish – amusement or annoyance.

'Not exactly; I was just trying to change the subject.' She lifted a shoulder, allowing the sheet to slip, an innocent look on her face.

He shook his head, and a mischievous grin widened across his face. Good, it was amusement – Jess really didn't want to mar a perfect Sunday morning with annoyance.

'That makes a weird sort of sense.' He paused before asking, 'Is that what you women talked about yesterday? Pregnant sex? I thought it would be all baby talk.'

Jess rubbed at her forehead. 'The first part was – and don't remind me about that. Talk about boring – and yet people think that they're endlessly fascinating. Babies, that is,' she clarified when the confused look was back on his face.

'You seem to be pretty fascinated with this one –
the amount of shit you've bought for it.'

She shrugged again and grinned as his eyes
wandered to the breast she'd exposed, darkening
with lust. 'Yes, but that's all part of my campaign for
godmother. This child needs someone who can help
them navigate the minefield that life can be.'

'And who better to do that than you.' His finger
circled her nipple.

'My thoughts exactly. I'm an independent woman
with my own business. I know first aid, and I can
teach Piglet all about the outdoors. Besides, the baby
will be an Aries, and I'm an Aries, so I'll know exactly
what tricks it uses to get its own way. When you put
it all together, you have to admit I'm the most perfect
person for the role.'

A chuckle rolled through Nathan's body. 'It's not a
job ad you're being interviewed for, you know. Besides,
who else would Richie and Max choose other than you
and Dan?'

'I suppose.'

He flipped onto his side and idly ran his finger
across the curve of her tummy, a trail of goosebumps
chasing his touch.

'Do you ever think about it?' he asked, fingers
circling her bellybutton.

'About what? Babies? Christ no. Do you?' The
goosebumps were now piling on top of each other.

'No, well, not yet anyway. I'll leave it to Ash and Reece to supply Mum with grandkids. Maybe one day …'

'I don't think I ever will,' said Jess. 'I'm way too selfish. Let's face it, I work too hard, and things have to be my way or the highway.'

'Really? I hadn't noticed.'

She punched his arm lightly. 'I know it's difficult for you to believe, but I'm not great with compromise, and babies take over your whole life – apparently, you have to fit in with them, rather than the other way around. So no, I'm a long way from that.'

Nathan stopped the finger tracing thing, and Jess really wished he'd start again.

'What else went on at this baby shower of yours yesterday?' he asked.

She screwed up her nose. 'You know, boring baby stuff. Once the others left and we broke open the champagne, it was heaps better – that's when we talked about other things.'

'Like pregnant sex.'

'Exactly. That was one bottle in. I had the best idea too – about Holly and Dan.'

'What about them?' His voice sounded guarded.

'You know how she's crushing on Dan?' When Nathan didn't reply, she added, 'You can't say that you haven't noticed.'

'I've noticed, but it's none of our business.'

It sounded as if he didn't want to talk about it. Whatever. 'I've decided that Holly needs some help with the situation.'

'No, Jess, just leave it alone. Leave them alone.'

If she didn't know better, it sounded very much as though he was issuing a warning.

Jess turned onto her side to face him. 'Holly didn't seem to have a problem with it.'

'Did you even give her a chance to say she had a problem?'

Jess pulled back and frowned. 'What's that supposed to mean?'

Nathan sighed and rolled his eyes. 'It means when you have an idea in your head, you don't stop and listen to other people's opinions. How do you know Dan wants to be matched with Holly?'

'What's wrong with Holly? She's lovely, and Dan doesn't know yet that he wants to be with her.' She tapped lightly at Nathan's chest. 'There's a difference.'

'All I'm saying is, be careful. They work together, and you don't want to upset that balance, do you?'

'Okay, you have a point there; I'll be careful.' He was right; they worked well together, but Jess was sure they'd be able to balance the two. 'Speaking of which, let's call by Beach Road for something to eat first.'

'Sounds good, but what do you mean by first? You know I need to be on the road by two-ish if I'm going to make the five o'clock ferry.'

'I thought we'd call in on Richie and Max – they're moving in today.'

'Which is exactly why we shouldn't call in on them today. Let them have some space.'

She tipped her head to the side to consider his suggestion. 'They'd be expecting us to go over. In fact, I'm convinced Richie would think I wasn't interested if we didn't go.' Narrowing her eyes, she said, 'I don't suppose you're going to tell me what the big secret is.'

'Maybe I will – later.' Then he grinned. 'But we're not going over there this morning.'

'I'll go on my own then.' She pouted.

He shrugged as if that didn't matter. 'Go for it. I'll hit the road early and catch an earlier ferry.'

Jess had to admit that him standing up to her was turning her on. A lot. He was the only person who had ever stood up to her. She chewed thoughtfully on her lower lip, and then when his eyes darkened, she moistened her lips and did it again.

'Okay then,' she said. 'If we're not going to Richie's, what are your plans for the morning.'

He danced his fingers up her leg and across her back, pulling her until they were skin to skin. 'Given how your fridge is again empty—' When she would have opened her mouth to argue that it wasn't really empty, it contained beer, wine and yoghurt which, she would have added, was still within its use-by date, he placed his finger to her lips. 'Instead of going to Beach

Road where you'll likely remember something you
need to talk to Dan about or something you'd meant
to tell Dayna and before we know it, you're right into
work mode; we'll go to that place in Arrowtown we
both love.'

'The one that does the Turkish eggs with yoghurt?'

'That one. And then we'll come back here to make
love again.' He pulled her leg up so it curled around
him, her foot resting on his bum, creating room for
his hand to slip between her legs. Jess couldn't help the
moan that escaped from her lips. 'Following which, I'll
head back to Stewart Island, and you can visit Richie
and Max if, after thinking about it, you really think
you should.' One of his fingers slid inside her. 'How's
that for a compromise?' He lifted an eyebrow, gaze
penetrating full of heat.

'It all sounds fine,' she managed with a sigh. What
this man could do to her. 'Except for the part about
making love later.'

'You're right,' he said. 'Definitely a flaw in the plan.'
He pulled his fingers away and watched her panted in
frustration. 'How about we reverse the order and make
love now and eat later?'

Jess put both hands to his chest and pushed until
he was on his back with her straddled above him. 'Now
that's what I call a compromise.'

CHAPTER FIVE

'Before I forget,' Nathan said, 'I know you're on track next weekend, but Tom was saying yesterday he's thinking of bringing the grapes in next weekend. If he does, I might come up and help.'

They'd finally made it to Arrowtown and were having what was now brunch rather than breakfast.

'Right.' Even though she'd urged him to feel at home here, Jess didn't know how she felt about Nathan visiting when she wasn't here. It was selfish, but she enjoyed knowing he came here for her. Although, she supposed, the more he felt he belonged, the less likely he'd be able to leave when the time came.

'Is that a problem?' He tilted his head slightly, his brow furrowed. 'I don't mind staying with Mum if it's weird.'

'No, it's okay, use the apartment – you have a key, and I'll be home on Friday afternoon so we can spend the evening together, but I'll be gone again at the crack of dawn on Saturday. It's just that you said you probably wouldn't be driving back and forth every weekend, so does this mean that you won't be here the weekend after?'

He frowned, pushed his fork through his nasi goreng, and Jess's heart did a strange little flip as he delayed his answer. 'I haven't decided. When I first took this project, you said you'd come down, but so far, you haven't, so why not the weekend after next? It's Bluff oyster season, and there are also some tramps we can do together. Because I've been here each weekend, I haven't had a chance to do any tramping down there – and everyone says the tracks are worthwhile.' His voice sounded hopeful, but his eyes skittered away from hers.

'I'm not sure,' she said slowly. 'It'll be getting close to the baby being born, so I probably won't be too far away in case Max needs me.'

'Fair enough.' Nathan shrugged, but Jess thought her response had disappointed him.

'Would you come here if I don't go there?' Jess hated herself for asking the question.

'As I said before, I haven't decided. It's still a couple of weeks away, so we can talk about it when you get home.'

'Maybe I'll come down when the baby's born,' Jess said, trying to sound optimistic.

'Yeah, maybe.' He pushed the rice around the plate.

'About this afternoon,' she started, 'perhaps I should let Max and Richie settle into the house before I visit.'

Nathan nodded his head once, slowly, a faint smile curving his lips. 'I think they'd appreciate that,' he said. 'They've waited so long to have their own space.'

'I suppose.' She heaved a deep sigh. 'I can't believe I'll be the last person to see the house, though,' she said, slumping in her chair. 'Especially since you know what the surprise is.'

His eyes crinkled at the sides as he laughed at her dramatics. 'Well, given Max would've seen it by now, I don't suppose there's any harm in telling you … if you ask me nicely, that is …'

His grin was wicked, and Jess's insides dissolved. Hoping it didn't show on her face, she shrugged. 'Are you going to tell me, or do I need to call in there and see for myself?'

He sighed deeply in mock exasperation. 'Seeing as you're so impatient … Richie's painted a mural on the nursery wall.'

'A mural?'

'A massive oak tree. It covers two of the walls. He's painted in birds and rabbits and blue flowers.' He shook his head as if he were seeing it again. 'I know Richie trained as a garden designer, and I know he's always sketching, but this is really amazing.'

Jess's eyes moistened, and she had no idea why. Perhaps it was how Richie was unafraid to show Max what she and their baby meant to him – that he felt comfortable putting so much of himself on the line.

He was a big softie where Max was concerned.

'Hey, are you okay?' Nathan asked, reaching across to run a finger lightly down her cheek. 'I didn't mean to upset you.'

Jess blinked away the tears before they could escape. 'You haven't upset me; it's just … I don't know …'

'Yeah,' said Nathan. 'I know.'

Jess met his eyes and knew that he did.

After Nathan left to drive down to Bluff, Jess caught up on some work. She loved her time on track, and while the extra money the guiding brought in helped over the summer when business wasn't as brisk as it was during the peak ski season, being out of the café put her behind. She was, however, aware that she wouldn't have been able to juggle both – Beach Road and guiding – if it wasn't for Dan. For about the millionth time since she opened Beach Road, she thanked her lucky stars. When she was away, he managed the kitchen and Dayna took charge downstairs. To be honest, the pair of them could run it easily without her these days.

After letting herself into the café, she took a minute to stand in the space and appreciate it with no one else there. Jess loved this time of the day – when the café was closed, and the crowds had gone. The counter gleamed, and the coffee machine glinted as a ray of late afternoon sun snuck through the window. Outside, the path that ran along the lakefront was busy with tourists taking a Sunday afternoon stroll, and the *TSS Earnslaw*, the steamship that took day-trippers across the lake to Walter Peak, a high-country sheep farm, was chugging back into the dock.

Even when she wasn't heading out on track, she often found herself back here on a Sunday afternoon after Nathan left. Not only did it allow her to get a clean start on the week ahead, but she also needed a break between Nathan leaving and her going home – doing the accounts for the café gave her the perfect distraction. It was as though his presence had time to leave before she stepped back through the front door of her apartment.

This afternoon, though, the accounts were done in no time. Beach Road was running well – too well, according to the accountant.

'It's time to expand,' she'd said when Jess visited her last month. 'You have the cashflow.'

'What do you mean by expand?' Jess had asked. 'I was thinking of adding catering to our services – bespoke canapés for events, afternoon teas, that sort of thing.'

'You could go in that direction, but I was thinking more about a new café or a new business venture. Perhaps Beach Road Too.' She chuckled at her creativity, but her laugh died when she saw the cautious look on Jess's face. 'I'll leave that thought with you.'

While Jess had initially dismissed it, the idea had lodged in her head and came out to look around whenever the coast was clear. Aside from the occasional problems that needed Jess to resolve, these days, any improvements to the business were tweaks rather than wholesale changes. Like the situation with the pies and sausage rolls. The simple solution would be to change suppliers – find someone who produced a more artisan product – but Jess wondered whether the time was right to hire an in-house baker and sell Beach Road bread as well. That option, however, came with its own set of inherent challenges.

While Holly and Dan could support each other, before Max came to work for her, Jess had been reliant on Amy – who wasn't reliable at all. Every time Amy was off sick, it potentially left Jess with nothing to sell customers to have with their morning coffee. Max had helped fill that gap. She didn't want to go back down the path of having a single point of failure again – which would be where she'd be if she employed a single baker. And that was before she upgraded the kitchen to deal with bread ovens and industrial mixers.

It mightn't make business sense – at least not yet – but she could see the cabinet stocked with a more rustic looking offering, bread baskets piled high with sourdough loaves and baguettes, the blackboard advertising pastries with a local twist. The market was there, she was sure of it.

Jess closed the laptop and stood, hunching her shoulders up to her ears on the inward breath and letting them relax with an audible exhale. She wasn't the type to sit still for any period. She ran her hand over the smooth stainless-steel benches. Even without the capital outlay needed, would there be room? Bakers worked ungodly hours and would start before the breakfast crew came in, so there was the possibility to stagger shifts. Jess thought it through some more. No, that had trouble written all over it.

What if … she surveyed the bench under the window where the baking happened. The setting sun cast soft pink light across the lake. What if she opened a bakery and used the product to supply Beach Road? It would be an enormous step – and a massive risk she wasn't convinced she was ready for or prepared to take – but what if …? It was an idea worth thinking about. But not tonight.

Jess closed her laptop and put it back into her bag. Switching off the lights in the kitchen, she went down the stairs into the café. What was it she'd forgotten to do?

Her phone pinged with a message – Nathan letting her know he was on the ferry. That's what it was – she hadn't told her mother about yesterday morning's stranger, the one who'd known her father. Before she could forget, she dialled her parent's number.

After greeting Milly, she said, 'I forgot to mention

it yesterday; there was a man who came in who said he was an old friend of Dad's.'

'Oh really? Who was it?'

'No idea. He didn't leave his name. He was English, though. One amusing thing, he called you Melinda – even I'd forgotten that was your real name!' Jess laughed, but when Milly didn't join her, she continued, 'I thought he looked familiar, but then I figured he must have one of those faces.' Jess balanced her phone between her ear and her shoulder and checked the back door was locked.

'You're probably right,' said Milly. 'What did he look like?'

Jess paused as she remembered. 'Tall, lanky, curly grey hair – but not white-grey, that dark grey that black hair sometimes goes. Actually'—she wrinkled her nose— 'he was good looking for an older dude – he would've had to be sixty, but still fit. Ring any bells?'

'No,' said Milly emphatically. 'Did he say how long he was in town for?'

'He didn't. I told him Dad and Richie ran Lakeview Landscaping, but he said he didn't think he'd have time to drop in.' Jess switched off the light over the stairs. 'He said he was just passing through – I got the impression he was doing the road trip thing; thought I'd tell you in case he calls by.'

'Thanks, Jess,' said Milly. 'You're away this week, aren't you?'

'Yes, I'm doing Routeburn from Wednesday. It's a back-to-back, so I'm heading out again on Saturday for Milford.'

'That's a pity – Tom's bringing the grapes in, so will do a barbecue over there on Saturday evening.'

'So Nathan said – he's coming back for it.'

'Kate was saying she's glad he is – even though she knows both Nathan and Ash like Tom, Nathan helping is a sign that he approves of her relationship with him.'

'He always has, hasn't he?' Nathan had taken immediately to Tom when they met on Milford Track last year. 'He told me that while Tom would never replace his father, he was happy they were together.'

'Yes, but he'll be in town expressly to help Tom – not just to see you,' said Milly. 'And that means a lot to Kate,' she added.

Jess grimaced as she silently acknowledged she hadn't given that perspective much thought at all. 'I'm sure it does. Anyway, Mum, I need to get home, so I'll see you later, eh?'

After she hung up, Jess stood where she was for a little longer. The conversation was, on the surface, the same as all her conversations with her mother, yet there was something odd about this one, something she couldn't put her finger on. Outside the lake had taken on the hues of a watercolour painting as the violet in the sky was reflected on the water. Shaking her head, she pushed it from her mind, shut the café door behind her and stepped out into the Queenstown twilight.

Milly struggled to maintain a calm facade when every organ inside her body was jumping about. From the minute Jess said, 'He called you Melinda.', Milly had known.

She placed the phone carefully back in its cradle and glanced across the kitchen bench at Cam who was putting away the last plates from the dishwasher.

As if he'd felt her gaze, he shut the cupboard door and said, 'What's wrong? Don't tell me Jess is already over at Richie's? I thought she might've given them some breathing space.' He shook his head, his smile wry.

Milly took her time in answering, her brain scrambling to find some thought to cling to, some piece of logic that would tell her this stranger was someone other than who she thought it was.

'Gary's in town.'

The smile died on Cam's face. 'What?' He wasn't asking her to repeat what she'd said. 'How do you know?'

'There was a man in at Beach Road yesterday asking about you.'

'That could've been anyone. How do you know it was Gary?' Cam flicked the switch on the kettle and took two cups down from the cupboard, his shoulders square and stiff. 'Did this man leave a name?'

'No.' She tapped at the stone counter with her

fingertips. 'Jess said he was tall and lanky with curly grey hair.'

'That description could fit any number of people, and it's been years since you've seen him.' Cam poured water over the tea bags and added milk to both cups.

'He was English and referred to me as Melinda.' Cam's hand stilled, a tea bag dangling above the cup. 'It's him, I know it is.' Cam's face had paled, and there was a pulse beating at the side of his jaw. He knew too.

Milly held her breath as she waited for Cam to say something, anything. When he remained silent, she said, 'Feel free to tell me it isn't Gary, that plenty of other people have called me by my real name over the years.' She stretched her mouth into a smile that wouldn't fool him.

'What do you think he wants?' Cam pushed her cup of tea across to her, managing not to meet her eyes.

'I've no idea. Maybe he's here on holidays and remembered we're here too.' If Milly told herself that often enough, she might even believe it. 'He told Jess he probably wouldn't have time to drop in.'

'Jess told him where to find us?'

Milly nodded sympathetically. 'She also told him Richie's working with you.'

Cam's head jerked up; his brow furrowed. 'Regardless of what he told Jess, he's not just passing through. He's here to find you.'

Milly didn't answer; she didn't need to. Like Cam, she believed Gary had come to Queenstown specifically to see her, which could only mean he wasn't here simply to say hello. No, whatever he was here for, it wasn't good.

CHAPTER SIX

A little wrought iron table and two chairs were tucked behind the greenhouse where the seedlings were nurtured. It was away from customers who could wander off the path and perfectly positioned to catch the sun. While it was too hot to sit here during the height of summer, it was perfect at this time of the year. Richie placed his sketchbook on the table, unwrapped his sandwiches, poured himself a coffee from the thermos and settled back into the seat with a sigh. It had been a busy morning.

Because one of the drivers had called in sick, Richie had helped with two deliveries of soil, taken orders for another few and had a video conference with a potential new supplier of garden ornaments. He now had thirty minutes of peace and quiet before he needed to get over to Bannockburn to discuss a garden design with a winemaker.

After speaking to the owner early last week, Richie had already done a few sketches based on the brief. The customer was seeking to create a space for visitors to eat picnic lunches accompanied, of course, by their wines. With his sandwich held in one hand, Richie flicked through his sketchbook with the other.

The climate around Cromwell and Bannockburn – although less than fifty kilometres from Queenstown – was drier and warmer; with the conditions more arid, it was perfect for pinot noir. An old alluvial gold-mining area, the landscape was dramatically pock-marked with the scars of the goldrush days. When he was a kid, he thought it looked like the landscape in those old movies set in the wild, wild west. He smiled to himself as he pictured it in his mind's eye.

Last November, he and Max had taken a drive out there. It had been years since he'd been and had forgotten how sparsely beautiful the area was. They'd walked hand in hand through the wild thyme – a leftover from the gold town days – that now grew as a weed through the sluicings. As they walked, the scent rose through the air, and Max reached down to run her hand over the little clumps of it, releasing yet more fragrance. If he could bring some of that wonder into his design, the client would be pleased – and if this client was pleased, he might get more referrals for design work.

Although his father had declared he was happy for Richie to expand Lakeview Landscaping into garden design, he was hesitant about doing so. The issue was that Richie's idea of design and his father's differed on one important level – scale. Fletch wanted to keep things small for now – do a few suburban gardens and build up slowly from there. Richie, though, wanted to design the gardens he'd been sketching for years – the spaces that flowed seamlessly from their natural landscape. He and his friend Brad, a designer based in Melbourne who predominantly did rooftop bars and corporate spaces, had spoken about it when he and his fiancé Abby had visited last Christmas.

'There's so much you can do here, mate,' Brad had said. 'The lake, the mountains, there's inspiration everywhere you look.' Brad specialised in, as Abby had put it, gardens you can live in, where the outside was brought inside.

'It's a bit cold here for rooftop bars, though,' Richie had joked.

'Perhaps,' said Brad, 'but you'd be surprised. You've got something down here we don't have in the city – the drama of the natural landscape. People come here to see that, so give it to them.'

It had sounded so simple when Brad had said it, and Richie had known that was exactly what he wanted to do – not that he'd said as much to Fletch yet. This job in Bannockburn was an opportunity for him to show Fletch what was *really* possible – to take his ideas and turn them into a reality Lakeview Landscaping (and his father) would be proud to be associated with.

As he contemplated this, Fletch strode around the

corner, a mug of coffee in his hand. 'I thought I might find you here,' he said, sitting in the empty chair.

'I figured I'd better grab something to eat while I could,' said Richie.

'Thanks for helping on the truck this morning,' said Fletch. 'Your mother and I had an appointment at the accountants I couldn't get out of.'

'You mean Mum wouldn't let you get out of,' Richie said, grinning

Fletch's smile was rueful. 'You know it. You're out in Bannockburn this afternoon, aren't you?'

'Yes. Flynn's Folly. They're after a terrace off the cellar door. I've had a few ideas.' Richie pushed the open sketchbook across the table towards Fletch and tried not to hold his breath as his father flicked through the pages.

'Have you seen the place yet?' Fletch asked, turning the pages over.

'No, that's what I'm doing this afternoon; those were just thoughts,' he said, his head tilting towards the drawings. 'I'm hoping there'll be some magnificent views of the cuttings from the winery – and even Mt Difficulty. I can picture it all – the terrace running down to the vines, contrasting with the almost desert landscape of the old cuttings and gold trails.'

'Hmmm.' Fletch rubbed the back of his neck, avoiding eye contact with Richie. 'It'll be a big job.'

'Perhaps, but we're ready for it.' Richie popped

the last of his sandwich into his mouth, chewing as he organised his thoughts. 'If we get it right, it's a gateway to more of that work.' He hesitated slightly before adding, 'It's what I've always wanted to do.'

Fletch nodded slowly. 'I know it is, Rick. I'm just concerned about biting off something too big to start with. If we get it right, it could make us, but if we don't …' He left the alternative unsaid, but Richie knew precisely what he wanted to say.

'It could break us,' Richie finished his father's sentence for him.

'Don't forget you're going to be a new father soon, too. Do you want to be taking on something the size of this when you have a new baby at home?' His eyes met Richie's, his tone serious. 'Don't underestimate that. You'll be operating on little sleep, and those first few months are exhausting – both physically and emotionally. Max will be a wonderful mother – there's no doubt about that – but she'll need you to be there for her when you also feel as though you've got no energy left to give. Her job is to nourish your baby – yours is to take care of her so she can do that.'

'You think I don't know that?' The tone and volume of Richie's words caused Fletch's eyes to widen over the top of his coffee mug. 'She's all I think about – you know that!' He took a deep breath to calm down. When Fletch didn't respond, he said, more quietly, 'You don't want me to do this, do you, Dad?'

Fletch exhaled heavily and slumped in his chair, suddenly looking older than he was. He bit his lower lip, causing him to grimace, his eyes squinting against the sun. 'I'm not saying that, son,' he said gently. 'I know it's always been your dream to design, and I know it frustrates you delivering soil and other supplies so other people's ideas can come to life.'

'It's not that—' Richie stopped talking when his father interrupted him.

'It is Rick, I know that. I'm not saying you can't take on more design jobs; all I'm saying is that maybe now isn't the time to be taking on something as big as Flynn's Folly.'

Heat burned within his chest. He understood Fletch's concerns about him taking on too much, but it sometimes felt to Richie as though he'd been waiting forever to come to this point – and now he wanted to jump into it. 'If not now, then when? You asked me to take the time to get to know the business – and I've spent the last six months doing just that. Now you're asking me to wait some more?'

'Just a few months, Rick. Just until the baby's routine has settled, and you and Max feel comfortable taking on something that size. You haven't stopped since you came back. Not only have you been getting used to how things work around here, but you and Max have been building the house and getting ready for the baby. If I know you, you'd also be eager to get a start on your own garden. All I'm saying is you need some breathing space, and you're unlikely to get that with a new baby.'

What his father was saying made sense, but that didn't mean he wanted to hear it. 'What if this is it, though? What if I turn this job down and I don't get another opportunity?'

Fletch drained the last of his coffee. 'You don't believe that,' he said. 'There'll be other opportunities, and I'm not telling you to turn it down.'

'What are you telling me then?'

'I'm not telling you anything,' said Fletch, speaking slowly like he did when Richie was a hot-tempered teenager who needed to be talked out of doing something that would have consequences. Richie bristled at his tone. 'I'm asking you to think about the timing and what you're looking to take on. I'm asking you whether you should commit to something like this.'

'The implication being that you won't support me if I do?'

Fletch sighed and closed his eyes briefly as if he were trying to control his own temper. 'That's not what I'm saying. This is my business, so if you commit us to a job, I'll have no choice but to follow it through.'

Richie recoiled as though his father had slapped him. Across the table from him, Fletch rubbed at his face with his hands. 'That's not what I meant to say,' he said. 'I didn't mean it to come out that way.'

'You mightn't have meant to say it like that, but somehow, Dad, you did.' He stood, balled up the wrapping from his sandwich and emptied the dregs from his mug onto the gravel. 'At least I know how you feel about it.'

'That's not how I feel … I'm just saying …'

'I know what you're saying, Dad, because you said it.' He picked up his thermos. 'I'd better be going. I'm due out there at two, and it's an hour's drive.'

'Richie—' Fletch started, but Richie didn't wait to hear what he had to say. He'd already heard enough.

Milly was on the phone when Cam stomped into the office and sat down heavily in his chair. She raised her eyebrows, and he half-shrugged, half shook his head.

'What happened?' she asked, finishing her call and laying the phone on the desk. 'Rick?'

He bumped into the corner of the desk, cursed, and rubbed at the side of his leg. 'How'd you guess?'

'Oh, I don't know,' she said with a faint smile. 'It could've been something in the way your son burst in here, slammed his coffee mug down, grunted a "see you later" and stormed out again. The chat about Flynn's Folly didn't go as well as you would've liked?'

'Something like that. I didn't handle it well. I tried to say that we'd support him whatever he decides, but it came out that if he dropped the ball, we'd pick up the pieces to save the reputation of the business.'

Milly stared at his solemn face, frowned. 'That doesn't sound like something you'd say, Cam.'

'I didn't exactly say it like that, but I think that's how Rick heard it.'

'Oh dear. Well, there's nothing you can do about it now.' She walked across the office to where he sat at his desk, the paperwork he'd been working on spread across it. Kissing him on the top of his head, she said, 'Another coffee?' She flicked the switch on the kettle that sat on the bench of the small kitchenette in the office.

'No thanks. I haven't long finished one, and I need to get that delivery of water features sorted.'

'Don't worry about Rick.' Milly dunked the tea bag in her cup, tossing it into the bin before adding a splash of milk. 'You always knew there'd be things the two of you wouldn't agree on with the business.' She smiled when Cam finally lifted his eyes from the paperwork, giving his full attention. 'I've never yet known a father and son to work together without there being some fireworks and differences of opinion. You know what's worked over the years, and he has his ideas about how he sees it working in the future. You're both opinionated, and you can both be stubborn so and so's when you want to dig your heels in – I'd be more surprised if it was completely plain sailing.'

'I suppose so,' Cam said, pulling at his ear. 'He's got a good head on his shoulders, and his designs deserve to be seen; it's just sometimes it seems he's in such a hurry and so damn sensitive.'

Milly leaned against the desk where he sat and ruffled his hair. 'Oh Cam, he's scared. He can't control what's happening with him and Max and the baby, so he's trying to take charge of what he can control.' Reaching over, she picked up the family photo sitting there. Jess was in her arms, and Cate had a firm grip on her skirt. Cam was holding Richie's hand, his little face gazing adoringly into that of his father's. She leaned back and looked down at him fondly. 'Don't you remember what you were like when I was expecting Jess?'

He let out a short laugh. 'I wasn't that bad – was I?'

'You were so much worse!' She chuckled at the look of disbelief on his face. '*So* much worse. Seriously though, love, let him go. He'll commit to this job, or he won't – who knows, they might not like his vision, and you'll be worrying about nothing.'

'They'll love his ideas,' said Cam as if there was never any doubt.

'In that case, we'll be here to take the pressure off if we need to.' She leaned in and kissed his lips. 'It'll be fine.'

He nodded and returned her smile. 'Yes, you're right,' he said.

'Of course I am. Now get out there and get those water fountains set up for display.'

Milly ushered Cam from the office, closed the door

behind him and slumped into her chair, releasing the breath she'd been holding. The smile slipped from her face as she rolled her shoulders. Through the window, Cam was sitting on the forklift, shoulders hunched.

While she'd been ecstatic when Rick and Max arrived from England at the end of last winter and even happier when it became clear they were staying, she'd always known there'd be some teething problems between him and Cam. While they both had a similar work ethic, Cam was, understandably, more set in his ways at almost sixty-five than Richie was some thirty years younger. There were always going to be clashes, but of late, they'd been more frequent, although today was the first time Rick had stormed off. She was sure it was just a very natural fear of becoming a dad, but Milly made a mental note to check in with Max in case there was anything else going on with him.

CHAPTER SEVEN

Richie had gone over and over his father's words on the drive out to Bannockburn. As the kilometres flew by, he acknowledged there were the tiniest of possibilities that he'd overreacted, that Fletch hadn't meant to say them in the way he had. By the time he was on his way back home – after a successful meeting with Flynn Murphy – he'd decided that the problem wasn't so much what his father had said, but that neither he nor his father were great at saying what they felt. Richie was better at talking about things since he and Max had sorted themselves out, but only with her. He let out a snort as he guessed his mother would probably say the same thing about his father.

They were very alike – he and Fletch. They had similar mannerisms, similar values, and a similar work ethic. They were both as stubborn as each other. There were, however, fundamental differences in their approach to business. Where Fletch was conservative, Richie was looking towards the future. Even as he acknowledged the wisdom of his father's approach, he couldn't help feeling frustrated. As far as Richie was concerned, he'd spent too long on the business side of gardens and not enough on what he really loved.

It was different while he was in Brookford and managing Blossoms and Buds. The owner spent most of his time in Spain and had given Richie free rein to expand the business in other directions. Working together, he and Max had introduced locally produced food such as jams, chutneys, cheeses, and smoked goods. They'd begun selling a small range of handmade gifts and garden accessories, and Max produced a monthly newsletter featuring seasonal produce and recipes. It had been enough to satisfy his creative urges and had also grown the business – unfortunately to the level where one of the national brands paid a good deal of money for it, leaving him and Max out of jobs.

Since he'd come home, though, it was all about the landscaping supplies. Sure, they also sold pots, plants, and larger ornaments such as statues and water features, but there was nowhere to stamp his personality on the business. His father had said he was happy to listen to Richie's ideas and to support him in some design work, but had, at the same time, cautioned him against rushing into it.

At first, he'd been fine with that – there was a lot to learn and building the lake house kept his artistic side busy. Now though, Richie had an almost irrational worry that if he didn't branch out and grasp the

opportunities to do some garden design, he'd wake up
in five years' time and be in the same position as he
was now.

While he'd talked his concerns over with Max,
he hadn't admitted to her that his fears of not using
his talent to their full potential were tied up with his
other worries – the ones about impending fatherhood,
being able to provide a secure life for his family, being
a good and involved dad – and about not letting his
father down. While he hadn't said it aloud, he thought
Max had probably worked it out – the way she worked
most things out.

He would, he decided, talk to his father about it,
though – properly talk. Maybe not now while tempers
were running high, but soon.

Today's meeting had been positive. Flynn had liked
the ideas Richie had presented to him. After seeing the
landscape and taking plenty of photos, and listening to
Flynn speak about his vision for Flynn's Folly, Richie
was aching to get back and let his pencil fly over the
page. If he ended up winning the commission, the
project would still take a few months to get off the
ground – leaving time for him, Max, and Piglet to settle
into a routine of sorts.

Taking a glance at the time on the dashboard, he
decided he'd have time to call in at the yard and, if
not apologise to his father, at least let him know he'd
calmed down, before he needed to be back in town

to pick up Max. Ten minutes – fifteen tops – plenty of time to let Fletch know Flynn was interested and that he'd taken his advice on board about potentially delaying the start of the project.

Milly was updating the order book when Dave, one of the drivers who helped in the yard, popped his head around the door. 'There's someone here to see you or Fletch,' he said, pushing his wide-brimmed hat back as he spoke. 'Gary, he said his name was – an old friend, apparently?'

Milly's heart stopped beating, and a chill spread across her body. From somewhere, she found a smile and nodded. 'That's fine, you can tell him to come through. I don't suppose you know where Cam is?'

'I saw him out in the yard,' he said. 'Do you want me to let him know?'

'If you could,' said Milly, gripping her hands together under the desk so Dave couldn't see them shake.

Once Dave had left the room, Milly forced herself to stand and check her reflection in the mirror above the little sink outside the bathroom. She tipped her head upside down and scrunched at her short curls to give them back the bounce that had been flattened during the day. Straightening, she pinched at her cheeks until they held some colour and pulled her t-shirt so it hung better over her tummy. Back at her desk, she dabbed a little balm onto her lips and pressed them together. Three deep breaths and she was ready.

At first glance, Gary hadn't changed as much as he probably should have after thirty-odd years and looked to be more in his early fifties than the sixty-three he was. Back when they were married, Gary had worked on his fitness a lot – he'd always been at the gym and had played soccer each weekend, competitively. So competitively that he'd been under contract in the state league. His tall frame was still lean, but now was rangy and wiry rather than strong. The denim jeans he wore were fitted in all the right places, and although his t-shirt was loose fitting, there seemed to be not an ounce of middle-age spread. She had hoped to find him in worse shape; it would've been only fair if the excesses he'd been prone to when they were together had caught up with him. Milly chided herself for the unkind thoughts, even though he deserved no kindness from her.

Gary smiled confidently and walked through the open door with that easy lope he'd always had. His confidence had always been so ingrained that he'd never needed to strut or display it; much of his charisma was in the ease of his movements, his lop-sided smile. The London accent, snappy suits and fast cars had been part of it, sure, but they weren't what attracted people (especially women) to him. It was something else, something Milly had never been able to put a finger on. He had a way of drawing people in – of making them feel as though they were the centre of his attention. It had always been his superpower, but Milly knew him well enough to be immune to it. At least she hoped she was.

Up close, the lines the years had left were more obvious, but they suited him. Looking at him now, Milly could see what Richie would look like in thirty years. Suddenly, she worried about how she appeared to him. These days she kept her brown hair short, with lighter foils blended through to help hide the grey she was too vain to grow out. While she carried a few more kilos than she had back then, she was still trim and fit.

Judging by the appreciation in his eyes – the same appreciation he'd give to any attractive woman – Gary thought so too. When he bent to kiss her cheek, Milly instinctively recoiled, offering her hand instead. He looked at it for half a second, deciding to shake it or not before taking it and holding it in his. When it became obvious he didn't intend to release her hand, she pulled it from his, ignoring the little flutters deep in her belly.

'You haven't changed, have you, Gary?'

His eyes travelled up and down her figure, and he smiled that lop-sided smile of his. 'Nor have you. You're looking good, Melinda.'

Cam burst into the room, the speed of his breath a sign he'd dropped whatever he'd been doing in the yard to rush back to the office. Milly winced at the smirk on Gary's face.

'Evans.' Cam's words were brusque as he held out his hand.

'Fletcher.' Gary shook Cam's hand. 'Nice place you have here.' Gary sardonically scanned the tiny office with its three cramped desks, two of which overflowed with papers. 'Business must be good.'

'We do alright,' said Cam, his chin firming and walking to where Milly stood to put his arm around her waist. Cam might've intended it as a sign of his protection, but judging by the narrowing of his eyes, Milly was sure Gary interpreted the action as ownership and a sign Cam was feeling threatened. She sighed inwardly.

'What brings you here, Gary?' she asked, briefly placing her hand on Cam's waist to let him know she appreciated his closeness.

'I was in New Zealand on holiday and remembered that Queenstown was where you ended up, so I thought I'd look in and see how you're going.'

If Gary had been anyone else, Milly would've accepted the innocent look on his face and believed what he'd said, but this was Gary – and the Gary she knew did nothing without a reason.

'As you can see, we're doing fine,' she snapped.

'And our children? What are Cate and Richie up to?' Gary perched himself on the edge of the only clean desk, Richie's, and picked up a piece of paper from the orderly pile in his tray.

Cam stiffened beside her. Milly snatched the paper from Gary's hand. 'They're doing well,' she said. 'Cate's married and living in Sydney, and Rick, as I'm sure you know, works here with Cam.'

A quick smile flashed across Gary's face. 'Aaah, Jess told you I'd called in.'

'She said someone fitting your description had called in at her café; I figured it was you.'

He shrugged one shoulder and made a show of looking around the office again. 'Where is he?'

'Out,' said Cam.

Gary raised his eyebrows at Cam's clipped tone. 'You don't seem happy to see me,' he said.

'Did you expect we would be?' Cam shot back.

Rather than making Gary uncomfortable, Cam's words seemed only to amuse him.

'It's been a while, mate, so yes, I thought you'd be more reasonable these days. After all,' he added, 'you got the girl.' Gary's eyes raked over Milly's figure again. 'Didn't you?'

Milly placed a calming hand on Cam's, which had tightened around her waist at the insolence in Gary's gaze. 'Yes, he did,' she said. 'And, as you know, that was long after you left me.'

'Was it?'

His smile was knowing, goading her into a response. 'You know it was. So, you've dropped in, said hello, and asked about the kids you've ignored for decades. I'd say that's your business done here.' Milly forced a dismissive tone into her voice. 'Thanks for dropping by; I'll let Richie know he missed you.'

'Will you?' His mask slipped for such a brief instant that Milly thought she'd imagined it.

'Yes, I will. How long are you in town for?'

A beat and then another passed as Gary's eyes stayed locked on hers. It was as if he was trying to work out what she was thinking. Finally, he said, 'I'll be in town for another week. I'm staying at the Novotel down by the lake.' He dug into his back pocket and pulled out a card. Swivelling around to the desk, he found a pen and wrote on the back of it. 'Here's my number. Richie can reach me on it anytime.' His gaze narrowed in on Milly's. 'I'll drop by again in a few days if I haven't heard from Richie.'

Wrestling her gaze from his, Milly allowed her chin to jut. 'Rick's a grown man; I'll leave it up to him whether he wants to contact you.'

He shrugged again as if it didn't matter to him either way, and Milly bristled inside. 'Fair enough. If I don't hear from him, though, I'll be seeing you.' He pointed a finger at Cam. 'You can let her go now; I'm hardly likely to be whisking her away with me.' The confidence in his voice showed that if he'd wanted to, he could.

Before Cam could react, Milly stepped away from Cam's arms, walked to the door and yanked it open.

'Goodbye, Gary.'

He smirked, then said, 'I'll be seeing you, Melinda. Fletcher.' He waved over his shoulder as he left and didn't look back.

Milly closed the door behind him, releasing her breath before turning to face Cam. 'Thank goodness he left before Rick came back,' she said, stepping into Cam's outstretched arms.

'Why? You heard what he said – if Rick doesn't call him, he'll be back.' Cam sighed and pressed a kiss to Milly's forehead. 'I should've known he'd turn up some day.'

'Who?' Richie asked as he opened the office door, tossed his keys onto the desk and straightened the papers Gary had dislodged. 'Who'll be back?'

Milly took a deep breath and walked across to her son. Taking his hands in hers, she looked up at him. 'Your father, Rick.'

'But?' Richie looked across at Cam, confusion on his face.

'Gary Evans,' said Cam flatly. 'He's just paid us a visit.'

Max sat back in the chair Dan had put into the corner of the kitchen, especially for her, and sighed deeply. And then sighed once more.

'Are you right there?' asked Holly, chuckling as she cleaned down the stainless-steel benchtop.

'You have no idea,' said Max.

'Does it hurt?' asked Dan.

Jess, who had been trying to concentrate on paperwork, couldn't control her giggles.

Max exchanged glances with Jess and then Holly and laughed. 'Are you asking if the baby hurts?'

'Yes,' said Dan, colouring beautifully, which made Jess giggle even more and earned her a glare from Dan.

Jess lifted her head and waited for Max's answer, biting at the inside of her mouth to hide her smile. 'It's uncomfortable,' Max finally said. 'At this stage, Piglet is sitting on my bladder most of the time and, just to remind me he or she is there, kicks me every so often, but that's weird rather than painful.' She laughed and added, 'You should see it when I'm lying down, and Piglet moves. I never know whether it's an elbow or a leg, but it ripples along my belly. Richie loves watching it – he thinks it looks like something out of *Alien* but in a good way.' She rubbed her hands on her belly and then looked at Dan and with a tired smile. 'That's probably too much information?'

Dan said nothing, his cheeks still tinged pink. Jess and Holly grinned at his discomfort.

'Seriously though, it's just tough being on my feet all day.' Max lifted one foot off the floor, turned it in circles, then repeated with her other foot.

'How about I make you a cup of tea, and I'm sure I can find you a cheese scone somewhere,' offered Holly.

'If you can, I'd love you even more than I already do,' said Max, sighing once more for effect.

'How's it finally to be in your own home?' Dan asked once Holly had disappeared downstairs. 'I bet you're missing having this one barging in at all hours of the day.'

'I'll have you know,' bristled Jess, 'that I've chosen to give them some space to settle in before I barge in.'

Max chuckled. 'You're welcome to visit whenever you want,' she smiled across at Jess.

'As long as I knock, right?' Jess abandoned all pretence of concentrating on her paperwork. 'But where would the fun be in that?'

'Ha! But to answer your question, Dan, it's wonderful finally being in our place. Richie has done a fabulous job – he even painted a mural in Piglet's room. If you can pass me my phone, I'll show you the photos.'

'You're not getting up from that chair, are you?' Dan grinned as he retrieved Max's phone from her workbench.

'Nope. Not for anything.' She scrolled through the photos on her phone. 'Okay, here you go. Flip through from here.' She handed the phone back to Dan.

'Wow, that's pretty amazing,' he said. 'And he kept it a secret?'

'Yes, although Fletch, Tom and Nathan were in on it.'

'Have you seen it yet, Jess?' asked Dan.

'No, not yet. I was going to go over on Sunday, but Nathan convinced me they might appreciate some together time on their first day.' She shrugged her shoulders and rolled her eyes. 'I've seen the photos, though, and I can't believe he kept it quiet.'

Holly bounded back up the stairs with food for Max. Jess frowned as Max set upon the plate gratefully. 'Did you take a break for lunch?' she asked.

Max shook her head, her mouth full of generously buttered scone. 'I was going to but somehow forgot.'

'You need to eat, Max. Richie wouldn't be happy if he knew. I promised him we'd look after you.'

'I know, but he's not going to know, is he? It was only today, and I'm eating now, so no harm done. Holly, have you seen the mural Richie painted in Piglet's room?' Her smile was sheepish.

'And changing the subject isn't going to make me forget,' chided Jess. 'I mean it, Max. How do I know you'll look after yourself when I'm not here if you can't do it when I am? I only agreed to you working so close to the due date because you promised you'd take it easy.' She turned her attention to Dan. 'When's Mia starting?'

Dan had hired Mia, a local girl running a pop-up bake stall at the lakefront markets, to replace Max.

'She starts tomorrow,' said Dan.

'Okay,' Jess said. 'Dad's in my ear about how if

we're not careful, Max will give birth on the floor in here.' She laughed loudly at the look of horror on Dan's face.

'Don't worry, Dan,' said Max. 'That's the last thing I want too!' Holding onto the arm of the chair, Max leveraged to her feet, the effort showing on her face. 'Okay, that's me done. Richie will be by to pick me up shortly, so I'll see you two tomorrow,' she said to Dan and Holly, 'and I'll see you next week,' she said to Jess.

Max blew them kisses and, clasping to the handrail, walked slowly and carefully down the stairs.

Jess watched her with concern. While there were still a few weeks before Max's due date, even though she didn't complain – if you didn't count the occasional relieved sigh as a complaint – Max was finding it more difficult to get through the day. Where Max had always been fit and active, these days, her walk was more of a waddle. Seeing the care she took with the stairs, she must be feeling as though her centre of gravity had shifted and was worried she'd miss a step and end up tumbling down. Max loved her work – and they'd all miss her while she was on leave – the sooner she hung up her apron, the more comfortable Jess would feel.

Soon after Max left, Holly finished cleaning down and said her goodbyes, leaving Dan and Jess in the kitchen.

Closing her laptop, Jess wandered over to where Dan was plating up toast and mushrooms. 'What are you working on?' she asked. 'Don't we already do toast and mushrooms?'

Dan looked up from the plate and grinned at her. 'Yes, but not like this mushroom toast.' He passed over a small bowl filled with a dark puree. 'Try this,' he encouraged, handing her a teaspoon.

Jess took a small amount from the edge of her spoon and licked it. 'Oh. My. God. What is that?'

'You like it?'

'Yes, I think so, but it's different from anything else I've tried.' Jess's brow furrowed as she attempted to isolate the flavours.

'It's mushroom ketchup – essentially a mushroom Worcestershire sauce. I've sprinkled some into creamed baked garlic and spread that on sourdough toast before finishing with the mushrooms – which I've cooked in butter and finished with lemon and parsley. I think I'll put it on the specials board this weekend.' He cut one slice in half and handed it to her, popping the rest into his mouth.

With her hand under her chin to catch any drips, Jess took a bite and nodded slowly. 'You should – this is great.'

'Thanks.' He smiled quickly and lowered his head before taking the frypan he'd used across to the sink.

'Is everything okay, Dan?'

'Sure, why do you ask?'

Jess hesitated over her reply. There was nothing

she could put a finger on, but Dan wasn't himself. If he was, he would've gone into more detail regarding the components of the dish – whether she was interested or not. If he was himself, he would've laughed harder at the baby banter, and rather than saying 'whatever you think best', he would've expressed more of an opinion about changing the supplier of their pastries when she'd asked him about that earlier today. If he was himself, he wouldn't have avoided meeting her eyes as he was doing now.

Maybe he'd been disappointed in love again. Dan, like her, had a habit of falling for seasonal visitors – the snow bunnies here for the winter or the backpackers here for the summer. They used to laugh about it, commiserating with each other over a beer at The Rugby Club, but it had been months since they'd done that. Not since Nathan came into her life. Dan had always been there to pick her up, and now that she had Nathan, he must feel as though she'd pushed him aside. Some friend she'd turned out to be.

'No reason,' she said now, frowning as his face fell, as if he were hoping for more from her. 'Hey, do you want to catch up for a beer when I'm back? At the club like we used to. We can even'—she shrugged one shoulder and grinned— 'talk about something other than work.'

A glimmer of something flickered in his eyes. 'Sounds good, Jess.' He finished wiping down the bench and took his apron off, hanging it on the row of hooks at the back of the kitchen. Collecting his backpack from the same place, he said, 'You tramp safely, eh?'

'I will.' Jess wasn't entirely convinced by the warmth of his smile but returned it anyway. 'Have a good night; I won't be far behind you.'

Dan slipped into his backpack and waved before disappearing down the stairs.

Jess slid her laptop into its bag, tidied her work area and switched off all the lights. Downstairs was empty – the café had closed, and the crew had left for the night. Locking the door behind her, she halted. 'Max, what are you still doing here?' Max sat on the bench seat out the front of the café, one hand on her belly, the other holding her phone. On hearing Jess's voice, she put her phone back into her bag. 'You left ages ago – at least forty minutes. Have you been out here the whole time?' She didn't give Max a chance to answer before asking, 'Where's Richie? It's not like him to keep you waiting.'

'He's on his way,' said Max. 'He's been out at Bannockburn seeing a potential client and lost track of time.'

Jess raised her eyebrows in disbelief. Richie never lost track of time where Max was concerned. 'Really? Do you want me to sit and wait with you?'

'I'm fine,' said Max. 'He'll be here any second. In fact, that's him coming around the corner now.'

Despite Max's protests, Jess hung around until

Richie pulled up beside them.

'What's going on,' Jess asked when she opened the passenger door for Max.

'Nothing,' said Richie. 'I just got caught up.'

Another one who wouldn't meet her eyes. What was it with Dan and Richie today? Richie leaned across to kiss Max's lips. 'I'm so sorry, Maxi,' he said.

'It's okay,' said Max, smiling gently. 'You're here now.'

'Have a good night, you two,' said Jess, shutting the door on them. As the car pulled away, she smiled; Richie would be already questioning Max about her day, whether she was too tired, and how Piglet had been behaving. With a little sigh, she admitted to herself that she envied their routine and their closeness. It was lovely having Nathan here on the weekends, but somehow that just made the evenings during the week when she had no one waiting for her at home seem lonely.

She reminded herself that it wouldn't be long before he finished his project and was here all the time. That time would pass in a flash, and Jess couldn't wait.

Max was aware something was very wrong. Richie had tried to look and act normally and had ignored the accusing look Jess had given him and her criticism of his tardiness; he didn't need to hear that from her; he felt bad enough for keeping Max waiting. He'd leant across and kissed Max on the mouth as he always did, enquired after her day, asked how Piglet was behaving, whether she'd stopped for some lunch, taken it easy. That was all normal.

When he started on a story about the customer who came in and wanted a hedging plant that never needed trimming, Max placed her hand on his knee. 'What's wrong?'

'What makes you think there's anything wrong?'

'Where shall I start? Because your jaw has been clenched since I slid into the car, your knuckles are white on the steering wheel, and you can't even look me in the eye.' She paused. 'Plus, you lost track of time, and that hasn't happened since we've been together. Mostly though, because I know you, Richie, and you've currently got the same look on your face as when you were getting ready to leave Brookford without telling me.' She paused and squeezed his leg gently. 'And if memory serves me correctly, that didn't go well. Whatever it is, you can tell me – I don't need wrapping in cotton wool.'

He took his eyes off the road for a second. Max's expression on her face told him there was no point in trying to hide.

'Fletch and I argued,' he said, sighing heavily. 'About Flynn's Folly.'

'I see,' said Max. 'Now tell me, what's really wrong?'

How did she know? 'Couldn't it just be that?'

THE LITTLE CAFE BY THE LAKE

'It could be,' she said with a hint of scepticism in her voice, 'but it's not. What's going on, Richie?'

'My father is in town,' he said simply.

Silence filled the car. He waited for her to say something like, 'What are you talking about? Your father lives here.' Instead, she touched his jaw lightly – right on the spot where the little pulse beat. Without taking his eyes from the road, he rested his cheek against her hand.

'Well,' she said. 'That's unexpected.'

His mouth curled into a smile and he snorted. 'That, my darling, is the understatement of the year.'

Fletch paced up and down the living room while Milly wiped down already clean benches in the kitchen.

'Tea?' she asked, flicking the switch on the kettle.

He stopped pacing long enough to smile briefly and say, 'No thanks.'

They both knew she'd only offered it to have something to do.

'Cam, please stop pacing.'

'And do what?'

'I don't know! Just stop pacing; it's doing my head in.' She walked into the living room and sank into the lounge. 'You've hardly said a thing to me since Gary left. How can I know what to say or what to do if you won't even talk to me about it?'

Cam stalled but didn't turn to look at her. 'What

do you want me to say, Milly? There's nothing I can say.' He shook his head sadly. 'There's nothing I can do.' He screwed his eyes tightly closed and tipped his head back. When he opened them again, he looked squarely at Milly. 'We have to tell them the truth. We should've known it would catch up with us one day – that he'd catch up with us.'

'We haven't exactly tried to hide away,' she said. 'Gary could've found us any time he wanted to – but he hasn't wanted to.'

'Until now.'

'I'm sorry, Cam.' A tear tracked its way down her cheek. The bleak despair in Cam's eyes seemed unfathomable. 'This is my fault.'

Cam was quickly on the seat beside her, cradling her in his arms. 'Oh, my darling, this is no one's fault. If anything, it's mine. I fell in love with you all those years ago. You were married to Gary, and I should've walked away, but I couldn't. And when he left, what else could I do but help you with Cate and Richie? This isn't your fault, Milly, and it's not mine. He's the one who cheated, and he's the one who left, and that's the only thing we need to remember.'

'But we're the ones who lied, Cam,' she said.

'Yes, we did. And now it's time to tell the truth.'

'What if we lose them?' Milly clung tightly to him as the unimaginable became real to her. 'Rick's only just come back, and he and Max are so happy. Then there's the baby.'

'We'll deal with it the same way we've dealt with everything over the years. Together.'

Milly pressed her cheek against his chest, but his words did nothing to calm the churning of her stomach. She needed to find out why Gary was *really* here – before he ruined everything.

CHAPTER EIGHT

Jess loved her job as a guide on two of what they termed New Zealand's "Great Walks". She'd begun with a summer job back when she finished school and had been guiding ever since. That first summer had been tough, and Jess still remembered how sore her feet were after her first tour, the blisters upon blisters, her leather boots taking time to mould to her feet. She'd learnt over the years to break in new boots gradually, in-between wearing her old ones. It helped too that she tramped all year round.

Blisters aside, she'd learnt so much about New Zealand's plant and bird life during her years on track – and even more about human nature. Tramping brought out the best – and the worst in people. Jess had figured out that most trampers on tour fitted into one of three major groups – and you could usually pick who would be in which category before they even set foot on track.

First up were the sprinters. These guys were competitive and had to be first – first out, first back to lodge, and first to get their clothes washed and hanging in the drying rooms each night. They took few photos, stopped rarely, and missed much of the birdlife and tranquillity found in nature. They tended to stick with their own kind in the lodge and not mix with their fellow walkers or guides.

Next were the regular trampers who pulled their boots and their packs on each morning and strode off with a smile and at a leisurely pace – one that rarely changed over the day. They stopped to appreciate their surroundings, talked good naturedly with anyone else they encountered, and enjoyed the company of others each evening, often bolstering the spirits of those who weren't coping quite as well. These guys, when younger, would've been freedom walkers – carrying everything they needed on their backs and staying in the Department of Conservation, or DOC, huts.

The third group were the recreational walkers. Most banded together with friends and partners to challenge themselves or tick off a bucket-list item, although some travelled solo, and others were there with partners (some obviously) under sufferance. This group tended to opt for the ensuite accommodation and private rooms at the lodge. It was also with this group where Jess found her job to be most rewarding. Watching people have breakthroughs, accomplish things they never thought possible, and seeing the wonder of nature through fresh eyes was a gift she never tired of witnessing. It reminded her of the tour at the end of last year when she'd met Nathan and Kate and had gotten to know Tom better. While Nathan and Tom were fit, Kate had been underprepared – for both the physical and the environmental conditions. Grief had also weighed her down – her grief as heavy as a backpack she could never take off. It had been a privilege to watch her and Nathan process that at the top of Mackinnon Pass; the experience cathartic for them both.

Today, the Routeburn trampers gave her no time to think about what might be going on with her friends and family back in Queenstown. A full group, it had the usual mix of participants, but there were a couple who were particularly challenging.

It hadn't helped that the rain had begun at Te Anau and, by the time the group had alighted from the bus at The Divide, had become steady. The regular hikers put their waterproofs and pack covers on and started walking while the newbies struggled with poles. One well made-up woman, who was walking with her husband as part of his sixtieth birthday challenge, wondered aloud if they might wait until the downpour had passed before starting. Jess bit the inside of her lip to stop smiling while she explained that where they were, in Fiordland National Park, was one of the wettest places in the world.

'We get almost seven metres of rain here a year,' she explained. 'And, given that it rains on average nearly two hundred days a year, if we stopped to wait for it to pass, we could be waiting a good while.'

She'd smiled encouragingly as the woman sent her husband a look that had daggers in it and would be capable of shrivelling the souls of many men in one glance. Steve, her husband, however, was made of sterner stuff.

'Come on Margot,' he said, 'the sooner we get walking, the sooner we'll get to the lodge. Besides, once you're wet, you can't get wetter.'

She'd sniffed, unconvinced, and Jess had said, 'I'll walk with you guys, shall I?'

The track climbed steadily almost immediately – as did Margot's complaints. 'How much further?' she asked after they'd been walking for around fifteen minutes.

'We'll be climbing for about an hour. It doesn't matter how long we take, though; there's plenty to see along the way,' Jess said, stopping to point out a waterfall through the trees. 'This is what I love about rainy days in this part of the forest – the sudden waterfalls.'

'I'm loving the green,' said Steve. 'It feels as though it's dripping from the trees.'

Jess smiled over at him and agreed. The beech forest was as beautiful in the rain as it was on a fine day – unfortunately, it did, however, make the track heavier going – especially after the lunch stop when the path was steeper and rockier.

'Wait till you see Earland Falls,' she said. 'It's at about the halfway point this afternoon, and it's truly spectacular. On a day like today, you'll come around the corner, and they'll be there – spilling off a mountain that you hadn't even been able to see a minute before.'

The DOC hut was their lunch stop, and Jess checked in with some of the other trampers. Another guide had already departed with the front-runners, and the middle group had finished eating and was about to do the same. Jess had a few words with Louise, the other guide.

'You head off with that group if you like; I'm happy to stay with these guys.'

'Are you sure?' asked Louise. Even though the policy was always to have one guide up front, one somewhere around the middle, and one at the end, usually the guides swapped their positions around throughout the day.

Jess gave a quick nod. 'It's fine. See you down there.'

After checking in with the other trampers in the hut to make sure no one had hot spots on their feet or were having trouble distributing the weight of their pack on their backs, Jess went to Margot and Steve who were sitting away from the main group.

Margot complained hers was too heavy.

'It's okay,' said Steve, 'I'll carry a few things.'

Jess almost laughed aloud at what Steve was

transferring from Margot's bag to his own – especially when it included a hairdryer and make-up bag. No wonder she was finding it too heavy.

While Margot was off in the bathroom, Steve said, apologetically, 'I know what you're thinking. They told us at the briefing to only bring one change of clothes – that we could wash everything at night – and that we shouldn't be carrying more than about seven kilos on our backs, but …'

Jess bit down on a grin but said nothing. There was no use for either make-up or a hairdryer out here.

'I know she doesn't want to be here – she's doing it for me,' he said as if that explained it.

'Let me know if you need help,' she said gently. 'That's what we're here for.'

His smile was grateful.

The rain had reduced to a drizzle by the time they'd climbed to the falls and was more like a heavy mist as they began the steep, rocky descent to the lodge. By now, the group with Jess had swollen to a half dozen trampers.

'Just take it easy,' Jess urged after checking their poles and lengthening them slightly for extra stability where necessary. 'Check where you're putting your feet and don't rush it.'

A few hours later, back at the lodge, Jess greeted the other guides, had a quick shower, dealt with her laundry and was back in the common room to help with dinner and the evening briefings. She was pleased to see that Margot looked happier. She and Steve were sitting with another two couples from this afternoon's group and were relaxing with glasses of wine. Margot was using her hands to make a point about something and laughed out loud about something else. Steve caught Jess's eye and gave her a quick thumbs up. She grinned at him and left them to it. It had been a tough day for Margot, and Jess hoped that after a hearty dinner, a good night's sleep and (fingers crossed) better weather tomorrow, she'd enjoy it a little more.

It was only later that evening, after everyone had retired for the night and the generators had been switched off, that Jess allowed herself to relax. She'd tramped this track more times than she cared to remember and knew it like the back of her hand, but today had been tough.

Forcing herself to think about something else, she remembered the phone call with Milly the other night. What was it about that? It was something about the man who'd asked after them on Saturday morning. While she'd thought nothing of it at the time, she could've sworn her mother had hesitated on the phone that night, that she knew the man who hadn't left his name.

There was something familiar about the stranger – even Nathan had noticed it. He'd phoned on Sunday night when he got off the ferry to tell her so.

'How do you know him?' she'd asked.

'I don't. I've never seen him before in my life, but there's something about him ...'

'He's probably one of those people who always looks like someone you know,' she said. 'It's like Dan – he says that everywhere he goes, people say he reminds them of their brother or cousin or someone they knew at school.'

'That must be it,' said Nathan, but he hadn't sounded convinced.

It was only now, lying in the dark, that the thought hit her. The stranger reminded her of Richie – or Richie if he was thirty years older. And given that her mother was an only child with no close living relatives, that could only mean the stranger was someone from Richie's father's side ... or Richie's father.

Jess had never seen pictures of Richie's birth father. It wasn't so much that Milly had kept it all a secret – it was common knowledge that Milly's first husband had walked out when Richie was only a few months old. Fletch was the only father Cate and Richie knew. It was more that no one was interested enough to talk about Gary Evans. It was as if he'd never existed. Richie had certainly never mentioned him and nor, to the best of her knowledge, had Cate.

Jess recalled her mother saying to Fletch, soon after Richie and Max had come back to Queenstown, how much he'd grown to look like *his* father. Fletch had agreed and then said, 'Thankfully though, he's nothing like him in other ways.' Milly had chuckled softly, and they had changed the subject.

Could the stranger have been Gary Evans? And if it had been, had she done the wrong thing to mention his visit to her mother? After all, the man had said he probably wouldn't have time to look them up. Maybe she'd jumped to the wrong conclusion, and he wasn't Gary but a brother or a cousin or something. After all, if it had been Richie's father, surely, he would've reacted when Jess had mentioned his name and surely, he'd want to make sure he made contact.

It was times like tonight when Jess wished they had cellphone reception out here. She could've called Nathan and talked it through with him. He'd make sense of it all – he always made sense of things, even when Jess felt as though she were spinning madly.

Jess couldn't explain what it was, but Nathan calmed the wild edges of her thoughts and put things into their proper perspective. She had a feeling that Nathan saw below the surface toughness she cultivated – and she wasn't sure whether that scared her or comforted her. He was getting too close; she was getting too attached, and where would that leave her if he went home at the end of this project? Even though that was something she'd refused to even consider during the daylight hours, here in the middle of the New Zealand wilderness in the pitch black and complete quiet, it was a possibility.

The way Jess figured it, if she refused to

contemplate the thought that he'd be going home sometime, it wouldn't happen. That if she only sent positive thoughts out to the universe, they would materialise. While she wasn't sure how she'd adapt to a life without him in it, there was no question of her giving up what she'd worked for to follow any man – not even one like Nathan. He had to stay. She refused to consider the alternative.

CHAPTER NINE

On Tuesday when Gary called by, Milly had been unprepared, but this morning, she deliberated for ages over what to wear. While she didn't want to be seen to be dressing up for him, there was a part of her that needed him to know he hadn't broken her, and yes, even to see what he'd missed out on by leaving. She spent longer applying her make-up and fingered some mousse through her hair to give her curls more lift. She'd slipped on her most flattering pair of jeans with an olive-green long-sleeved t-shirt and a scarf that picked up the autumn colours outside and brought out the green-gold tints in her hazel eyes.

Milly had arrived at the café early, walking inside to check that Gary wasn't waiting, before coming out again and feigned interest in the other tenancies. Glancing at her watch for the twentieth time, she sighed inwardly when she realised just a few minutes had passed since the last time she'd checked it. From the corner of her eye, there was movement. Gary walked along the footpath until he reached the door, ignoring her outstretched hand to shake; instead, kissing her cheek. The half-smile on his face showing he registered her discomfort. She reminded herself (again) that Gary was just someone she used to know – and any power he may have once held over her was long gone.

'It looks like we need to order at the counter, so why don't we do that and find somewhere to sit,' she said, her eyes scanning the café to avoid meeting his.

'Sounds fine. Then we can catch up.' He raised one eyebrow. 'I assume that's why you wanted to see me?'

There was no reason for Milly to be flustered, but, she reasoned, it wasn't every day you met up with the man who had been your first real love and who was the father of two of your children. Cam's face swam before her. She shook her head to clear the vision, smiled tightly and led Gary to a table at the back of the room, feeling his knowing grin on her back as she walked.

'I take it you don't come here often?' he said once they'd sat down. When her brows raised in a silent question, he added, 'You didn't know whether it was table service or not.'

The café, in a business park in Frankton on the road towards Shotover, was far enough out of town, she'd figured, that she was unlikely to see anyone she knew. Milly shrugged one shoulder, the movement deliberately light.

'Does Cam know we're meeting today?'

Milly pushed away the guilt and ignored his question. 'Why are you here, Gary?'

He tilted his head slightly to the side. It was something he did that made anyone in his orbit feel as though they were the complete focus of his attention. It was a trick that used to work on her too, but not anymore. 'Because you asked me here,' he said, matter of fact.

'You know what I meant,' she said.

He half-smiled, his eyes set on her determined expression. 'As I said the other day, I found myself in Queenstown and remembered you and Cam had moved here, so thought I might look you up.'

Milly narrowed her eyes. There was no reason not to believe what he said, but there was something … She remembered hearing somewhere how everyone has a "tell" – something they do all the time when they were lying. Milly hadn't worked out what Gary's "tell" was until the end, but she'd never forgotten. His was a slight tilt in the corner of his mouth, the tiniest of movements, but it was there. 'Now that you've looked us up, you can continue with your holiday then.'

'That was before I knew Richie was here. Again, as I said the other day, I'm prepared to wait around to see him.'

'You obviously haven't given a thought to either Richie or Cate over the past thirty-odd years, so why start now?'

'How do you know I haven't thought about them? Of course I've thought about them; they're my children.'

Milly searched for the "tell" as coffees were placed in front of them, and Gary flashed the waitress, a tired-looking middle-aged woman, one of his best smiles. Milly groaned inwardly and tutted to herself as the woman beamed in the face of it, making her look years younger. 'All I'm saying is you haven't tried to contact us in the past, so why now? I wrote to you when we left Australia and told you what we were planning and heard nothing from you. I even sent you details of where we'd settled in case you ever wanted to see the kids and heard nothing, so why now?'

Gary tore open a sachet of sugar, stirred it into his coffee and took a sip before answering her. 'Because I'm getting older. Rachel and I didn't have children together—'

'Didn't she have her own children?'

'Yes, two daughters, and they have children of their own now, and I wondered whether I might be a grandfather and not know it.'

Milly snorted in disbelief. 'And you thought you could swan on into our lives?'

'No. It just made me realise how much I'd missed out on when you took our children away.'

'When I took?' Milly shook her head and forced herself to take a breath and lower her voice. 'When I took the children away? You moved to the other side of the country with another woman and her family.'

'And you took my children out of the country.'

'You could've stopped me but chose not to.' Her stare was steely, and he dropped his eyes first. 'You made your choice Gary, and it didn't involve our kids.'

'You've certainly grown a backbone since we separated,' he said, his tone even, lifting his coffee cup to take a sip.

'I had to,' she retorted. 'I had two children under two I needed to look after.'

'Touché.' Gary clapped his hands. 'How long have you been waiting to say that? Besides, Cam was quick to step into my shoes. He'd been sniffing around you from the minute I introduced you both. How do I know Richie isn't his?'

Milly sat back in her chair, her eyes wide. 'You can't be serious?' she said through clenched teeth.

He shrugged one shoulder and then laughed shortly, mirthlessly. 'I know Cam had too much integrity to make a move on you – even when he knew what I was up to while he was covering for me. How long did it take after I left? One month? Two?'

'Two years.' Milly's tone was expressionless.

'Two years? You made the poor bastard wait that long?' Milly had forgotten how much Gary used to enjoy laughing at other people. Cam had borne the brunt of a few of his "jokes" while they were "friends". Milly later learned that Cam had tolerated Gary so he could stay close to her and be there to support her when Gary finally broke her heart – as Cam had known he would.

'What about you?' she asked. 'Are you and Rachel still together?'

He shook his head. 'No.'

'What happened?'

'Do you have to ask?'

Milly shook her head and laughed ruefully. 'No, I don't suppose I do. As they say, leopards can't change their spots.'

Milly wondered how long Gary had lasted before he'd cheated on Rachel – or how long Rachel had put up with his cheating – but wasn't going to give him the satisfaction of asking.

They finished their coffees, giving Milly a minute or two to catch her breath and gather her thoughts. 'Seriously, though, why are you here?'

'I really am here to find out about the kids. I hurt you a long time ago, Melinda, and I don't blame you for hating me, but I've missed out on my kids, and I want to get to know them.'

Milly stared at him for a few long seconds, almost believing him, but remembering that this was Gary and everything he did had a reason. She shook her head and straightened her spine. 'You could've done that – as per our deal, I sent you regular updates until they turned eighteen. I would never have stopped you from seeing them, and now they're both grown adults and can make up their own minds.'

He leaned forward, resting his hands on the table. 'Tell me about them.'

Milly hesitated. As illogical as it was, telling him about Cate and Richie was letting him into their lives, and Milly wasn't sure she wanted to do that. But she didn't know whether she had the right to exclude him either.

'Please,' he added, so quietly it was barely a whisper.

She bit her bottom lip before nodding – after all, he was their father. 'Okay, well, Cate lives in Sydney now. She did an economics degree in Auckland, and then the bank she was working for transferred her to Sydney. She's been there for about ten years, I'd say.'

'You said yesterday she's married?'

'Yes, to Harry. No children though, I think they both decided not to – Harry travels a lot.'

'And Richie?'

'He's always been creative and always loved gardens, so he studied in Melbourne – landscape design. His dream is to design a garden for Chelsea Flower Show one year.' She smiled at the thought. 'He travelled a bit when he graduated and has spent the last five or six years in England. Now he and Max are back; he's working with Cam – the plan has always been for him to one day take over Lakeview Landscaping.'

'And who's Max?'

'Richie's partner.' When his eyebrows rose, she added, 'It's really Maxine, but everyone calls her Max.'

'They're not married?'

'Not yet. They're engaged, but they've delayed the wedding until after the baby comes.' Milly closed her eyes briefly as she realised what she'd said.

'They're having a baby?' Gary sat taller; a smile spread across his face. 'I'm going to be a grandfather?'

'Of sorts. You might be Richie's father, but Cam is his dad. This is our grandchild, not yours.' Her nerve endings bristled, and she squared her shoulders, her chin jutted out.

'Blood is thicker than water,' he said, shrugging as if what she'd said meant nothing to him.

'Not in your case.'

'We'll see. Have you told him I'm here?' She nodded. 'And that I want to see him?' She nodded again. 'What has he said about it?'

'He hasn't decided if he wants to see you yet.'

'Are you going to encourage him to?'

Milly held his gaze, pursed her lips and shook her head slowly. 'No, I don't think I will. He can make that decision for himself.'

'I see. I'd suggest you might want to encourage him a little, sway him in my direction.' There was a gleam in his eye that Milly didn't like at all.

'Why would I want to do that?'

'Because my dear Melinda, I have some papers

you've wanted me to sign for some time, and I might finally be ready to do so.'

Late on Thursday afternoon, Richie was working on some preliminary sketches for Flynn's Folly when Fletch entered the office and sat heavily in his chair.

'Sometimes I think I'm getting too old for this,' Fletch muttered with a heavy sigh.

Richie looked up from his pad and grinned cheekily. 'Old bones, Dad?'

'Something like that,' he said ruefully, rolling his left shoulder forward and back.

'Are you alright? Your back's not playing up again, is it?'

'No,' said Fletch. 'I'm just a bit stiff in the muscles back there. It's been a big week for deliveries.'

'Yeah, it's been a big week all round.'

'Sure has,' Fletch said, nodding slowly before releasing a deep sigh and leaning back in his chair. After a few seconds of silence, he asked, 'In all the drama of Tuesday afternoon, I forgot to ask how you went out at the Folly.'

'Good,' said Richie. 'I think the job is mine as long as he likes the final design, and the price comes in where I think it will. Flynn also indicated yesterday he'd be looking to do the project in stages with a kick-off in July – which would suit my timing.'

'That's good,' said Fletch. 'Have you got anything

I can look at?'

Richie recognised the question for what it was – his father offering him an olive branch – and passed across the sketch book.

'I like what you're doing here,' he said. 'Using the thyme, lavender and rosemary with the local rock will help the garden blend into the landscape while still being attractive – especially as it drops away to the vines.'

Fletch leafed through the pages, making other comments. When he shut the book and handed it back to Richie, he said, 'I'm sorry for what I said on Tuesday, Rick. I didn't mean it to come out the way it did.'

'It's okay, Dad. I overreacted too.'

'Your mother suggested I might be a bit set in my ways – just a wee bit, you understand.'

Richie chuckled. 'Oh, I understand. Maxi suggested I might be a bit that way too – although she used the word stubborn, and I don't think I'm that.'

Fletch laughed with him. 'Funnily enough, that's the word your mother used too.' He sobered and said, 'In all seriousness, Rick, we're going to have our disagreements; I just want you to understand that it's never because I doubt your ability.'

'Thanks, Dad; I appreciate you saying that.'

'Everything else okay? With you and Max?'

'We're good. While we appreciate you guys putting us up for so long, we're loving having our own space. It's just all a bit …'

'Overwhelming?'

'Yeah.'

'I remember,' said Fletch with a grimace. 'I was shit-scared even though I'd been around for you and Cate, but watching your mother go through it with Jess …' He shook his head. 'It's okay to be scared, though. I reckon it'd be worse if you didn't care.'

Richie hesitated before asking, 'What was my … What was Gary like? When Mum was pregnant with me?'

Fletch sucked in a breath. 'Now, there's a question. To be honest, I don't know. He didn't talk about it, and if anyone asked, he'd say what was expected and change the subject.' He met Richie's eyes. 'Your mother doesn't talk a lot about those days, so I only know what I saw and the few things she said at the time. It's fair to say she struggled with being pregnant and having Cate toddling about; I don't think she got the support I gave her when Jess came along – and that I see you giving Max now.' He paused and added, 'Your parents had a different relationship to what you and Max have and what your mother and I have had. That's all you need to remember, Rick. The best thing you can do for Max is to continue to love and respect her.'

That was the longest speech his father had ever given. 'Thanks, Dad.' He tapped his finger against his jaw. 'Do you think I should meet him? Gary, I mean?'

Fletch's eyes skittered away. 'That's up to you.'

'What does Mum think?'

'That it's a decision you need to make,' Fletch said quietly.

'Will you be hurt if I do?'

Fletch shook his head and met Richie's gaze. 'No, son. I won't be disappointed whichever way you go.'

Richie opened his mouth and shut it again. 'Okay.'

'Now, don't you think you should get home to Max?'

'Yeah, I'll hit the road.' Richie stood and packed up his paperwork until the desk was as neat as it had been when he started that morning. 'Thanks, Dad.'

As he turned to go, Fletch said gruffly. 'I know we've had some differences of late, but your mother and I couldn't be prouder of you, you know.'

Suddenly choked up, all Richie could do was smile tightly and squeeze Fletch's shoulder on the way out.

CHAPTER TEN

'Gary's in town.' It was early Friday morning, and Milly
was at Cover To Cover helping Kate stock the shelves
with the new releases she'd received the previous day.

Kate hesitated for only a second before saying in
an even tone, 'Gary, as in first husband, Gary? The one
who cheated on you when you were pregnant and left
when you had two babies under two? That Gary?'

'Yep. That Gary.'

Kate slid the last book into its spot on the shelf
and climbed down and off the stepladder. Meeting
Milly's eyes, she said slowly, 'I see. Let's take this into
the garden.'

'I don't want to hold you up.' Milly pretended
to straighten some books before turning back to her
friend. 'But I'd really appreciate a friendly ear.'

Kate closed the stepladder, resting it against the
bookshelf and smiled sympathetically. 'It's fine, Milly.
We don't open until ten, and I can get Sandie to do
that. Besides, after unpacking those boxes, I think we
both need a cuppa.'

Milly let out the breath she didn't realise she'd been holding. Although she'd only known Kate for a few months, the two women had fast become friends, and Kate was the only person she felt she could confide in. After a few days of going through the motions and trying to tiptoe around Cam and Richie, she desperately needed to unburden on someone.

While Kate made tea, Milly wandered into the little courtyard where Kate had set up some tables and chairs. Kate intended for Cover To Cover, or C2C as they'd all begun to call it, to be a place where people could sit and read, sit and work, or just sit and be still. Pots and planter boxes contained herbs and salad vegetables, and quirky garden ornaments were randomly placed amongst the greenery. On the lawn beyond the courtyard was a long timber table with bench seats which Kate intended to utilise in the warmer months for pop-up supper clubs, and she'd earmarked the free-standing studio for small classes – something she'd launch later in the year. Kate had accomplished so much in the two months C2C had been open that Milly had to remind herself it had only been two months.

While the morning was cool, the sky was blue, and the sun had turned the autumn hues in the trees to bright flame-like shades of gold and red and orange. The hill behind where she sat was alive with the colours. A tui sang in the branches, the little white tuft of feathers at its throat looking like a ball of cotton wool. Milly sat and listened to its complicated song while she waited for Kate.

'A penny for them?' Kate placed a tray with a pot of tea, two vintage china cups and a plate holding a couple of slices of lemon drizzle cake on the table.

'I was thinking how much you've accomplished since you've been here.'

Kate's eyes wandered around the courtyard, and she smiled with quiet pride. 'I wouldn't have thought it possible either,' she said. 'And while the bookshop is up and running, there's still plenty I need to do, but that will come.'

'I bet this time last year you wouldn't have thought you'd be here.'

Kate shook her head, her look pensive. 'No. This time last year, I was in Sydney in the middle of wedding planning for Ash and Reece. Nathan was in Cairns doing whatever he does up there, and Neil was alive and with Vanessa.' She leant forward and poured tea in both cups. 'Since then, everything has changed. Neil and I got back together, Ash and Reece married, Neil passed away, and Nathan and I came here to do a simple little hike and climb a mountain; and ended up staying.' She let out a short laugh, smiling at the irony and random nature of life. 'I suppose Vanessa will have had the baby by now too,' she mused. 'For a while, that consumed me and now? I haven't thought about her and what she tried to do to our lives in such a long time. It feels like it all happened to someone else in another lifetime.' She sipped at her tea. 'Which brings me to you and your ex-husband and what he's doing here.'

Milly broke off a piece of cake and popped it into her mouth, letting it dissolve on her tongue, savouring the sweet tang of lemon. 'I don't really know why he's here. He says he was in the area; knew we were here and thought he'd catch up.'

'But you don't believe him?'

'No. I've made no secret of where we were, but Gary has wanted nothing to do with any of us for all this time. Now he says he wants to get to know Rick and Max and intends to stay around to meet the baby. He hasn't said much about Cate – not that I've told her as much – and he's not at all interested in Jess, but then why would he be? She's Cam's daughter.'

'How's Richie taking it?'

Milly shrugged. 'He's putting a brave face on it and Max is holding him together – or it could be that he's holding himself together for her sake. I'm not sure which.' She laughed mirthlessly. 'At first, he was adamant he wanted nothing to do with him, and now he's playing the wait and see game as far as I can tell.'

'Has he met Gary yet?'

'No. Jess has though – not that she knew it.' Kate raised a brow in silent question. 'He went into Beach Road last weekend when Jess and Nathan were in there.

He said he was an old friend of Cam's, but he didn't leave his name, and Jess had no idea who he was.' She took another sip of her tea. 'As soon as she described him, I knew, though.' She placed her teacup back on its saucer and scratched idly at her collarbone. 'He called in at the garden centre on Tuesday. Rick, by chance, was out seeing a client.'

'How was it?'

Milly hesitated before answering. 'He's the same Gary, just older. He still looks fit, and he still has his own hair, and he still has that cockney cheekiness I fell for all those years ago.' She let out a short laugh and shook her head at the memory. She'd been so young and so ready to fall in love.

'How was Fletch about it?'

'He's hardly said a word since. Gary has always made him feel … I don't know, less than himself. Cam hasn't said as much, but I know he's beating himself up being on the back foot and not saying the things he always told himself he'd say one day.' She lifted one shoulder in a half shrug. 'But that's how Gary makes you feel. He never really had many male friends – and those he had were there to support him, cover for him and make him look good. I doubt if that's changed.'

Kate topped up the teas. The tui was still singing, its chirp joined by the chime of a bellbird. 'What did they say when Gary said he'd stay around for the birth?'

'Who?'

'Fletch and Richie.'

Milly dropped her eyes, her fingers crumbling the remaining cake on her plate. 'I haven't told them,' she said in a small voice.

Kate looked confused. 'But you said Fletch was there and ...' The penny dropped. 'They don't know because you've seen him since then.'

Milly looked away briefly, her lips pursed. 'Yes. I met him yesterday.'

'And you didn't tell Fletch.' Milly shook her head. 'Oh, Milly.'

Milly let out the breath she'd been holding in a heavy sigh and attempted a smile that didn't quite work. 'I know I should've told him, but he's so worried that somehow he's going to alienate Rick – they've been arguing about work – that I didn't know how to tell him I was meeting Gary. And now that I have met him, I'm worried that if I tell Cam about it, he'll wonder why I'd kept it from him in the first place.'

'You can't blame him for that.' Kate's tone was gentle, but she was chiding her.

'No, I know, but I needed to know why he was here.'

'So you reached out to him?'

Milly nodded miserably. 'We met at a coffee shop in Frankton. It was strange seeing him again after all those years. I'd wondered how I'd feel, but when I looked at him, other than a little tummy tremble – which I put down to memory – I felt absolutely nothing. I thought I might still hate him – even though, in hindsight, he did me a favour in leaving. Cam was a far better partner for me and father for the kids than Gary ever was – and as far as role models go, I hate to think how Rick might've turned out if he had Gary to look up to.'

She took a thoughtful sip of her tea as she struggled for the words to help Kate understand. 'I was pregnant with Cate the first time I caught Gary out in a lie; I suspected he was having an affair, but I didn't want to know because I didn't want to have to *do* anything about it. When you're pregnant with your first child, it's supposed to be a special time.'

She smiled quickly when she realised what she'd said and that if anyone understood, it would be Kate – who had confided the circumstances of Nathan's birth soon after they'd met. Having discovered she was pregnant with Nathan after splitting with his father, she'd kept his birth a secret from Neil for several years.

'I had dreadful morning sickness – or rather, all day sickness, was tired, emotional and convinced that once the baby came, everything would be fine. I told myself that this was just Gary dealing with the idea of fatherhood his way.'

'By cheating on the mother of his child?' Kate's tone was derisive.

'I know how it sounds, but I was making excuses for him. Gary was always a bit of the man about town with his North London accent, snappy clothes, and fast cars. I remember the argument when he had to get rid of his two-seater sports car for a more family-friendly sedan. But I was an only child; my parents had both died in a car accident the year before I met Gary, and he made me feel whole again. I feared being alone, so'—she shrugged again— 'I pretended I didn't know. When Cate came along, he seemed to settle a bit; he liked to show her off to all his friends and even though he wasn't interested in doing the hands-on father type of things – I don't think he ever changed a nappy – that was just because of the way he'd been brought up. It was how his father was, and I understood that.

'When I was pregnant with Rick, it happened again, and this time I couldn't pretend not to know. She was the wife of one of his colleagues. Cam told me later he'd known but hadn't wanted to interfere in case I turned on him too.'

'That must have put Cam in an awkward position,' said Kate.

'It did. I know I would've taken it out on Cam – even though it wasn't anything to do with him. When I confronted Gary, he swore it was over, and he'd never do it again. A momentary lapse of reason, he called it.' She laughed derisively. 'Naturally, it was all a lie, and he moved out with her when Richie was about eight weeks old.'

'And Cam helped you out?' Kate's elbows were on

the table, her cheeks resting on the back of her hands.

'He did. I didn't know, of course, that he felt anything for me other than friendship; I was just so grateful he was there. Gary sent money, so at least he was responsible in that respect, but we didn't see him. He called me once to tell me he was moving to Perth with the woman he'd left me for and that, I thought, was that.'

'When did you and Cam get together?'

Milly had to think about that. 'I told Gary it was about two years after he'd left, and I suppose that's right; although it happened so gradually, I couldn't tell you for sure. At first, he was available if I needed help with anything, and then he began coming with us on picnics and walks and was there for birthdays and Christmas. It stopped being the three of us and began being the four of us, and I hadn't even noticed. He kissed me for the first time when Rick was about two.' Milly smiled at the memories. 'He was so afraid he'd overstepped the mark, but for me, it was as if all the pieces had slid together. I didn't so much fall in love as know I was already there – and had been for some time.'

'How was Gary when he found out?'

'He went ballistic. He immediately stopped maintenance payments and said Cam had been undercutting him the whole time, that we'd still be together if it weren't for Cam. Gary didn't want me, but it was such a blow to his ego that I'd fallen for someone who used to be his friend.' She paused. 'Then he told me if I wanted a divorce, I'd need to go to court for it, and if I did, he'd fight me for the kids. He said he didn't want to get married again, so it was no skin off his nose if officially he stayed married to me.'

'And you believed him?'

Milly nodded and sighed. 'I did. I couldn't risk a custody battle, so Cam and I decided to let it rest and see what happened. We thought he'd calm down – after all, he was still with *her*. But then I fell pregnant with Jess, and Cam wanted us to get married so he could adopt Cate and Rick. He wanted there to be no doubt he loved them all as his own.'

'And Gary finally agreed.'

'No.'

Kate's eyes widened in shock. 'But—'

'He agreed to a financial separation – so that side was all sorted – but he said he'd never sign the divorce papers, and he'd never consent to his kids having Cam's name. He also threatened the custody thing again and said he'd say I was sleeping with Cam before he left. He said he'd insist on a DNA test for Richie even though he knew it was all a lie.'

'What did you do?'

'I couldn't do it. I couldn't go through the court case, and I couldn't risk the kids going to him – they didn't even know who he was. Cam was the only father they knew – how could I send them to the other side of the country to visit with a stranger?' She shrugged. 'So, we did nothing.'

'But I thought—'

'That we're married? We are in our hearts, but we don't have a piece of paper. People refer to me as Milly Fletcher, but all my legal documents are still in Evans. I think people assume I kept my maiden name or didn't want to go through the palaver of changing it again, and I've said nothing different. We had a commitment ceremony once – before we moved out here. We knew it meant nothing legally, but it meant the world to us. Legally we're life partners, and for all intents and purposes, we're married, but we're not *actually* married.'

'I see,' said Kate, frowning as though struggling to understand what she'd just been told. 'Did Gary tell you the real reason for his visit?'

Milly nodded. 'He wants to get to know Richie, and if I help him do that, he'll sign the divorce papers.'

'Which gives you a few new problems?'

'Exactly. How do I tell Cam that I met him secretly? He'd be devastated if he knew. There's the tiniest part of Cam that has never forgotten that not only did I love Gary first, but that I made excuses for his behaviour and continued to stay with him. That same tiny part of him wonders whether if I met him again if I'd fall back under his spell. Then there's Rick – surely it should be up to him if he wants to meet his father without me putting him under pressure – or worrying about Cam's feelings if he does so. Finally, there's the biggie – we've never told the kids that we're not married, and neither Cam nor I know how to tell them now.'

First one and then another tear ran down her face, and soon she couldn't stop the flood. 'It was all so long ago that even Cam and I had forgotten we weren't married. And I know these days it doesn't matter that we're not legally married, but it still did in the eighties and the kids think we are. I even have the "wedding" pictures around the house.' She swallowed hard and swiped at her tear-streaked cheeks. 'I'm so frightened, Kate. We didn't mean to lie, but we have, and now it's going to all come out, and I'm scared I'll lose both Cam and the kids.'

'Oh, Milly.' Kate reached out a hand and laid it over her friend's, squeezing gently. 'That's a fine pickle you're in.'

'I have no idea what to do,' sobbed Milly.

'I can't tell you what to do.' Kate smiled gently. 'But I know how Nathan was when he found out I'd kept Vanessa's threats from him. And that was nothing compared to how Ash reacted when she found out. Trust me, when Ash has a tantrum, she makes it a good one.'

'You're saying I should just tell the truth.'

'I'm saying treat your family the way you'd like them to treat you. There might be some short-term fall-out, but at the end of the day, you told them – they didn't find out from somewhere else.'

Milly gave her a watery grin and a slight nod. 'You're right; I know you're right. I just don't know how.'

'You'll figure it out.'

Milly forced a smile and finished her tea.

CHAPTER ELEVEN

'How was your week?' Jess asked as she twirled the pasta around on her fork. The food at the lodges was great, but she never had time to sit and enjoy it. As a result, it had become a ritual that her first meal back after time on track was (whenever possible) pasta with red wine – and plenty of both. Bread dripping with garlicky butter was an optional but appreciated extra. It was even better when shared with Nathan, who'd been waiting to meet her when the bus pulled up earlier that afternoon. She'd stepped off the bus and into his arms – she was becoming such a cliché.

'Awesome,' said Nathan, wiping some spaghetti sauce from his chin. 'I did my first cage dive.'

Jess met his eyes, which were twinkling. 'With great whites?' Her stomach flipped at the thought. 'How was it? Were you scared?'

He thought for a minute and then said, 'Actually, no. I thought I would be, and then once I thought about it logically, I was fine. We'd been through all the safety stuff; the cage was secure, I had plenty of air.' He waited for a beat, his face split into a magnificent smile. 'I was so excited, but not scared at all.' He leaned over for another piece of garlic bread. 'I get why people do it, though; it was a massive rush. They're *awesome* animals – you can't fathom how big they are until you're down there with them – and they're more agile than you'd expect. The power is just—'

'Awesome?' finished Jess with raised eyebrows.

'Yes.' His grin was broad. 'That's the only word I can use. One of them swam past the cage – a large female. She would've had to have been four metres long. They have these black eyes that make you feel as though they're staring right through you. It's impossible to move or look away.' He leant towards her. 'Awe-inspiring.'

'I suppose that's at least a slight difference from awesome.' Jess grinned at his enthusiasm. Nathan really was in his happy place when he was in the ocean. Not for the first time, a tinge of guilt squeezed her heart at the fact that he was compromising that – at least to an extent – to be with her.

'What about you? Good walk?' he asked, wiping another piece of garlic bread around his bowl.

'Not bad at all. Just the one wet day.'

'Not like when we did Milford?' His grin was lopsided as if he were remembering those days when the rain had appeared it was coming down in curtains rather than drops. While rain in Fiordland was expected, there had been rather a lot of it the week that Kate and Nathan tramped the track. Since then, it had, on balance, been a remarkably fine summer.

'There were a couple of people in the group who struggled, so I certainly had plenty to do.'

Margot, in particular, had struggled on the switchbacks – or zigzag track – up to Ocean Peak Corner, but once up there, she had marvelled at the view. The day was unusually clear, and they'd been able to see down to the coast. Margot had also had some nervous moments on the narrow, exposed path across Holyford Face and above Lake Harris. Walking through the valley, though, she'd seemed to relax and almost enjoy herself. And this morning, once the initial rocky descent from the lodge was done, she was a completely different woman. She'd taken Jess aside at Routeburn Shelter as they prepared to board the bus for the return trip and thanked her.

'I couldn't have done it without you,' Margot had said.

'I'm sure you could have,' Jess had replied. 'You just didn't know it.'

'It changes you, doesn't it?' she'd said with a smile towards Steve. 'I was so scared to begin with, but now I can do anything.'

Jess's throat had tightened with emotion at Margot's words. It was why she loved her job.

'You would've loved that,' Nathan said after she'd

shared Margot's story.

'The challenge or the breakthrough?' she asked.

'Both. Equally.' He propped his chin on his hand and grinned at her. 'There's nothing worse than when you have nothing to occupy yourself – that's when the trouble begins.'

'Oh, ha ha. I had been hoping for some downtime to put some thought into how I can get Dan to notice Holly,' she said.

Nathan tipped his head back and exhaled his exasperation. 'You're not still on about that?'

'Absolutely. They'd be perfect for each other. Don't you think?'

'What I think doesn't matter; it's their lives you're messing about in.'

'I'm not messing about,' she said indignantly, 'And I haven't done anything yet. I'm simply considering giving them a helping hand. It's what I did for Richie and Max, you know. I told them he needed to knock her up so she'd stay in Queenstown, and I'd have someone who was a fabulous baker who I could also trust to run the shop when I was on track. Win for them and win for me.'

Nathan grinned at her arrogance. 'I hate to tell you, Jay, but I'm pretty sure you can't take any credit for Max being knocked up – judging by when this baby is due, that boat had well and truly sailed by the time they landed here.'

Jess lifted her shoulders as if his logic had no place in her world. 'Do you want to know how I'm going to make it happen?'

'No. Are you going to eat that garlic bread?'

'I certainly am – and I'll fight you for the last piece on the plate. As for Dan and Holly—'

'Jay,' said Nathan, shaking his head. 'You know I love you, but do you really not see?'

'See what?'

'Dan's not interested in Holly – you're the one he wants. If you're planning on doing anything in that regard, let it go.'

Jess frowned and sat back in her chair. 'That's ridiculous. Dan's like another brother to me – he's always treated me the way Richie does.'

'Maybe he does, but you haven't seen the way he looks at you when he doesn't think you'll notice – although why he thinks you would be beyond me.'

'Why he thinks I would what?'

'Notice.'

Jess chewed at her bottom lip, frowned some more, and then shook her head. 'No, you're wrong. I'd know if Dan felt anything for me other than friendship.'

'I don't think I'm wrong, Jay.' Nathan shrugged. 'Maybe it's more that you don't want to consider the possibility he might feel something more for you – after all, he's your head chef.'

Jess continued to think about it and didn't even

notice when Nathan used her distraction to steal the last piece of garlic bread. Nathan was wrong about Dan; he had to be. Dan had always been there dusting her off after she'd gotten into some scrape or another, tramping with her on weekends when Richie was in England, listening to her when yet another seasonal boyfriend packed his bags and left to go back to wherever he'd come from. If Nathan was right, it could cause her a lot of trouble; surely he was seeing something that wasn't there. But there was something else he'd said …

'You said that you loved me,' she said, her smile beginning in her heart and spreading across her face and all the way to her eyes. 'Just then when you said, "You know I love you but …" Did you mean it? Because you've never said it before.'

He grinned sheepishly and looked down at his now empty plate and then back up into her eyes. 'Yes, I meant it, and no, I haven't said it before – to you or anyone else.'

Her grin became cheeky. 'Strictly speaking, you still haven't said it.' She snatched the half-eaten piece of bread from his hands and waggled her eyebrows.

'Sure I have.'

'Nope.' She shook her head, her thick chestnut ponytail swinging. 'You told me I know you do, love me, that is, but you haven't actually said it, and unless you actually say it, you can't assume I know it.' If she were ten, she would've added: "so there".

His smile widened playfully, his eyes flaming as his initial discomfort turned into something much more fun as far as Jess was concerned. 'You say it first,' he said.

'Yeah ... nah.' She said the words slowly, and under the table, her foot stroked up and down the length of his calf. 'You first.'

His eyes momentarily fluttered closed as she slid down in her seat a little, enough for her foot to reach up into his lap. 'No one's watching,' she said. 'But I'm listening.'

'I love you,' he finally said, the last word a groan as her toes found their target.

Filled with a sudden rush of what could only be pure joy, she felt the same way about him – for the first time in her life, she was truly in love too. But she couldn't say it yet; the feeling was too new and needed to be savoured for a little longer.

She pulled her foot away, slipped it back into her shoe and stood up. Laughing at the look of both surprise and disappointment on his face, she walked around to where he still sat and nipped at his earlobe before sucking it lightly.

'Let's go home,' she whispered.

Tom had lit the barbecue and fire pit, handed the beers around, and decanted the red wine. On the surface, it was, thought Richie, very similar to this time last week. Then they'd been celebrating the imminent birth of his and Max's baby – the male equivalent of a baby shower (was there even a name for that?) – and now they were refuelling after a long day of picking grapes. Even the weather had been the same. After a few cooler days during the week, the day had been mild and sunny – more like the start of March than the end. Tom and Ryan, Tom's winemaker, both had a feeling that when the weather broke, it would do so suddenly, so all hands were on deck to get the grapes off the vines and into the vats.

Yes, on the surface, it all seemed the same, but things were very different underneath. Fletch was talking to Tom and Ryan as they all stood guard over the steaks sizzling on the barbecue. Even from a distance, the tension in his father's stance was obvious. It was in the way he gripped the stem of his wineglass, the set of his jaw, the slight slump in his posture. Mostly, though, it was in the way his eyes kept darting around the yard to find Milly – even though it was apparent he was attempting to avoid her.

As for his mother, she was making a good show of it but hadn't met his eyes when she kissed him hello and had headed straight into the kitchen where Kate and Max were putting together bowls of salads. His parents had had an argument, and you didn't need to be Einstein to figure out what or who they'd had words over.

With a start, he realised Nathan had been talking to him and was expecting a response.

'Sorry mate, what were you saying?'

'I was just asking how you'd both settled into the new house. Was Max happy with the mural?'

At least here was a subject Richie didn't need to pretend with. 'She was over the moon. I tell you what, it's great finally having our own space and knowing that my sister can't come charging into our bedroom without notice whenever she wants to!'

'I think she'll miss being able to do that,' said Nathan, grinning.

Now he thought about it, Nathan had been doing an awful lot of grinning today. 'You seem pretty happy today – things going well?'

As he thought, there was another grin. 'Yep. I did my first cage dive and spent some time underwater in the kelp forests, so I've had a good week.'

'Rather you than me on the shark front,' said Richie, not even bothering to hide his shudder of fear. 'Judging by that grin, things are going well with Jess too.'

He nodded, rocking back on his heels. 'Yes, I think they are.'

Richie slapped him lightly on the back. 'I'm pleased to hear it. You two are good together.'

'Thanks mate.' Nathan's cheeks coloured slightly, and he took an embarrassed mouthful of beer. 'What's new with you?'

Richie almost didn't tell him. He almost said what he'd been saying to everyone else he'd caught up with over the last few days, saying everything was sweet and Maxi was blooming, and yes, we're excited. But he needed to tell somebody, and preferably somebody who wasn't part of the family – although Richie hoped Nathan would be part of the family someday. Richie hadn't known Nathan for long but instinctively knew he could trust him. He tilted his head toward the vines and suggested Nathan should follow.

'Dude, what's going on?' Nathan said once they'd reached the row of vines they'd been working on earlier that day.

'My father's in town,' Richie said, his tone expressionless, his gaze fixed on the mountains. When Nathan looked confused, he clarified, 'My birth father, Mum's first husband.'

'Whoa. Have you seen him?'

Richie shook his head.

'Are you going to see him?'

'That's the thing – I can't decide whether I want to. Apparently, he wants to see me, and he wants to meet Max. I have no idea whether he knows there's a baby on the way or if he'd care about that. Part of me wants to meet him, to face him and ask how he could do what he did – not just to Mum, but to Cate and me. If Mum hadn't ended up with Fletch, things could've been very different for us.' He picked a leaf off the vine and rolled it between his fingers. 'I don't understand it, I can't understand it. When you meet the one, she's all that matters, you know? You don't treat her the way he treated Mum.'

'Yeah,' said Nathan, and with that one word Richie knew he knew – that Nathan felt about Jess the way Richie felt about Max.

'And then when you're going to be a father, well, it's huge, but if I'm scared, I know Maxi's even more scared. What she's got to do – with the birth, I mean – is terrifying, but she has to do it, and my job is to be there for her. How can you say you love someone and do to them what my father, Gary Evans, did to Mum and us?'

'I was furious with my father when he and Mum split – especially when he took up with Vanessa – but at no time did he disrespect Mum. I can't imagine how I'd feel if he had.' Nathan took a mouthful of his beer before asking, 'What's stopping you? From confronting him?'

'Mum and Dad.' Richie shrugged. 'I worry that me seeing Gary might bring it all back for her and that Dad might see it as a betrayal – after all, Fletch is my dad, Gary's my father.'

'What's Max said about it?'

Richie grimaced and shrugged again.

'You have spoken to her about it?'

'Sort of. I told her Gary's here and wants to see

me. I don't want to stress her out, though. This isn't her issue, and I want her to enjoy these couple of weeks before the baby comes, to chill and do the nesting thing – in between baking for my sister and your mother, that is.' Richie forced a laugh, and while Nathan smiled tightly, he didn't join in.

'You need to tell her – you know you do. If I know anything about Max, it's that she'll know something's not right, and that will worry her just as much. Jay told me what happened last year – when she was worried about your ex-girlfriend, and you were worried about her ex-husband. The way she tells it – and knowing Jay as I do, there would've been some dramatic licence in the telling – that one nearly ended badly.' He raised his eyebrows to emphasise his point.

'Yeah, you're right.'

'Speaking of which, does Jess know?'

Richie shook his head. 'No, but she's met him – he came into Beach Road on Saturday morning, apparently.'

'The tall bloke? We thought he looked familiar.'

Richie closed his eyes and rubbed his forehead. 'Mum called Cate, and she wants nothing to do with any of it. She's coming over when Maxi has the baby, but Mum said Cate doesn't want to meet him. I spoke to her last night too, and she's adamant she doesn't want to know.' He paused, and his shoulders slumped. 'So now I don't know what I should do.'

'It's not about what you should do, but what you want to do – and that's got nothing to do with your parents or either of your sisters.'

Richie's smile was sombre. 'Thanks, bro.'

Nathan patted him on the back. 'All good. Another beer?'

'Yeah,' said Richie, and the two men made their way back through the vines to rejoin the others.

Nathan was right – he needed to talk to Maxi about it. She wouldn't tell him what to do; she'd listen while he talked it through – she'd be there for him regardless of the outcome.

While Nathan searched for more beers, Richie went to Dan who was standing off to one side, deep in thought.

'Not a bad effort,' Richie said after greeting him. 'Up at the crack of dawn to cook breakfasts for half of Queenstown, and you still found the energy to spend a few hours helping here.'

'You know how it is, mate, all hands on deck. I told Tom last weekend I'd get here if I could.' Dan took a long draught from the beer bottle he was holding. 'Besides,' he said with a grin, 'there's a rumour he'll crack open some of last year's harvest later on.'

'You could be right,' said Richie. 'I reckon he'll wait till the pickers head back into town, though.'

Dan chuckled. 'I'd say so.'

'When's Jess back?' Richie asked.

'Thursday morning. The weather's forecasted to be great on track, so that's bad for us.'

'How so?' asked Richie. 'It makes for an easier tramp for everyone.'

'And that's the problem,' said Dan. 'If the conditions are good and everyone has the right level of fitness, and nothing goes wrong, it means Jess has all of that time to think.'

'Ah.' Richie could see where this was heading.

'And this has been a back-to-back – three days on Routeburn and five on Milford. At least Routeburn is three full tramping days, but days one and five on Milford have way too much thinking time,' added Dan.

'Which means she'll burst into work on Thursday with an entire set of new ideas,' said Richie.

'Yep,' said Dan. 'Last time she did a back-to-back in fine weather, she hit upon the idea of basket deliveries – where offices could order morning teas delivered to their doors in baskets. The time before that she reorganised front of house, and the time before that—'

'Okay, I get the gist.' Richie grinned as he contemplated what his whirlwind of a sister would come back with this time. Knowing Jess, though, she wouldn't have factored potential failure into her plans – she never did – so any unintended consequences wouldn't even occur to her. As far as Jess was concerned, a consequence was something fun that hadn't happened yet. 'Well,' he said. 'Let's hope someone needed extra attention on track, and she's been distracted.'

Over by the barbecue, Nathan was talking with the three older men. Nathan said something that made Fletch laugh and slap his back lightly.

'What's going on there do you think?' asked Dan quietly. 'With Nathan and Jess. He's given up a lot for her.'

Richie nodded slowly. 'He has. He's due to go back to his job in Cairns at the end of next month, but ...' He shrugged.

'It's Jess,' Dan finished the sentence.

There was something in Dan's voice that made Richie glance over and catch his friend's eyes. Dan dropped his first, and Richie groaned inwardly. Max had been right – Dan had a thing for Jess. She'd warned Richie about it, and he'd dismissed it. 'You're right about a lot of things, my darling,' he'd said, 'but not this one. Dan's been like an extra brother to her – especially while I was away – and she's his boss. He knows her too well for it to be anything more. Besides, he's my best mate, so I'd know if he had a thing for my sister.'

While Richie adored his reckless, feckless, and totally impetuous sister – she was such a force of nature she was impossible to resist – he was fully aware of her failings. Nathan, he suspected, had fallen for her before he'd worked that out, but there was no excuse for Dan; his eyes had been opened to Jess years ago.

'Anything I need to know about, bro?' Richie said.

Dan shook his head and scratched the back of his neck. 'It's sweet.'

'You sure?'

'Good as gold,' he said, taking another large swig of his beer. 'Do you think Jess feels the same? About him?'

Dan focused his gaze on the vines as he asked the question; Richie didn't think he was doing so out of any appreciation for how they looked under the setting sun.

'Yeah, mate, I think she does,' Richie finally said.

'Good to know.' He drew in a deep breath and switched his attention to the group around the barbecue. 'Nathan's a good bloke. He'll treat her right.'

Richie nodded again. 'I think so.' Christ, this could get complicated.

CHAPTER TWELVE

In the kitchen, Milly had ordered Max to a chair where she sat and sipped herbal tea and watched Milly and Kate put together bowls of salad.

'This is my first harvest,' said Kate, 'so I have no idea what to expect.'

'Mine too,' said Max.

'Well, it's not mine and let's just say as lovely as these salads are, they'll barely be touched. Most of the pickers are going to be happy with a snag or steak sammies,' said Milly. 'And, I have to say, who isn't happy with a sausage or piece of steak in between a couple of slices of bread. I just hope all the cheese rolls aren't finished by the time we get out there.'

'I'd never heard of cheese rolls before I came here,' said Kate. 'And the first time one was offered to me, I was surprised when it wasn't a bread roll filled with cheese, but something entirely different – a rolled-up slice of white bread filled with a cheesy oniony sauce and toasty brown on the outside.'

'It was a surprise to me too,' said Max.

Milly laughed at the look on their faces. 'The cheese roll is very much a south of the South Island thing – Southland, really. The main problem is you can't just make a couple – you have to make a whole loaf of bread worth – which is why they're perfect for occasions like this.'

'I know. Tom keeps them in his freezer now and just brings out a batch when he needs to.' Kate tossed a green salad and added some salad servers to it. 'Another wine Milly?'

'Please.' While she had to drive home, she could have another one. Milly turned her attention to Max. 'How's Rick doing?' When Max looked sideways at Kate, Milly said, 'It's okay, I've spoken to Kate about what's going on.'

Kate handed her the wine and gave her a comforting smile.

Max stared at her hands resting on her belly. 'To be honest, I don't know. He's not talking about it – although I just noticed him and Nathan standing off to one side, so maybe he's confiding in him? I'd say he doesn't want to worry me, but …' Max shrugged. 'I'm worried about him.'

'Yes,' agreed Milly. 'So am I.'

'Do you think Richie will see him? Gary, I mean?' said Kate.

'I don't know, but I think he should,' said Max.

'You do?' Max's reply surprised Milly.

'Yes. I know one fear Richie has is that he'll be a bad father. From the few photos he's seen of Gary, he knows there's a physical resemblance, and while he hasn't said as much to me, I think he's concerned he's more like him in other ways too. As an aside, I love you, Milly, but you should seriously have taught Richie to use his words more often.'

Richie's tendency to keep things he was anxious about to himself was a frequent cause of exasperation for both Max and Milly.

'He gets that from Cam – he's just as bad. You know he's hardly spoken to me in days. I'm giving him another day or so to get over it before I'm forced to pick an argument to get it out of him.' Milly shook her head and laughed, even though she didn't feel like laughing. If it was obvious Cam was actively avoiding her, surely it was obvious to their friends as well.

Yesterday he'd left home early, citing paperwork that needed to be done. He'd smiled and kissed her goodbye, but his smile didn't make it to his eyes – which hadn't met hers – and his kiss landed on her cheek rather than her lips. The same thing happened this morning, although this time he said (again without meeting her eyes) that he'd promised Tom he'd be here early to help him get set up for the day.

At first, she fretted that someone had seen her and Gary in Frankton, but then she reasoned that the likelihood was very low. She was, she decided, worried over nothing on that count. Then she wondered whether Cam was concerned about the argument he'd had with Rick before Gary turned up, but that wouldn't normally be enough to prompt this sort of behaviour – they'd argued in the past and would do so plenty more times in the future. No, she thought, whatever was going on with Cam was his concern, not hers.

Max laughed along with her, her hands cradling her belly as she did. 'I do the same with Richie,' she said. 'He gets two days tops, and then I'll pick an argument. It tends to work.'

'Neil used to be the same,' added Kate. 'Tom's very different though – he likes to talk through *everything.*' She rolled her eyes to illustrate her point. 'Anyway, let's take these salads out and get these hungry workers fed.'

As Milly picked up a bowl of salad, Max used the table to help her stand and placed her hand on Milly's arm. 'Is there anything I should know before I talk to Richie?' she asked softly.

Milly hoped her surprise didn't show in her face. Max reminded her of herself – but a much wiser version. She could read a situation and see things that others didn't. There was scarcely a day that went by since she'd come into their family that Milly wasn't grateful her son had chosen this woman to be his partner.

'There are,' she admitted, 'but Rick needs to make his mind up without them.'

Max searched Milly's face and then nodded. 'I see.'

'Yes,' said Milly, 'I really believe that you do.'

They were in the Land Rover coming home from Tom's when Richie announced he intended to contact Gary Evans – he still couldn't think of him as his father – and arrange to meet. Max had nodded in agreement and said she was glad and thought it was a good idea.

When they arrived home, he helped Max from the Land Rover and pulled her into his arms, the baby bump snuggling between them. Resting his head against her forehead he said, 'I might stay out here for a bit.' She'd nodded, seeming to know he needed some thinking time.

Once he'd seen her into the house, he wandered down to the boundary fence of their section so he could lean on it and look across the foreshore to the lake. The lake in the twilight was his favourite time of the day – the muted shades of pink and purple, each blending into the next. He'd once told Max that you could gaze at the lake for only a few minutes and see it change and take on a different mood, but at this time, it was a whole different personality – and one that suited his thoughts.

As he settled against the fence, the "what-ifs" played out in the last of the twilight. What if Gary had come back to cause trouble? What if either of his parents were upset because he'd reached out to Gary? They might've thought they'd been doing a good job of hiding it, but his father had an almighty sulk on about something – and that something could only be Gary Evans.

As for his mother, Milly was doing her best to ignore Fletch's mood, but if Richie knew anything about the cycles of his parent's relationship, it was only a matter of days before something blew. What if him seeing Gary was what pushed them both over the edge?

Behind all the other what-ifs was the biggest one. That one didn't jump around for attention, it just stood there in line behind the others, taller and straighter and harder to shift. What if he actually liked his father? What if Gary wasn't the ogre he'd spent his life believing he was? What if he was just an ordinary man who'd fallen in love with the wrong woman and had sacrificed his family for that? It didn't make what he did right – not by a long shot – but it made it understandable. After all, he knew what it was like to fall in love with someone you had no right to love. If he'd been in Gary's shoes, would he have done the same? Given up everything for the woman he loved? If that woman was Max, Richie knew what his answer would be. What if Richie had spent all his life hating his father for something he might have been tempted to do, too?

The moon was coming up and the temperature had dropped by the time he let himself back into the house. Max was sitting on a stool at the kitchen bench, her nightly cup of tea in front of her. What was the saying? You can take the girl out of England, but you can't take England out of the girl? He slid onto the stool beside her and smiled a tired smile.

'All good?' she asked, scratching at his favourite spot at the back of his neck.

He ran his knuckle down her cheek and said, 'Sweet as.' Before he changed his mind, he pulled his phone from his jacket pocket and sent a text to Gary suggesting they meet for a late breakfast the next morning. Even as he tapped send, there was a part of him that hoped his father wouldn't respond or that he'd say something like, "Sorry, I can't do tomorrow, in fact, I've decided not to hang around, and I'm going back to Australia instead."

Of course that hadn't happened, and a response had come through immediately.

Sounds great. 10 am? How about The Bath House on the lake?

'What did he say?' Max asked.

Richie slid his phone across the bench for Max to read. Max squeezed his hand and pressed a kiss to his temple. She slid off the stool and flicked the switch to turn on the kettle.

He stared through the glass sliding doors into the darkness, his forefinger lying across his top lip and his thumb under his chin. The what-ifs he'd locked away had somehow got out and were again crowding his brain.

Maxi placed his coffee on the bench and stood behind him, gently kneading the taut muscles in his shoulders and across the top of his back. Richie closed his eyes and groaned as her fingers eased the knots of his troubles and stroked them away – at least for now, anyway. She always knew – when to calm him, when to stand strong, when to pick an argument with him, and when to let it go. She knew him better than anyone else did or ever would. On the other hand, he was learning more about her every day, and just when he didn't think he could feel more for her, he fell a little bit more in love with her.

He reached up and caught one of her hands, bringing it to his mouth, planting kisses on her palm. 'I love you Maxi.'

She bent slightly and rested her chin on his shoulder, her cheek next to his, her baby bump pressed into his back. 'Take me to bed?'

They made love languorously, in long, slow strokes, Maxi arching into him, tightening around him, the little noises she made thrilling him as they always did, her pleasure fuelling his.

When they curled into each other, him spooning her from behind, his arms wrapped around her and resting on her belly, she said, 'Tell me.'

So he did.

'I don't know if I'm supposed to feel angry,' he confided. 'I know what Gary did to Mum was wrong, but Fletch is my dad, and I can't regret that. If Gary hadn't left, we wouldn't have Fletch, and we wouldn't have Jess – and the way I figure it, we got the better deal.'

'Are you angry?' Max asked, holding his hands fast to her tummy.

Vanilla and coconut filled his nose as he pressed a kiss behind her ear. 'I want to be.'

'But you're not,' she finished for him. 'Something else is worrying you, though?' she asked gently.

'What if I like him and if Dad feels I've betrayed him?' Saying the words out loud robbed them of some of their power over him. 'We've been arguing a bit of late, and even though we cleared the air the other day, I don't want Dad thinking I'm rejecting him for Gary.'

'It's okay to like Gary,' said Maxi. 'And if you did, both Fletch and Milly would understand, I'm sure.'

'Maybe not at first.'

'No,' she conceded, 'maybe not at first.'

'I'm scared, Maxi,' he said after a lingering silence.

'About the baby?'

'I'm not sure, I think so. I love you so much, but what if I don't have enough left for Piglet?'

'It's a different kind of love,' she said. 'And you're going to be a wonderful father. I know it.'

'How do you know?'

'I just do,' she said, and Richie believed her.

CHAPTER THIRTEEN

Richie's resolve wavered as he walked along the lake path away from Beach Road. While Max understood he'd be fine and would prefer to do this first meeting without her, the moment she and Dan got chatting in the kitchen, he'd regretted that decision.

'Under no circumstances is she to work,' Richie had instructed his friend.

'No problems, bro. She can sit here in the corner and issue instructions. I've told Dayna to send up tea on the half hour—'

'And cheese scones,' cut in Max.

'And cheese scones,' said Dan. 'But we've ordered her to stay put.'

'The way Piglet is dancing on my bladder, I'll need to get up for that,' said Max.

Richie had laughed as he was supposed to – Maxi had known he was nervous about the meeting and had been gently teasing him all morning. 'Okay, you can get up for the bathroom, but that's all.' He kissed her lips, lingering. 'I'm doing the right thing, aren't I?' he whispered.

She rested her palms on his cheeks. 'I think so. You'll regret it if Gary leaves town and you miss your chance to ask him what you need to.'

'Yeah.' He kissed her again, this time on the tip of her nose. 'I know. It's just ...' He shrugged.

Max smiled in understanding. 'It's not too late for me to come with you.'

'No, I'll do this first meeting alone, and if there's a next time, I'll introduce you.'

After one last kiss, he was down the stairs, out the door and striding purposefully onto the path that ran around the front of the lake.

The Bath House was on the lake beach – although his friend Brad had laughed uproariously when he first saw the pebble-filled beach when he and Abby were here last Christmas. 'You call this a beach?' he'd said. Aside from its prime position right on Lake Wakatipu, the Edwardian crown-like architecture of the building with its sunny terrace made it a popular spot for breakfast and lunch.

Richie sighed at the thought of the upcoming meeting, shoved his hands into his pockets and kept his pace brisk. What he needed right now was a good, long tramp. If Jess was in town, he might've suggested they tramp a leg of the Routeburn or even Ben Lomond. It had been months since he'd been out on track. The time he'd been stranded in terrible weather without cellphone reception last year meant Max wasn't keen for him to be going out on his own. Hell, right now he wasn't keen on being too far from her either. That didn't take away from the fact he needed to let off some steam and have some thinking time in the best way he knew how – by tramping in nature. Maybe when Jess came back, they could do something local – Queenstown Hill, perhaps. It was steep enough to require concentration but not technical and had the added advantage of only needing the commitment of a few hours.

Gary must've been watching for him as he stood from his place on the timber terrace and walked towards him, hand outstretched. Even if he hadn't, Richie would've known him anywhere. As his mother had said, it was like looking at an older, lankier version of himself. Gary was as tall as Richie was and had Richie's blue eyes. Although it was steel-grey now, Gary's hair would have once been as dark as his son's. Richie took the hand offered and shook it.

'It's good to see you, son,' said Gary.

'I don't know what to call you,' Richie admitted, slipping his hands back into his pockets.

'Gary will be fine.'

Richie followed Gary to the table he'd been sitting at, and they sat in uncomfortable silence. 'I thought we could order breakfast, and then you might tell me what you've been up to.' He smiled and handed the menu across the table. How could Gary appear so calm and not at all awkward – especially when he should've had a lot to feel awkward about? Perhaps it was an act?

'For the past thirty-odd years?' Richie asked, failing to keep the sneer from his voice.

'I deserve that,' said Gary. 'And I'm happy to answer questions you have for me, but not before coffee.'

They placed their orders, and when the coffees were served, Richie asked, 'Why are you here?'

Gary sipped at his black coffee before answering. 'What has your mother told you?'

'She said you wanted to catch up with us, but it's a long way to come if you didn't know if Cate or I would be here.'

He shrugged. 'Perhaps, but after all these years it seemed the right time. I knew your mother and Cam were here and figured they'd tell me about you and Cate and where I could find you.'

'Cate doesn't want anything to do with you,' said Richie flatly. 'And to be honest, I don't blame her – I'm not sure I do either.'

'If you feel that way, why meet me today? Did your mother tell you to?'

For someone whose sole reason to come to Queenstown was to catch up with his son, Gary was acting as though he didn't care either way, as if nothing Richie had to say could phase him. Yet, something in the set of his jaw told Richie that what he thought of him *did* matter.

'Mum left the decision up to me – neither Mum nor Dad,' Richie emphasised the word Dad, 'know I'm here. I wanted to meet you because I want to know why you think *you* have any right to know me. I thought you abdicated that right when you left Mum to bring us both up on her own. It was Perth, wasn't it? Where you moved to?' Richie met Gary's eyes and forced himself to hold the stare.

'Which of those do you want me to answer first?' The corner of Gary's mouth had lifted in a sardonic half-smile.

Richie should be angry – for his mother's sake, if not his own, but Gary's attitude had unbalanced him. 'In order would do fine.'

Gary straightened in his chair. 'In order it is. I probably have no rights at all, but as your father, I'm interested in knowing what you're doing – I've always been interested, you just haven't known about it. And yes, it was Perth where I moved to with Rachel. Did you want to know why I moved there?'

'No,' said Richie quickly, but now Gary had mentioned it, he really did want to know. 'Unless you have a burning need to tell me.'

That half-smile was back as if Gary could see inside his head and hear the questions and what-ifs that lived there. 'We moved because Rachel's husband wasn't exactly overjoyed at the thought of her leaving him for me – it was important we got as far away as possible, so Perth it was.'

'She had children too, didn't she?' The implication being he'd ruined the lives of two families.

Gary didn't rise to the bait. 'Yes – they came with us.'

'Did they get to see their father?'

'Once things settled down, they could see him every so often.'

'But you brought them up.'

'For all intents and purposes.'

'Instead of us.'

'That's right.'

Richie fisted his hands under the table, pain in his jaw from clenching it as he struggled to maintain control in the face of Gary's no-nonsense replies. He could at least have embellished his answers, pretended he'd regretted his actions. 'Why?'

'Why what? Why did I bring them up but not seek to have contact with you two?'

Richie nodded slowly, the answer too important for words.

'Because they were Rachel's children, and I was in love with Rachel. Having no contact with you was the price I paid to be with her. That doesn't mean I haven't thought of you over the years, and it doesn't mean I haven't missed you.'

The arrival of breakfast bought Richie some breathing space. He'd expected to meet a man who, if not the uncaring monster Richie had always assumed that he was, was at least someone who pretended to be apologetic for his past actions. This man was simply telling it as he knew it – laying it all on the table for Richie to take – or leave.

'Just look at that, a perfect egg,' Gary said, placing a knife through the egg on his plate and watching the yolk mix into the hollandaise sauce.

'The best eggs benedict in town is the one Dan, the chef at my sister's café, does.' Richie said, more for something to say than anything else.

'Aaah, yes, I was there last weekend. I met your sister.' He took a mouthful of his breakfast, chewing slowly. He put his fork down and looked steadily at Richie. 'You're wondering why I haven't apologised to you?'

Richie considered his answer. He'd thought he wanted an apology, but now he wasn't so sure. 'I'm not the one you should be apologising to,' he finally said. 'Cate, Jess and I have had a great father – we've never known any different.'

If Gary was surprised or offended by the reference to Fletch as Richie's father, it didn't show. 'You think I should apologise to your mother?'

Richie studied Gary's face, then asked, 'Don't you?'

He put his cutlery down. 'There's a lot you don't

know that went on between us – I knew she'd be fine with Cam.'

And just like that, the heat of anger Richie had been hoping to feel spread across his chest. 'How could you know that? They weren't together when you left.'

'Weren't they?' He raised his eyebrows. 'Maybe I was mistaken about that. This is a very good breakfast – how's yours?'

'It's good,' lied Richie, who had tasted nothing he'd eaten. He leant forward, his forearms resting on the table, his hands balled into fists, his stare fixed on Gary. 'You know damn well Mum and Dad didn't get together until well after you'd gone, so don't even try blaming her to justify what you did.'

Gary raised his hands in front of him in mock surrender. 'I'm not trying to blame anyone. All I'm saying is I've always known Cam had a thing for your mother, that's all. I also know they spent a lot of time together.'

Richie sat back, and he narrowed his eyes, his mind working through what Gary had said. Could his mother and Fletch had got together before they say they did? A flicker of a smile played around Gary's mouth. Richie pushed aside the thoughts that were skipping about in his brain. His mother had said Gary liked to play games – he wouldn't oblige him.

'You said before that not seeing Cate and I was the price you paid. What did you mean by that?'

'Things go on inside a marriage, and deals are made. The version you have is your mother's – and that's as it should be in the circumstances. It's her story to tell you, not mine. All I'll say is I would've liked to have been involved in your life, but it didn't work out that way – I couldn't have the woman I'd fallen in love with and my children.'

'So, you chose her instead of us.' Richie's tone was flat but accusing.

'Yes. I didn't go looking for it, but you're with someone now – Max or Maxine, I think your mother said.' When Richie nodded, he said, 'So you know what it's like to fall in love with someone and what you'd do to stay with them.' It wasn't a question.

Richie thought back to last year when Max had been pregnant with James's child. While she'd sadly miscarried that baby, he would've been happy to raise that child as his own – the same as what Fletch had done with him and Cate, and the same as Gary had done with Rachel's children. He loved Max, so in Richie's mind, it followed he'd love her child – even if it wasn't his.

'I'm not here to cause you or anyone else any trouble, Richie, but I'd like to get to know you, and I'd like to meet your partner. Your mother mentioned that she's pregnant – you're not married?' There was something in Gary's tone that made Richie bristle.

'I've asked her to marry me, but we wanted to

move into our place first and will wait until the baby's born and things have settled back down before we get married.'

Gary's smile was small but seemed genuine. 'Probably a wise decision. Now, tell me about your design work. Your mother said you studied in Melbourne?'

'I didn't realise Mum had a chance to tell you so much about me the other day,' Richie said.

'She didn't. We caught up for coffee on Thursday morning. Didn't she mention it?' Gary's forehead was furrowed as if it surprised him Milly hadn't shared that information.

'No, she didn't.'

Why hadn't his mother said anything to him, and had she said anything about it to Max or Kate? Had Milly said anything to Fletch? – and if the answer to each of these was no, why? And then, because it was far easier to talk about his work than it was to wonder about why his mother had hidden her meeting, Richie took the easier option.

Max was taking a batch of scones from the oven when Richie walked in.

'You've been busted, my sweet,' said Dan, laughing as he poured hollandaise sauce over a perfectly poached egg.

'I couldn't just sit here and drink tea while you

guys were working, could I? And I behaved myself for ages,' she said, flashing Richie her best I-tried-to-be-good smile. It worked, as it always did, although he tried to keep his stern face on for a little longer to make his point. Her smile was the perfect distraction from the conversation he'd been replaying since leaving his father at The Bath House.

'Did you at least have breakfast before they put you to work?' Richie mock-scowled at Dan, who flicked the tea towel over his shoulder in triumph.

'She cleaned up two serves of Holly's crumpets with ricotta and honey,' he said. 'I have to say, Max, your appetite is beyond amazing!'

Max grinned cheekily. 'They're excellent crumpets, and one day when we're not as busy, Holl, you must show me how you get that perfect rise. Don't worry, darling,' she said to Richie, 'I haven't been doing much at all – just a tahini banana bread, some white chocolate and raspberry muffins and these cheese scones. Nothing really. Are you ready to go?' What Max was really asking was, 'Are you okay?'

He nodded. 'If you can drag yourself away from the oven, that is.'

'I've already wiped the bench down, so I'm all yours.'

He wrapped his arms around her expansive middle, pulling her back into him and kissing the side of her neck. 'I thought you were already all mine,' he whispered.

'I am.' She arched her neck so he could nuzzle into that sensitive spot behind her ears.

'Okay, Max,' said Dan, laughter in his voice. 'Stop making out and turn that oven off. And as for you, bro, you've already knocked her up, so at least try and keep your hands off her in my kitchen.'

With one last kiss, Richie released her. 'We'll be off then.' Turning back to Dan and Holly, he said, 'I'll see you guys later.'

Max waited until they were in the car and on the way out to Tom's winery before asking the question she'd been dying to ask. 'How was it?'

He hesitated for a beat before replying. 'It was not bad. Awkward at first – he openly admits he feels no guilt about what he did, and I found that difficult to understand.'

Maxi turned to him, her eyes wide. 'You mean he didn't apologise for leaving you?'

'Nope, not even for leaving Mum. And he had no apology for his lack of apology. It hurt until I realised he could've pretended to feel something he didn't in order to make me feel better, but had decided just to be straight with me instead. I suppose I've got to respect that.

'There was one point where he hinted Mum and Fletch might've been together *before* he left, and I was angry about that, but if my anger worried him, he certainly didn't show it.'

'Why do you think he said that?'

'No idea.' He rubbed the back of his neck. 'It's the only thing he said that seemed like a cheap shot.'

'Did he say why he was here?'

'Yes – I think he really does just want to get to know me. He strikes me as being someone who says it like it is.' He pressed his lips together as he searched for the words he needed. 'To be honest, he's nothing like I thought he'd be, and I'm finding it difficult to match the man I met this morning with what I've heard from Mum – or rather what I haven't heard from Mum.' He paused briefly and added, 'Do you think it's strange she and Dad have never really spoken about him? All we know are the facts – Gary cheated on her and he left. That's it. She never mentions him, never talks about how they met or what their relationship was like before it went wrong.' He let out a breath. 'The image I have of him is one I've created.'

While Milly had never hidden the fact she'd been married before – his and Cate's surnames were the giveaway there – nor had she spoken about it. In the absence of any factual information, Richie had attempted to fill the gaps himself and now wondered whether Cate had done the same.

'I don't think it's at all strange,' said Maxi. 'He'd hurt her badly and hadn't been there for any of you – but Fletch was there for you all. I can understand why she hasn't talked about it. You were a baby when it happened, so when would the right time to tell you have been?'

'I guess,' he conceded. 'Gary said Mum had told him what I studied, about how I spent some time in England; she even told him about my dream to exhibit a garden at Chelsea one day.'

'Riiiight?' Maxi elongated the word, turning it into a question.

'I don't have a problem with her telling him any of that, but …' He paused before asking, 'Has Mum said anything to you about meeting him separately, without Dad?'

'No, she hasn't.' Max manoeuvred in the seat to face him. 'If Milly had met Gary, why hadn't she said something?'

'Apparently, they met for coffee on Thursday. Mum hasn't said anything to me, and neither has Dad, which means—'

'That she hasn't told Fletch,' Max finished his sentence.

'Exactly.'

The hum of the radio filled the silence. Richie took his eyes off the road for a second. Max was staring at the road ahead, chewing on her bottom lip in the way she did when she was thinking about something. It used to drive him crazy – all he ever wanted to do was kiss those lips until she was so distracted that she'd forget what she'd been doing. These days, though, he was lucky enough to kiss her lips every day. Right now, though, the lip chewing was over something a little more serious.

'I can try and find out for you today,' she said. 'Kate and Milly will probably do what they did yesterday – take it in turns to have a break and keep me company.' Richie had asked if she wanted to spend the day back at their house, but she'd declined, saying she'd rather be with everyone else.

When Richie smiled his unspoken thanks, she said, 'Did you like him?'

He took a few seconds to consider his reply – it wasn't a simple question to answer. He hadn't wanted to like Gary. He'd hoped he was the man he'd always pictured – a faithless, untrusting, unfeeling bastard. The type of man who could cheat on his pregnant wife and shoot through as soon as the babies were born without looking back. But he hadn't found that man.

'I think I did,' he finally said, barely able to hear his own voice.

'And … you didn't want to.'

'No darling, I didn't want to like him.' He squeezed Max's hand that had come to rest on his thigh. 'He wants to meet you – he says he'll be staying around until Piglet is born.'

'I'm happy to meet him, but as for him staying around?'

'I know.' He didn't say as much, but they both knew that Gary staying around could only mean trouble.

CHAPTER FOURTEEN

Milly watched with fondness as Richie held and kissed Max goodbye before he headed down to the vineyard. Anyone would think he was leaving her for a week rather than just the few hours he'd be helping Tom's team of (mostly seasonal) workers to finish picking the last of the grapes.

Cam was out there somewhere too, although he certainly hadn't farewelled Milly in the same way. Until the last few days, their mornings always began the same way: she'd make him breakfast while he packed his lunch; they'd chat about what each had in store for the day, he'd kiss her goodbye and tell her to have a great day, she'd tell him to drive carefully and that she loved him. He'd say he loved her back, and they'd get on with the business of the day.

Today, for the third morning in a row, there was no chat, and the kiss goodbye was a graze on the cheek rather than her lips.

Yesterday they'd driven separately to the vineyard, Cam saying he wanted to be there to help the crew get set up. After dinner had been cleared away and Richie, Max, and Nathan had left – the pickers long back in town – she'd suggested they leave too.

'You go on ahead, Milly,' he'd said. 'I'll see you there.'

It had been almost midnight before he arrived home. He'd crawled into bed beside her, mumbled good night and gone to sleep. Unable to relax and not wanting to disturb him, Milly had taken her book into the living room to read. When she woke on the lounge this morning, a blanket was over her, and Cam had already left.

What had begun as a niggle of worry had grown until it threatened to consume her. It had to be Gary; there was no other explanation. In the early days, they'd never argued about Gary, although Cam had always been afraid Gary would reappear and she'd go back to him – regardless of how he'd treated her in the past. It was a combination of the way she'd ignored Gary's earlier indiscretions and the way Gary made Cam feel less than he was. She'd known that and had ensured she'd never given him any cause for concern.

The first time Gary drove a wedge between them was soon after they were together. Cam was keen to finalise the divorce so he and Milly could marry, but Gary insisted on speaking with her in person and alone. It was at that meeting Gary told her she could have either a divorce or her children – but not both. He'd reminded her she'd made an "until death do we part" promise, and he intended fulfilling that vow.

'How can you say that?' she'd demanded. 'What about the forsaking all others part?'

'If memory serves me correctly,' he'd drawled, 'we didn't say those words. As far as I recall, it was love, honour and respect that you insisted on.'

'In which case you've broken your promise to me. You've shown me neither love, honour, nor respect in what you've done.'

'Who said anything about not loving you? I've never stopped loving you,' he said. 'I simply love her as well. And in my own way, I think I'm honouring and respecting you as a mother by making this deal. You're the one who wants to break the "till death do we part" vow, not me. I'm quite happy to stay married to you.'

'So you don't have to marry her?'

'Perhaps.'

'I don't understand – we've settled the property; why don't you want to finalise everything else?'

He'd smiled that annoying lop-sided smile of his and said, 'Because I don't want to be free of you.'

'Don't you mean you don't want me to be free of you?'

'No, that's not what I mean.'

And then he'd looked at her in the way he used to look at her, the way that had made her blood bubble in her veins and her tummy flip. She'd shaken her head.

'We're not doing this, Gary. I'm with Cam now. I love Cam.'

He'd taken a step towards her and slid his finger lightly down her arm. Despite all her good intentions, and despite knowing what she did about him, her body had reacted the way it always reacted, and she'd swayed towards him.

That night when she got home, and Cam asked how the meeting had gone, she'd simply told him Gary wouldn't agree to a divorce – not yet anyway. He hadn't asked her anything else, but she'd known he'd wondered what had happened and what had been said.

It wasn't long after that when she'd discovered she was pregnant with Jess. Again, she'd attempted to secure the divorce she and Cam wanted. Again, Gary insisted on meeting face to face, just the two of them. 'This has nothing to do with Cam or Rachel,' he'd said. 'It's between us.'

He'd listened to her, and he'd declined her request. 'I don't think you really want a divorce, Melinda,' he'd said. 'Your head says you do, but …' He let his eyes finish the sentence as they ran slowly down her body, clinging to every curve, lingering on her mouth and her breasts.

She'd been later than expected getting home, and Cam had looked up from the show he was watching and said, 'I was expecting you before this, love.'

She'd ignored the worry in his eyes and said, 'He

won't agree, Cam. Can we just go on as we have been? Do we really need a piece of paper to prove to the world that we love each other?'

'What if I'd like a piece of paper?' Cam had said. 'I want all of us to be a family.'

'We can be.' She'd held his arm and looked up into his dear face. 'Even if we have different surnames, we can be a family. I won't risk losing them, Cam, and I won't have them shuttled across to the other side of the country every time he decides he wants to see them.'

He'd nodded and said that he understood, but Milly wasn't sure he did. Part of her hoped he didn't, that he couldn't read her mind. Cam was afraid of losing her to Gary – she just hoped he didn't know she was afraid of the same thing.

They'd had their version of a wedding – Cam called it a commitment ceremony, she referred to it as a hand-fasting – but whatever it was called, it had confirmed their intentions as strongly as if they'd signed a marriage certificate. And they'd been happy over the years – content with their lives, their children, and their love for each other.

And now Gary was back, and it was starting all over again. Surely Cam couldn't think Gary would still tempt her? But if she didn't believe that, why had she met Gary in secret, why had she not told Cam about the meeting, and why was she now so afraid that somehow Cam had found out that she *had* met Gary? It was all such a mess.

Shaking her head slightly to send the thoughts back to where they belonged, she walked across the lawn to greet Max.

'I wondered if you'd stay home today,' she said. 'Are you sure all this isn't too much for you?'

'I'm fine, Milly. I want to be out and about; as it all gets closer, I'm too inclined to worry about the logistics of it.'

'Big head, small hole sort of stuff?' grinned Milly.

'That's a good way of describing it, but yes. During the week, our final prenatal class talked about pain relief options and different birth positions, and while Richie wants me to think about it and have a plan, I truly just want to see what happens.'

Milly smiled and rested her hand on Max's tummy. 'Yes, this child is going to come out, and you have little say in how that's going to unfold. Rick's right in one respect, though – it's good for you to understand your options so you can react when you need to, but also be prepared that the choices might get taken away from you anyway.'

Max rubbed at the top of her belly. 'Part of me wants Piglet to stay in there where he or she is safe, but at the same time'—she rolled her eyes— 'it's getting really uncomfortable.'

'I remember just how uncomfortable it can get. Not long to go, though.' She didn't tell Max that one day she'd be standing here saying the same thing to her daughter or daughter-in-law, and it would feel like days rather than years had passed. 'You two were later than I thought you'd be this morning? Taking advantage of no Jess tearing through your bedroom door to have a well-deserved sleep-in?'

A flutter of panic churned in Milly's stomach when Max avoided her eyes; then, with a small shake of her head, Max said, 'Richie met his father for breakfast.'

There was no mistaking she was referring to Gary. 'I see.' Trying to breathe normally, she hoped the panic didn't show on her face. 'How did that go?'

Max smiled kindly at her and took her arm, leading her slowly back up to the house. 'He already knew a lot about Richie,' she said gently. 'You've seen Gary and talked to him too, haven't you?'

Milly barely nodded, unable to meet Max's eyes. 'Does Richie know?'

'He does. Gary told him.' Max hesitated briefly. 'Richie's mostly concerned that Fletch doesn't know about the meeting.' She spoke slowly, quietly, as if she didn't want to say what she had to say. 'We both are.'

'I see,' Milly said again.

'It's not our business, but—'

Milly cut her off. 'Actually, Max, it's very much your business – and Cam's business and Richie, Cate's and Jess's business. It's everyone's business.'

'Is that why Cam …?'

'Why he's avoiding me?' She rested her head on Max's shoulder and sighed. 'I thought you'd noticed. I think Cam suspects, and it's driving him mad not knowing – but at the same time, he doesn't want to ask.'

They stopped walking, and Max turned to her, concern written all over her face, and said, 'You have to talk to Cam … and Richie.'

'I know. But I also have things I need to say to everyone, and I don't know how to do it. I only want to do it once. I was hoping it could wait until Jess is home.'

'And Cate?'

'I'll ring her separately. She's made it clear she doesn't want to meet Gary and won't be coming home while he's here.' Unlike Richie, Cate had vague memories of her father and was adamant she wanted nothing to do with him.

'That could be awkward,' said Max, grimacing. 'He told Richie he doesn't intend on leaving until the baby arrives, and Cate has said she'll be on the first plane over here when the baby arrives.'

Milly exhaled slowly. 'Yes, Gary said the same to me. I'll call Jess and tell her to come for dinner on Thursday night.'

'I have a better idea,' said Max. 'She hasn't seen the house yet, and I know she'll be dying to, so come to ours instead. I'll cook.'

'Are you sure that's not too much for you?' Milly's protest was half-hearted.

'Heavens, no, it'll be something simple. But please, Milly, talk to Fletch.'

'I will,' she promised, her fingers crossed behind her back. After all, she'd only promised she'd talk to Fletch; she hadn't made any promise about when she'd do it.

CHAPTER FIFTEEN

The weather on Milford Track was about as good as it got. The group, on the whole, was a well-prepared one – except for one solo traveller, a middle-aged Australian woman named Rose. She'd managed a steady pace on days one and two but struggled – from both a fitness and a confidence viewpoint – with Mackinnon Pass on the third day. To make matters worse, she'd stumbled on the way down, twisting her lower back, so Jess had had to help with her backpack.

Despite her difficulties, Rose had gritted her teeth and carried on without complaint, one foot after the other on the long, steep descent, her smile rarely slipping. Jess had chatted easily with the older woman and surprised herself by telling Rose about Beach Road, Nathan, and how much she was looking forward to seeing him the following weekend.

'He told me he loved me,' she said, 'and I wanted to tell him I felt the same way, but …'

'It was a shock to you to realise it?' guessed Rose.

'Yes,' admitted Jess, keeping an eye on Rose as she

picked her way forward, choosing each step carefully. 'Also, though, it's the first time anyone's said it to me, and it surprised me a bit.'

'Do you think he was disappointed you didn't say it back?'

Jess thought for a second or two and then said, 'Yeah, I think he might've been, at first anyway – not that he said so.'

She mightn't have said the words, but as they'd made love that night, Jess had *shown* Nathan exactly how she felt about him in the best way possible. Before she'd left the next morning, she'd kissed him awake and said, 'Thanks for telling me.'

With his groggy morning voice, he'd replied, 'You're welcome,' and had sat up in bed watching her pull her boots on and jam her waterproof into her backpack.

She'd stood to go, kissed him again, and said, 'I feel it too.'

He'd smiled slowly. 'I hoped you did,' he said. 'Even if you can't say it yet. We'll talk next weekend, eh?'

Remembering the conversation brought a wistful smile to her face that Rose, walking ahead of her, missed.

It wasn't until day five of the tramp that Jess allowed her thoughts to drift. After breakfast, they began the day with a cruise on Milford Sound. Jess had lost count of the number of times she'd done this cruise, but the sight of Mitre Peak and the sheer scale of Stirling Falls never ceased to render her speechless. Usually, Jess used the hours on the boat – and then later on the bus back to Queenstown – going through her to-do list, working through ideas in her head for the café, breaking down problems that needed solutions, coming up with "what-if" scenarios. Today, though, her thoughts were all on Nathan.

Something had changed between them on Friday night – it wasn't just that he'd said, "I love you", it was a shift into something that was more committed. Was committed the right word? Whatever it was, they'd moved there.

At first, at least on the surface, Nathan, tall broad-shouldered and fit in an outdoorsy sort of way, was like every other man who'd broken her impetuous heart over the years. Not that she ever allowed anyone to see she was bruised; all her family and friends saw was the way she shrugged and jumped in again next time with the same amount of enthusiasm, the romantic equivalent of getting back on the horse.

Like many of the ones who'd come before, Nathan was only in town for a short time and a good time – and a very good time they'd had. When he left to go back to Australia, despite the words they'd exchanged and the (quite frankly fabulous) sex they'd had, Jess firmly believed that would be the last she'd hear or see of him – even though right from the start it had felt different for her.

The first inkling that he might break the pattern of a lifetime was when he called her as soon as he arrived back home in Cairns. Then he called her the next night. And the night after. Even before his mother had decided to settle in Arrowtown, Nathan had planned to come back to Queenstown for a long weekend, and Jess had dared to hope that this one would last longer than they usually did.

Nathan differed from her usual type in other ways too. He was adventurous, but not recklessly so. He would tramp any track she wanted but drew the line at some of the other activities Queenstown offered, such as bungy jumping and skydiving. 'I'm not interested, Jay,' he'd said. 'They're just about quick thrills, and that's not who I am.'

As he'd said it, he'd looked deeply into her eyes, and she'd known he wasn't just talking about adrenaline activities.

Most visitors came here for the skiing or the tramping or to launch themselves off a platform to see if they'd bounce back – and then they'd go home to their desk jobs and their gyms. Nathan, though, loved nature and the outdoors as much as she did. Being a marine biologist, he was interested in the birds, plants, and the environment. All of it. He was the first man she'd been with who was happy to tramp in silence, allowing the sounds of the forest to surround them; standing statue-still to allow a titipounamu to hop around on the track in front of him without being tempted to take a photo to post somewhere to prove it had happened. For him, it was enough to observe the little bird and enjoy the experience.

He was patient, kind and reliable, yet prepared to stand his ground with her when he needed to. His kisses blew her mind, and she burned at even the thought of his touch. When he proposed taking three months' leave of absence from his job in Cairns and giving New Zealand a chance, Jess began to hope this could be *it*. That she could have what Cate had with Harry, what Richie had with Max, and even what her parents had together.

'We have a window, Jay,' he'd said. 'A few months where we can explore this thing – see whether we can make a relationship work – but we can't do it with me in Cairns and you in Queenstown.'

Before she could tell him she had a business and a family and way too many responsibilities to think about uprooting herself – even for a few months – he said, 'There's a voluntary role going on a research project with Otago University's Department of Marine Science on Stewart Island – Rakiura, I think they call it. It's seasonal, so the timing's perfect, and it's only a few hours away if I time the ferries right. I can be here most weekends – and you might come to me some weekends.'

She'd shuddered when he'd told her what the project was about. 'Great white sharks,' he said, 'don't have the same public relations machine as humpback whales and sea turtles do yet are in just as much danger – actually more danger. The problem is we don't know enough about them or their patterns of migration.'

'You can't possibly like them more than the animals you get on the reef.'

'Perhaps that's because I don't understand them. Besides, I've always wanted to dive in kelp forests, and there are some great ones down there. I've seen videos of the sea sponges below them – you've got to see it to believe it, Jay. They look like little villages of marshmallows. It's incredible. Have you ever been diving?' She'd shaken her head. 'Snorkelling?' She shook her head again. She'd hardly even swum in the ocean, not that she told him that. 'You must try it sometime – maybe snorkelling on the reef at home, man, you'd love that.' She'd smiled at his enthusiasm but had been noncommittal.

'Please tell me you don't have to get in the water with the sharks.' Jess had tried to keep the fear out of her voice.

'I do, but it'll be in a cage, and it's all perfectly safe. I'm excited to give it a go.'

'That's alright then.' She'd pretended a nonchalance that she didn't feel. The image of Nathan in a cage at the bottom of the ocean in the dark with a monster shark coming at him was one she pushed to the back of her mind.

As if by unspoken agreement, they'd avoided the subject of what would happen when Nathan's leave from his job was up. Jess had secretly hoped by the end of the three months he'd be tired of the travel, but so in love with her, he'd hand in his notice in Cairns and decide to stay in Queenstown. After all, that's what Max had done for Richie; there was no reason Nathan wouldn't do the same for her. Even the fact he'd come up last weekend when he knew she wouldn't be here just to help Tom with the harvest, well, that showed he was becoming a part of the community, didn't it?

So when he told her he loved her on Friday night, Jess had had to struggle to hide her elation. She was sure that was why the sky seemed bluer on track this time, the trees greener, the view across from Mackinnon Pass clearer than she recalled it ever being, and the food in the lodges was even tastier and more plentiful than usual. As for the trampers, Jess didn't think she'd ever walked with a more agreeable group. When she said it was a pleasure to have shared the experience with them, she truly meant it.

As she was sitting on the bus back to Te Anau, she decided this weekend they'd talk – really talk. Jess had never actually asked Nathan not to go back to Cairns, but this weekend she would. She'd tell him how she felt about him, and she'd ask him to stay. He'd need to go over for a week or so and unwind what was left of his life up there, and she might even take a week off work and go with him, but after that, they'd be able to get on with planning their life together. If Jess decided to expand the business and buy another café or a bakery, he could manage it. Even if she didn't buy another business, they'd find something for him to do. He might even find work with the Department of Conservation. It might have nothing to do with marine biology, but it was in nature, and Nathan loved nature. They'd work it out, she was sure of it.

At Te Anau, Jess switched on her phone while everyone stretched their legs and looked for coffee. Flicking through the texts as they pinged through, it surprised her to see only one from Nathan – confirming he'd got back to Stewart Island okay the previous Sunday and was already missing her. Usually when she was on track, he'd text once a day even though he knew she had no cellphone reception.

As she pondered this, another text landed – from Max, inviting her to dinner the following night. After sending a reply to Max in the affirmative – Jess really couldn't believe she'd be the last one to see their house – the only person she wanted to talk to was Nathan. Friday and Nathan suddenly seemed too far away, so she picked up her phone and called him even though he'd still be working – or whatever it was you called the work that he did. (He'd tried to explain how it wasn't all diving and outdoors, but a lot of observation and data collection and analysis – which was when her eyes had glazed over, and she'd tuned out). She wanted to hear his voice, even if it was his recorded message.

Getting his voice message as expected, she left one of her own. 'Hey you, I'm back in civilisation, well Te Anau anyway. I'm about to get back on the bus, so will lose reception again. Anyway, I just wanted to say hello. So, hello.' She nearly said it then, almost told him she loved him back, but she wanted the first time to be face to face, not in a voice message. 'Anyway, call me?'

Jess tried Nathan again when the bus pulled up in Queenstown, but again got his message rather than him. Not wanting to go home and wait for him to call, she pulled her backpack on again and began walking to Beach Road instead.

The café was, as she'd known it would be, closed, but Holly was still in the kitchen.

'What are you working on, Holl?' Jess asked, dumping her backpack in a corner and walking across to the bench where Holly was standing.

'I didn't expect to see you this afternoon,' Holly said, giving her a quick hug.

'Yeah, I thought I'd drop in and clean my emails out so I can get a fresh start tomorrow.' Jess peered at the plates Holly was fiddling with. 'These look great. What are they?'

'Profiteroles with goat's curd and rosemary-scented local honey. Try one.'

Jess bit into one, closing her eyes as the flavours melded together. 'This is so good.'

Holly's pale cheeks flushed bright pink. 'I'm putting together a Taste of The South menu,' she explained. 'When you said you wanted to look at a canapé-style menu to launch in spring, I thought I might get a head start on it.'

Jess nodded in approval. 'If you're going in that direction, check out what they're doing at Rātā,' said Jess, naming one of the destination restaurants in Queenstown. 'They even do a posh version of the cheese roll. Nathan thought it was one of the best things he'd ever eaten.' At the thought of Nathan, her mood dipped – he still hadn't returned her call. Deliberately dragging her mind from him, Jess said, 'What does Dan think of this?'

'He loves it – it was his idea to smoke the curd lightly and to use the rosemary.'

Unusually, Holly didn't colour at the mention of Dan.

'How are you two getting on?' asked Jess.

'Really well. He's always listened to my opinions, but lately, he's treating me as an equal rather than his apprentice. We bounce ideas off each other.'

Oh. While Jess was pleased to hear that, she was disappointed no headway seemed to have been made

on the romantic front. Even though she didn't believe
Dan had feelings for her, it certainly wouldn't hurt if
he was diverted towards someone else who had been
under his nose the whole time. Perhaps Dan and Holly
needed to move out of the kitchen and into a more
social situation.

'I know,' she said. 'Why don't the two of you go
to Rātā? It can be my treat, seeing it's for research. You
can see firsthand what they're doing there and get to
know each other better outside of the kitchen.'

It was such an inspired idea; Jess was amazed she
hadn't thought of it before now. She was, therefore,
surprised to see Holly drop her head and shuffle her
feet.

'I don't know how to say this, Jess, and I know you
think we'd be great together, but ...'

'What?'

'I've had a couple of dates with someone I might
really like. In fact, we're going out again tonight.'

Jess sat back in her chair, her eyes wide. This was
unexpected. 'So you've gone off Dan then?'

'Obviously not just like that,' said Holly. She picked
up the pen she'd been using to sketch plating styles and
tapped it against the notebook. 'It's been a little while
coming. I tried everything to get him to notice me,
but nothing seemed to work, so I decided enough was
enough, and I couldn't wait around any longer.'

'I see.'

'I know you wanted to see us together and thank you for that, but'—she shook her head—'Dan and I, well, it's just not going to happen, and I accept that now. To be honest, I was even wondering whether he felt something for you, but then I figured he's like an older brother to you – and you have Nathan.'

Jess forced herself to meet Holly's eyes without wavering. 'Yes, he's like another brother to me – although when your brother is Richie, one brother is absolutely enough!' She screwed her nose up and rolled her eyes.

Holly chuckled at the look on Jess's face. 'That's what I thought,' she said. 'Anyway, if you don't need me anymore, I'll head off – legs to shave and all that.'

'You get yourself date-ready,' said Jess. 'And have fun.'

Holly's blush was answer enough.

After Holly left, Jess made a cup of tea, snuck one of the profiteroles and settled in to go through her emails. Nothing had gone amiss while she'd been away, and Jess was almost disappointed about that. It was becoming apparent she'd need to make some wholesale changes sooner rather than later – and not just for financial reasons. With the tramping season about to end, and the café entering its peak tourists time, it was business as usual – and business as usual was no longer enough to challenge her.

After rinsing out her tea mug, Jess picked up her

backpack, switched off the lights, locked up, and began the walk up the hill to her house. The sun had barely dipped behind the mountains, leaving a wash of orange and yellow against the darkening sky. She pulled up the collar of her coat as the chilled air buffeted her face. A change in the weather was forecast by the end of the week and possibly even some early snow on the peaks. Jess shivered at the thought of it.

Everything looked in order as she slid her key into the door of her semi-detached townhouse, which was spread over two levels. After hanging her waterproof from the hook in the entrance, she emptied most of the contents of her backpack straight into the washing machine. She toed off her boots and stripped off the rest of her clothes, throwing them into the machine too. After adding the detergent and switching it on, she walked naked up the stairs to the main living area.

Once showered and dressed, Jess wandered into the kitchen in search of food. There was, unsurprisingly, nothing resembling fresh food in her fridge, so she tore open a frozen ready meal, pierced the plastic with a fork and popped it into the microwave. Pouring a glass of wine, she sat on a stool at the kitchen bench while she waited for the microwave to do its thing and gazed around the room.

Jess rarely gave much thought to her home – it was somewhere she slept and (occasionally) ate. She was rarely there between work and tramping, so it hadn't seemed important to pay much attention to how her house looked. As a result, it was practical rather than stylish. The L-shaped charcoal modular lounge was comfortable enough to sleep on if she did just that when watching TV, and she'd chosen the cushions more from a need to have cushions than by design. Although she had family photos scattered around here and there, there was no art on the walls. The same went for her bedroom – it was a place to sleep and a place to make love with Nathan, and that was that.

Maybe, she thought as she ripped off the plastic and ate her dinner, she should do something about that. Perhaps she could paint a wall or two, buy some art and some throws. Make the space more homely, put more of her personality into it. If Nathan was going to move in here, if they would make a life here, this should be a place they wanted to come home to.

As she was pondering this, her phone rang. Nathan, finally.

'Hey you,' she answered, loving the way her blood was suddenly dancing along in her veins.

'Hey yourself,' he said. 'Good walk?'

'Yeah, the weather was perfect, and the air was so clear.'

'That's good.' He sounded weirdly stilted, and Jess's heart skipped a beat for all the wrong reasons.

'What's wrong?' she asked. Then, hearing an announcement in the background, 'Where are you?'

'In ... Brisbane,' he said after a brief silence. 'Waiting for my connection to Cairns.'

'What?' The breath left Jess's body, and if she hadn't already been sitting, her legs wouldn't have held her upright. 'Why? When?' she asked, and then, 'Why didn't you tell me?'

'It happened suddenly, and you had no reception.'

'What happened suddenly?'

'Ferg called — you know, my boss.' When Jess said nothing, he continued. 'My leave isn't up for another month, but he wants to talk through some options with me. There have been some changes at the foundation, and Ferg wants me to interview for one of the vacant positions. There are some other opportunities too, and ...'

'When did this happen?' Jess demanded, her voice squeaking past the lump in her throat.

'Yesterday. Ferg emailed me through a ticket, and I've been travelling since early this morning. Invercargill to Christchurch, then to Brisbane. I still have one leg to go.'

Jess caught her top lip between her teeth, pushing down on it until it hurt.

'Jay, say something, please.'

'What do you want me to say? I thought we were going to talk about this before you went back to Australia.'

'We *will* talk about it,' he said. 'I'm only staying

a couple of days, and I'll be back. I'll have more of an idea about that in the morning after I've spoken to Ferg. Why don't you come out here and stay for a week? It'll give you a chance to look around.'

The lump in her throat plummeted into her belly. 'I can't just up and leave, Nathan. I have a business to run—'

'Which you have no problem leaving for a week when you're on track,' he pointed out.

'And Max is about to have a baby,' she finished. 'It's completely the wrong time for me to leave the country.'

'Okay, I understand that, but we need to talk properly, Jay – about what's going to happen when my leave is finished.'

'I know,' she mumbled. 'Does this mean you're definitely going back?' Her words sounded small, as though they'd come from a place she didn't know. 'If you're going back to interview, it sounds pretty definite.'

'No, Jess, it doesn't. It means I'm exploring the options.' His voice sounded rough, tired.

'I see.'

'Anyway, they're calling my flight. I'll text you when I land, eh?'

'Okay,' she whispered.

'I love you, Jay,' he said and then hung up before she could answer him.

'I love you too,' she whispered to the empty screen.

CHAPTER SIXTEEN

Jess slumped on her stool as if the conversation had taken all the breath out of her. She'd been so sure he'd stay. So confident that she hadn't considered the alternative. Cheeks burning, she pushed her stool back so hard that it fell over. She took a deep breath and shook herself. He hadn't *gone* gone; he'd only gone for a few days – a week at the most. He'd miss her – just like she'd miss him – and he'd be back. He said he would be. And once he was back, it was up to her to make sure he stayed.

That decided, she poured herself another wine, settled into the lounge, switched on the telly and tried not to think about Nathan. And it worked too – at least it did until she was tucked up in bed and snuggled into his pillow.

He'd asked her to go to Cairns for a week to have a look around. What he really meant was for her to see if she liked it, if she could live there with him. But how could she go when Queenstown was her entire life?

It was common knowledge what everyone said

about her, how they all laughed at her flightiness, her impetuousness, her wilfulness, her flashes of temper, and the way she dusted herself off after each heartbreak. The labels had been part of her for as long as she'd been able to understand them, and they dated back to when she'd been desperate to be included with Cate and Richie, to prove she was as strong and as fearless and wouldn't slow them down. Cate and Richie were older, more mature, responsible. Yet she, Jess, was the one who had stayed behind in Queenstown when Cate and Richie had left. She was the one who had secured herself a place in the community and built a successful business.

Jess had got her first part-time job when she was fourteen and had been working ever since – usually more than one job – scraping together money until she had enough to pester the previous owner of Beach Road to accept a deal worth far less than he should've accepted to secure the café. With Cam's help, the bank had come to the party. Then she'd worked every waking hour to turn the café around, to prove to her father she knew what she was doing, to create the destination café it had the potential to be. Each time the café featured on Instagram or in an article listing the top places to eat in Queenstown, while she may not have created the food or the pictures, she'd been responsible for it all.

Buying Beach Road was a risk, but it was one she'd been planning towards for a long time. She'd done the numbers, created a business plan and a strategy and documented all the risks she could think of – with mitigation for each. It might have appeared to her family and anyone else following along that she was flying by the seat of her pants, but the truth was very different.

Going to Cairns with Nathan was just plain dangerous. So much could go wrong and, if she wasn't careful, she could lose everything she'd worked so hard to build. She loved him, there was no question about that, but did she love him enough to walk away from Beach Road and her family? That was a different question indeed – and one Jess didn't have any answers for.

The following afternoon Jess was sitting at her little desk in the back corner of the kitchen going through accounts – more for something to do than out of necessity. The café was closed, and Holly had left as soon as she cleaned her section down. She'd confided to Jess her date the previous evening had gone so well they were going out again tonight, and this time she thought she'd ask him home with her.

Jess was happy for her – of course she was – so she tried to show a level of enthusiasm and interest that, in all honesty, she was incapable of feeling now. At least not while Nathan was away exploring opportunities for his life after her. Without realising she was doing it, Jess squared her shoulders as if preparing to dust herself down and get back up – something she'd need to do when Nathan left for good. On every other occasion, though, her heart hadn't been broken, just a little bruised. This time would be different.

'You're here late, Jess.' Dan's voice broke into her thoughts. 'Lots of catching up to do?'

'No, not really,' said Jess. 'I just—'

'Don't want to go home because Nathan's not there?' Dan guessed.

Jess's head jerked up from her paperwork, surprising a look on Dan's face she hadn't seen before. His mouth was in a straight line, his face taut and his blue eyes were, there was no other word for it, sad. Why hadn't she seen it before? Had it been there, and she either hadn't realised or hadn't wanted to see it? Even if she had noticed, Jess acknowledged, she still wouldn't have done anything about it – Dan was a friend and the closest thing she'd had to a brother during the years Richie was away. If he felt more for her than that, she was sorry for it, but she couldn't reciprocate.

'Something like that,' she admitted. 'Although I'm due over at Richie and Max's tonight for dinner, so I'm just filling in some time. To be honest, everything here'—she waved her hand at the spreadsheet on her laptop—'is in perfect order.'

'I saw Nathan at Tom's the other evening – he was telling me about the work he's doing.' He shuddered.

'Rather him than me – as far as I'm concerned, sharks can have the oceans all to themselves.'

Jess laughed at the look of horror on his face.

'He mentioned he only has another month left on this project. What's going to happen with you guys then?'

As hope flared across his face, a heart-shaped lump rose into her throat, and she swallowed hard, but it wouldn't shift. Then she blinked, but the tears wouldn't stay in her eyes. A choking sob escaped her lips.

Dan was beside her in an instant, pulling her out of her chair and into his arms and letting her cry. It would've been so easy to stay like that, but it wasn't fair to him. Reluctantly, she pulled herself from his embrace and wiped her eyes with the back of her hand.

Still sniffing, she said, 'I'm sorry Dan, I don't know what came over me. I'm alright, really I am.'

'You know I'm here for you, right?' he said, catching a stray tear on her chin.

'Sure, after all, what are friends for?' Jess forced a strangled laugh and turned away from the hurt on his face to perch her bum on the side of the desk and to rummage in her bag for a tissue.

After a few seconds of silence, he inhaled deeply and said, 'Jess, I know now isn't the best moment, but it's time I left and worked somewhere else.'

The shock of his words forced her head up.

'What?'

'I've got a job in Melbourne,' he said, his eyes focussed on the floor. 'I need a break.'

Dan's voice was so soft she strained to hear. 'Is this because of me?' Her words sounded squeaky and high-pitched.

Still, Dan stared at the floor and thrust his hands into his pockets. 'Yeah,' he said. 'Even if Nathan isn't here …'

'I'm so sorry, Dan,' said Jess. 'Truly I am, it's just—' She stood and walked to where he was standing.

'I know – I'm like another brother.' He looked up then and met her eyes; his mouth curved into a sardonic smile. 'It's all a bit weird, eh?'

Jess gave a short chuckle. 'It is a bit – after all, you know the worst of me.'

'And the best.'

'Maybe.'

'I'm just sorry I didn't realise it until I saw you with Nathan, the lucky bastard.' There was a pause before he added, 'He's good for you, Jess. Really good, don't let him go.'

Jess's throat closed again. 'I don't seem to have a choice in that,' she choked. 'He's already gone.' She bit the inside of her mouth and pushed her nails into her palm – anything to stop the tears threatening to overflow again.

'Oh, Jess.' She turned away from Dan as his eyes

were full of pity, sadness, and resignation. 'He didn't say anything on the weekend.'

'No. He left yesterday. It was a sudden thing. He'll be back, though, I'm sure of it.' Jess forced a weak smile.

'Why don't you go to him?' Dan said quietly, resting a hand on her shoulder. 'If you care about him, don't let him go.'

Jess swept her arm around the kitchen. 'How can I? I have all of this. Plus, now my chef is buggering off over the ditch to Australia.'

'You know as well as I do, this place runs itself now. Holly can manage, and Blake's settling in well; it's fortunate we took on a new apprentice when we did.' He smiled ruefully. 'Things won't fall apart just because you and I aren't here.'

Jess waved his words away. 'How long will you be in Melbourne for?' she asked. 'You can't be thinking of leaving forever – Queenstown's your home.'

Dan shrugged. 'As long as it takes to get you out of my head,' he said flatly. 'I can't stay here and see you every day and know …' He shook his head. 'I won't do that to myself anymore.'

'I'd hoped you and Holly—?'

Dan cocked his head to the side, a sheepish grin on his face. 'You figured that because Holly used to have a crush on me, you could arrange it so we'd all be happy?'

'You knew about that?'

'Yeah, it's why I've always been careful not to let her think we could ever be anything else.' He exhaled and rubbed at his chin. 'In that regard, I've been kinder to her than I have been to myself.'

'I thought—'

'You thought you had it all worked out, therefore, that's exactly what would happen?'

Jess hunched one shoulder.

'It doesn't work like that, Jess. You don't get to decide that I'll be attracted to someone just because you want me to be, or that I'll lose interest in you just because it doesn't suit you, or that Nathan will give up everything he loves just because you've decided that's what he'll do. I know you have a way of making things turn out the way you imagine they will, but you can't make those assumptions with people's emotions. There are consequences.'

'But consequences are fun things that haven't happened yet,' said Jess, forcing a smile and hoping he'd share the old joke with her.

'Not when it comes to relationships,' he said, holding her stare until she broke the connection. 'Anyway, I said what I needed to say, but think about going with him, Jess – you have a chance to be happy, don't waste it because you're scared to try.'

'I'm not scared; I just have responsibilities,' said Jess indignantly, her chin jutting out.

'If you say so.' He reached for her hand and placed a kiss on the back of it. 'Take a chance, Jess, and go with Nathan.' He took a deep breath before adding, 'Or ask me to stay for you.'

She took a step back, shaking her head slowly, unable to meet his eyes. 'I'm sorry Dan.'

His eye's closed briefly and, with a slight nod, said, 'Yeah, so am I.' He forced a smile before turning and calling over his shoulder, 'See you tomorrow?'

'Yeah, see you tomorrow.'

Dan trudged down the stairs, shoulders slumped, head bent. In that moment, she wished she could love Dan as more than a friend and quasi-brother – it would make everything so much easier. The problem, she acknowledged, was that Nathan already had her heart.

CHAPTER SEVENTEEN

'I can't believe I'm the last person to see your house,' said Jess with a pout.

'You're hardly the last person,' said Max, stepping forward to give Jess a welcoming hug.

'You've been away since we moved in,' added Richie, smiling at his sister's dramatics. 'So, it's not our fault.'

'I wanted to come over on that Sunday when you moved in, but Nathan told me I needed to give you some space.' She gave a short laugh and rolled her eyes in an "as if" way.

'Thank god for Nathan,' muttered Richie.

'I heard that! Admit it, big brother, you're going to miss having me barge into your bedroom.'

Richie shook his head and laughed. 'Yeah, nah,' he drawled. '*That* we won't miss, will we darling?' He reached for Max and cuddled her to his side.

Jess watched them, a picture suddenly coming of her and Nathan someday in the doorway of their new home. She shook her head slightly to clear it of the image. It was way too early to be thinking like that – or was it too late? 'Am I going to stand here at your front door all evening – as lovely as it is – or are you going to show me around?'

Max linked her arm through Jess's. 'Come on through,' she said, leading her into the kitchen and living room.

'Just wow,' Jess said, her eyes widening and darting over every inch of the space. 'You've done an amazing job – it looks like something out of one of those real estate design shows.'

'Let me guess, underfloor heating in the concrete?' she asked.

'You got it,' said Richie. 'We can't be doing with cold toes in the winter.'

'Those views!' Jess walked across to the full-height sliding doors, her gaze captured by the lake and the mountains, The Remarkables, rising high above it.

'Come and see the bedrooms,' said Max, leading her down the long side of the L to the three bedrooms, a study, and the main bathroom. 'This one is ours.'

'There's that view again,' gushed Jess. 'I love how the colours you've used in the cushions and throws makes it all feel as though the outside is inside – if that makes sense.' She ran her hand across the beautifully textured wallpaper and raised her eyebrows at the free-standing bath. 'I know about you two and your baths – do you even both fit in there?'

'Sadly no,' said Max, her trademark blush colouring her pale cheeks.

'Which is why we have a walk-in shower built for two,' added Richie with a wicked grin.

Jess shook her head in mock exasperation.

The other bedrooms were as beautifully decorated as was the main bathroom. The nursery, however, left her speechless for longer than Jess was usually without speech. 'Hooley dooley!'

'What?' Max burst out laughing at the expression.

'Sorry, it's something I picked up from Nathan, but wow just doesn't cut it. This nursery is flipping awesome! You did this, Richie?'

What he'd created on the wall of Piglet's room defied description. Jess's eyes filled with tears, and she shook her head to push them back. This in love thing had made her more sentimental – or what Richie and Max had was contagious. She figured you couldn't be around that much love without catching some of it – or at least wanting to catch some of it.

Richie was trying not to smile too broadly, and he was standing taller, his chest out. 'It's not too bad, eh?'

'Yeah, not too bad at all.' On impulsive, she pulled him into his arms and squeezed him tight. 'You must've gotten all the creative genes on offer – I couldn't do anything like this.'

A flush of pink spread across his cheeks. 'Max is pretty good on the design front too,' he said.

'That's true,' said Jess, twirling the mobile hanging over the cot.

'And your creativity goes into your business.' Richie paused. 'Dan and Holly are worried about what big new ideas you've had after so long on track.'

'Well, come to think on it, I came up with something pretty special while on Milford,' Jess lied, not wanting to think about how she was going to deal with Dan's departure. And it was all her fault.

Max laughed. 'I knew it! Anyway, your parents will be here soon, so let's get a drink while I get dinner ready.'

'Mum and Dad are coming too?'

Max's gaze flicked away, and a frisson of something not quite right scooted through Jess's tummy. 'Yes, we hadn't had everyone here yet for a meal, and it seems a pity not to give that oven a proper workout before Piglet comes.'

Max led the way back to the kitchen where Richie was already pouring Jess a wine, Max a sparkling mineral water and himself a beer.

'I suppose the next project is the garden,' said Jess. 'Any ideas?'

'Any ideas?' scoffed Richie. 'I'm glad you asked. I've got the designs right here.'

Jess was fascinated with his sketches, including a lawn for play, a kitchen garden for Max, some fruit trees, and various other plantings. Thankfully, the arrival of her parents saved her from Richie's boring plant explanations.

They'd already had the tour of the house, so they settled into the kitchen to chat while Max dealt with dinner.

'Did you know about the mural, Mum?' Jess asked.

'No, it was a complete surprise to me. Your father and Nathan were in on it though – and Tom too, I think.'

'I still can't believe Nathan said nothing to me.' Even saying his name aloud sent a fresh wave of pain crashing through Jess.

'He's a man who can keep secrets when needed,' said Richie. 'Besides, it does you good not to know everything.' As he said it, he turned away, as did Milly.

Cam, who, it now occurred to Jess, had said very little, walked out onto the deck off the lounge. Richie joined him, the two men facing the mountains. Her father seemed somehow smaller, diminished beside Richie.

Her mother was also watching them, but with a slight shake of her head, brought her attention back to her glass of wine. *What was going on?*

'It smells amazing, Max,' said Milly. 'Roast chicken?'

'Yes, but with a difference. I'm using the fat and chicken juices to make a sauce that I'll toss through some pasta with shallots, herbs, and parmesan. Then we'll tear the chicken into it.'

'Roast chicken pasta?' said Jess. 'I've never heard of it, and I can't understand why – it sounds incredible. What's for pudding?'

'My chocolate bread and butter pudding.'

Milly looked up quickly, meeting Max's gaze. *Something is definitely up.*

'Isn't that the one Richie reckons is like a chocolatey truth serum – it eases the path to say things that need to be said?' Jess asked.

Max laughed as she pulled the chicken out of the oven to rest, but it sounded high-pitched and very unlike her usual laugh. 'I have known it to do that, but it's also just very yummy. Jess, can you do me a favour please and chop that parsley and Milly, do you mind grating some parmesan? I need to pee *again.*'

'Did the picking go well?' Jess asked her mother.

'It did. We got the grapes in at the right time – they're forecasting a change tomorrow night and possibly some early snow on the peaks,' Milly said. When the cheese was grated, she asked, 'How's Nathan enjoying his job? He'd have to be two months into it now, wouldn't he? I imagine the driving's getting him down.'

Jess scraped the chopped parsley into a little pile on the board. 'He hasn't said so. I think he's enjoying it, though. He's full of talk about it every time I see him, so that's a good sign.'

She couldn't bear the pity in her mother's eyes if

she mentioned Nathan was in Australia. It surprised her that Kate hadn't already told her mother.

Max was soon back, rubbing the top of her belly. 'Sorry about that. Piglet seems to be sitting on my bladder.'

Milly narrowed her eyes. 'More like headbutting it I'd think by the way the baby looks to be lying. You look like you've dropped.'

'Do you think? I have an appointment tomorrow afternoon, so I guess he'll tell me then whether the baby has engaged.'

Milly nodded thoughtfully. 'I think it has.'

'I'm still two weeks away.'

'Hmmm,' said Milly. 'Is there anything else I can do for dinner?'

'No, I'm about to put all of this together, so if someone wants to set the table and get Richie's attention to freshen drinks, we can eat.'

To lighten the tension around the table, Jess chattered about the canapé menu Holly was creating. 'Holly has some great ideas and I think the timing's right to give her some more responsibility. I'm also considering expanding the bakery side.' She ignored the look Max was giving her.

'Plus, you think Dan will notice Holly if she's not by his side all day?' Milly voiced what Jess knew Max was thinking.

'No, it's not my place to interfere in their lives,' she

said as if the idea of bringing them together had never occurred to her. 'The way I figure it, it's a two birds thing: I get to expand the business and give Holly the recognition she deserves.'

'They're such a well-oiled team, though – Dan and Holly. Do you want to mess with that?' Richie asked. 'And since when do you have a bakery side of the business?'

'I don't yet, but I'm thinking about it. As for Holly, she could run that kitchen now if I needed her to. Dan's not going to be here forever. In fact'—she forced herself to keep her eyes raised and a smile on her face— 'I wouldn't be surprised if he was thinking about a change of scene now.'

So she didn't have to respond to Richie's open mouth, Jess stood and began stacking the plates. When Max moved to help, she said to her, 'No, you sit there. You cooked dinner, and besides, I'll be done by the time you manage to get out of that chair. Richie can help.' She raised her eyebrows and inclined her head to motion Richie into the kitchen with her.

Under the cover of packing the dishwasher, she whispered, 'What's going on?' When he would've opened his mouth to tell her nothing was going on, she said, 'And don't tell me nothing's going on, because there is. Dad's hardly said a word, and Mum's been shooting Max looks all night. If it wasn't for the fact you seem happy enough and she's still blooming –

although currently has the world's worst bladder'—she grinned as Max excused herself again— 'I'd think there was something wrong with her or the baby.' She raised her eyebrows and looked at him suspiciously. 'Have Mum and Dad argued or something?'

'Speaking of something going on, what's this business about Dan moving on? What have you done?' he whispered, ignoring Jess's questions.

'Who says I've done anything?' Jess's voice grew louder.

'Are you two alright over there?' Milly called. 'Do you need my help?'

'We're fine, Mum.' Richie stood and closed the dishwasher door. 'In fact, now that Maxi is back, we'll serve the pudding.'

There was silence as everyone oohed and aaahed over the first fudgy mouthfuls of pudding.

Jess couldn't bear it any longer. Something was going on – something everyone but her knew. After Nathan's shock announcement last night and Dan's bombshell this afternoon, she wasn't in any mood to deal with anything else. It was time to rip the Band-Aid off.

'Okay, what is it that none of you want to tell me?' Her eyes went around the table; no one met her stares. 'Dad's hardly said two words all night – and none to Mum. Don't look at me like that, Dad; you think I don't notice these things? What's the deal? Have you two had a massive fight, or is it something else?' When everyone remained silent, the dread that had peeked its head out for a look earlier in the evening came back and crept through her body. 'Please tell me you're not divorcing because I won't believe it or, oh god, one of you isn't sick, are you?'

Not only was the cold presence of dread making itself comfortable, but the back of Jess's eyes burned, and she was afraid she might soon cry, and that just wouldn't do.

'No one is sick or divorcing,' Milly said, sending a look to her husband that did nothing to put Jess's mind at rest. She paused before adding, 'Gary Evans is in town.'

Jess frowned. 'Who the fuck is Gary Evans?'

'You know I don't like that language at the dinner table, Jessica,' scolded Milly.

Jess waved it away, and then she understood. 'Christ. So it *was* Richie's father that we saw at Beach Road that day.'

She looked across at Richie, then at her mother and finally her father, who nodded slowly.

'Yes,' said Fletch, 'Richie's father and your mother's husband.'

Milly's face drained of colour, and she sat unmoved, like a deer in headlights.

'Don't you mean Mum's ex-husband,' said Jess.

'No,' Fletch said. 'I meant what I said.'

CHAPTER EIGHTEEN

After Fletch dropped his bombshell, he slammed his chair back and went to stand at the kitchen windows, peering into the twilight across the lake and towards the mountains. Milly's face was ashen, and she still hadn't spoken. Richie looked as if all the wind had been knocked out of him, and Jess was speechless. Stunned.

Max seemed to take in the situation and the emotional carnage that her dining table had become littered with in her stride. Using Richie's chair as leverage, she pulled herself up, took a second to rub the base of her back, and walked into the kitchen to get four glasses and a bottle of scotch. Without a word, she poured a measure into each of the glasses and set one down in front of Milly, Richie and Jess.

Moving across to where Fletch stood, his hands shoved into his pockets, his shoulders slumped as if from a weight that was too heavy for him to bear any longer, she laid a hand on his arm and handed him a glass. He took it and forced a sad smile, nodding once in thanks. While Fletch might naturally be a man of few words, Max must've known none were needed here. Not yet anyway.

Back at the dinner table, the whisky had done its job, and colour was coming back to Milly's face, although a slight tremor in her hand remained. Richie had straightened, his eyes fixed firmly on Max, pleading with her to either make sense of what had just happened or to take charge of what would happen next.

Max gently laid a hand on Jess's shoulder, and before she sat back down, she leant down to kiss Richie lightly on the lips. 'Love you,' she murmured into his ear. Jess watched as he squeezed her hand tightly in response. She wanted to go to her father – but was held back by a warning look from Max.

'Anyone for another whisky?' Max asked.

Over at the window, Fletch shook his head.

'No, I need to drive,' said Jess, feeling resentful that they had kept this secret from her.

Milly and Richie nodded, so Max refilled their glasses. When Max briefly laid a hand against her lower back, Jess was concerned at the slight strain around her mouth that Max wouldn't want anyone to see.

'It's true,' said Milly, swirling her whisky in the glass. 'What Cam said. I *am* still married, officially anyway, to your father, Richie. To Gary.'

'I don't understand—' began Jess, but another look from Max had her closing her mouth before she could finish the sentence.

'Let's hear what your mother has to say,' suggested Max, 'and then ask questions later.'

Milly smiled faintly. 'Thanks, Max.' She inhaled deeply. 'Gary and I never actually divorced – he wouldn't agree to it. He was fine with signing all the financial bits and pieces – not that we had anything, we'd been living in a rental and didn't have much between us to settle – but he said no to the divorce. I don't think it was because he still loved me, but more that Gary didn't want me to be free to remarry. I got some legal advice, and they said I didn't need his agreement to divorce, but I would need a court ruling.' She swallowed hard, her voice catching. 'And that meant custody arrangements would need to be sorted.'

'And I'm guessing he'd say that he wanted custody,' said Richie, who had found his voice.

She nodded. 'You had to prove that any children were taken care of and that you had adequate support and, I was on my own. I had Cam, but he didn't qualify as family. You were just a baby Richie, and Cate was toddling around; I couldn't risk losing you both.'

Richie's eyes gleamed as he reached for his mother's hand. 'I can't pretend to know what it was like for you, Mum.'

'What about me?' asked Jess. 'What about when you were pregnant with me?' *Why had no one asked that question?*

'Cam and I wanted to get married, so I tried again

to get Gary to agree, but it was the same response.'

'So I'm the bastard.' Jess didn't know where the word had come from, but it was out before she could stop it. Even as she said it, it sounded like she was the heroine in a Victorian drama. Who used that word these days?

Milly let out a gasp, but Jess's flat statement was enough to bring Fletch back to the table and the conversation finally.

'That's unfair and wasn't our intention,' he said, pulling his chair out and sitting. 'I wanted to marry your mother and adopt Richie and Cate, but Gary wouldn't let that happen. He didn't want any of you having my surname.' He smiled tightly at Jess and reached over to hug her with one arm. 'But he had no power over you; you had nothing to do with him.'

'There are photos though – of your wedding day. I used to look at them and think you looked so pretty.' Jess turned to Max, desperate for affirmation. 'You've seen them, Max?' Max nodded. 'Mum wore a calf-length champagne colour slip dress, with this fabulous baby tummy – which was me.' Jess wiped away tears as she spoke. 'She had a little see-through cardigan that tied under her boobs and above her tummy, and her hair was longer, shoulder length and flicked back a bit, sort of Courtney Love grunge – not that Mum was ever grunge, but that early nineties look – and I thought she was the most beautiful free-spirit ever in that photo.

And you're telling me that was all a lie?'

As a child, she used to pester Milly to tell her about the wedding, and Milly would say how she didn't have a mother or a father but that everyone important to her was there. Jess had always sworn that if she ever married, it would be like her mother's wedding – although, she assumed, minus the pregnant belly and the two other children. She wanted something casual and meaningful like they'd had.

Tears were rolling down Milly's cheeks, and Max looked as though she was trying to attract Fletch's attention to indicate that he should be holding her hand, doing this together. When Max met Fletch's eyes, he shifted his. Richie had also noticed, surprise mingling with concern on his face.

'Dad?' Richie said. 'Was it all a lie?'

'No, son, we had a commitment ceremony. It was important to both of us that even if we couldn't be officially married, that we'd said the vows to each other – and we meant them. I don't know about your mother, but to be honest, I'd almost forgotten we weren't really married. It was such a long time ago.'

For the first time since his bombshell, Fletch met Milly's eyes and tried a smile. It was, Jess thought, as if in saying the words out loud, he'd reminded himself of their importance.

'I'm sorry, Milly, I've been unbearable since I found out Gary was in town, and I've been blaming you – and none of this is your fault.'

Milly's answering smile was watery.

Everyone was so understanding about this, but they'd forgotten it affected people other than themselves.

'I still can't believe you lied to us,' said Jess, with a trace of venom in her voice. 'I remember when I had to get my birth certificate to get a passport; I asked you why your name on that was Melinda Evans, and you told me it was because you'd never gotten around to formally changing your surname. And don't tell me that technically it wasn't a real lie because it was. You could've told me then that you and Dad had never gotten married, but you fobbed me off with a lie. What else have you lied about? And please don't tell me you didn't want to hurt me, or the time wasn't right or any of that shit. I'm twenty-eight years old, and I don't need to be protected. For Christ's sake, I run my own business, and on track, I'm responsible for the safety of people, some of whom, quite frankly, are woefully underprepared. I'm all grown up and I can handle it.' Jess's voice rose as she continued to speak. 'And as for you, big brother, thanks a lot for not telling me about this before now.' She glared across the table at Richie.

'When exactly was I going to tell you? You've been away and out of cellphone reception for over a week.'

'How about last Friday? You knew he was in town by then, and I was home—'

'For a couple of hours – which you spent loved up with Nathan – and then you left again the next morning.'

'You could have told me Friday night.' She was spinning out of control and couldn't stop.

'Well, forgive me for having other things on my mind, and unlike you, I don't barge into other people's space.' Richie was leaning forward, palms on the table and glaring back at Jess. 'Besides, I hadn't met him then, so what would I have told you?'

'That he was in town would've been nice,' she bit back.

'So you could do what with the information? Worry about it the entire time you were on track? I suppose it might've been a more useful occupation than spending your time working out how you can get Dan and Holly together when anyone with even half a brain can see that Dan isn't interested in anyone other than you.'

'That's bullshit,' she yelled back. 'I gave up on that idea ages ago.'

'Well, what the fuck have you done to piss Dan off so much that he's leaving town?'

'Who says he's leaving?'

'You did!'

'I did not. I said he was thinking about leaving – there's a difference.' Jess was on the edge of her chair and leaning across the table to yell at her brother.

'For you to even know he's thinking of it, it means he's told you he is.'

Richie had a "told you so" look on his face Jess hadn't seen in years – and it only made her blood boil. As she opened her mouth to fling another insult, her mother interrupted.

'Rick! Jess! That's enough!'

Jess flounced back in her chair and crossed her arms as if she were an unruly teenager rather than the responsible adult she professed to be. Richie exhaled loudly as if he were the innocent party, and she was the instigator.

'When did you see him?' Fletch asked quietly into the ensuing silence. 'You just said, "I hadn't seen him then".'

'On Sunday.' Richie broke his glare at Jess and focused on his mother, who lowered her head. 'We had breakfast at The Bath House.'

'And you didn't say anything?' Fletch sounded hurt.

Richie shook his head. 'I'm sorry, Dad, I didn't know how to. I was still working it out for myself, and it was obvious you and Mum had fallen out, so I thought it would upset you if I mentioned it.'

'I can't blame you for thinking that,' Fletch said. 'Seeing him has brought back a lot of painful memories, and I haven't dealt with it well, I admit that.'

'Neither have I,' added Milly, smiling tenderly

across at Fletch and then turning towards Richie. 'What did you think of him?'

Richie glanced at Max before speaking; he took a sip of his whisky. 'He was different from what I expected,' he finally said. 'I wanted to hate him and to look him in the eye and ask him why he left us, why he left you, Mum, but when it came to it, I couldn't hate him. He had no guilt and no apologies for what he did. At the end of the day, I suppose I understand how you can't control who you fall in love with.' He smiled across at Max, and it again reminded Jess of Nathan's absence. 'I think under different circumstances, I could like him.' He shrugged and mouthed "sorry" to Milly.

'You don't need to apologise; Gary has always been likeable – it was his charm that attracted me in the first place,' Milly admitted.

'And I was his friend,' said Fletch. 'Don't feel that you need to dislike him just because of us.'

Throughout this conversation, Jess said nothing, but the tension within her bubbled away, threatening to explode at any second. She fought desperately to smooth it down, to think logically and deal with this rationally in the way Richie seemed to be doing. But then, she reminded herself, Richie had Max, and she had no one. Not anymore.

'I told him I'd introduce him to Max,' Richie was saying. 'That was the other thing, he's talking about not going home until after the baby arrives.'

Fletch rolled his eyes and said, 'Well, I suppose we'd better get used to having him around for another few weeks then. Do you know where he's living now or what he's doing?'

'No,' Richie shook his head. 'Come to think of it, every time I brought the conversation around to his circumstances, he changed the subject – but really subtly. I've only just realised that.' He sounded surprised.

'Yes,' said Milly, 'he's always been a master at that.'

'On the upside,' said Fletch slowly, 'there's nothing to stop us from applying for a divorce now. We don't need his permission, and he can't hold custody of the kids over us.'

'And we can get married for real,' said Milly, a broad smile crossing her face.

'If you'll have me, that is,' said Fletch.

'Cameron Fletcher, are you asking me to marry you?' Milly dabbed the corner of her eye with a serviette.

'I rather think that I am.' They sealed the proposal with a clink of their glasses.

Something Richie said earlier was jumping around in Jess's head with its hand up in the air. Something about Nathan knowing about Dan. Richie saw Nathan on the weekend – did he confide in him too?

'Does Nathan know?' Jess asked suddenly. 'About Gary?'

'Yes, I told him on Saturday.' Richie was matter of fact in his reply; the glare was back.

'And he said nothing to me about it.' She vaguely noticed her parents exchanging worried glances, but her focus stayed centred on Richie.

'To be fair, Jess—' began Max.

'No. Not you too,' said Jess. 'Don't make excuses for Nathan. He could've texted me during the week, so at least I was warned before I got here tonight.'

'I'm just saying, don't take this out on him. He hasn't been able to talk to you, and you can't tell someone something like that in a text.'

Max tried to calm the conversation down, but Jess was in no mood to be calmed down. It had gone too far for that. There was no getting around the fact that they had deliberately excluded her from what had been happening here in Queenstown while she was away. Despite all her accomplishments, they were still treating her as the baby of the family. No one had said anything to her, but she'd bet good money they'd told Cate.

'The way I figure it,' said Jess, 'is that I'm the last person to know. Again.'

'This isn't about you,' said Richie.

'Actually, it is. It's as much about me as it is about you and Cate. Speaking of which, does she know? Is she coming over?'

'She knows,' said Milly. 'I called her, and no, she's not interested in meeting him.'

'And the not married thing – does she know about that?'

'No. Your father and I will phone her later and tell her.'

Jess nodded, the movement short and sharp. 'As I was saying, you're all making out that Richie and Cate are the ones affected by this guy being in town, but you've all forgotten that this is just as much about me. Gary Evans might be your father, but he's stopped my parents from getting married, and that makes me a bastard, and it makes a lie of the happy family life we've all been living.'

'Who cares whether Mum and Dad were married when you were born? Plenty of people have babies the opposite way around these days,' said Richie. 'Max and I are doing it now, and it doesn't worry us. I'd like to take a bet that it won't worry Piglet either.'

'Why is that? Why haven't you done the deed yet?' Jess demanded. Max sent a warning glance to Richie.

'Because we decided to build the house first,' Max said. 'We'll get married when the baby is born. We're not in a hurry.'

'Doesn't it worry you?'

'No, not at all. Richie and I are as committed to each other as we're ever going to be, and I'm sure that's how your parents felt when they faced the issue.' Max hesitated before adding evenly, 'Frankly, I'm surprised it worries you.'

'Well, it does.' Jess muttered, knowing it wouldn't worry her under normal circumstances. That if anyone else was carrying on the way she was tonight, she'd roll her eyes and tell them none of that mattered. The problem was, she'd gone so far down that road now she had no way of turning back.

'What was that?' asked Richie belligerently, shrugging his shoulders when Max shot him a look that clearly said, "let her be".

Jess let out a breath and shook her head in exasperation. 'I said that it probably doesn't worry me but the lies they told do.' Why didn't Richie get that? They had lied to him as well. 'It also worries me that my brother, who I thought I trusted, spoke to my boyfriend before he spoke to me and that my boyfriend hasn't told me what you've all been trying to keep from me.'

'We haven't been trying to keep anything from you, Jess,' said Milly. 'I'm surprised you haven't spoken to Nathan today, though.'

'Perhaps he's doing an evening dive,' said Max.

'I don't even want to think about that.' Milly shuddered. 'It's bad enough that he's down there with those things without it being dark. I don't know how Kate deals with the worry.'

'And that, I suppose, is my fault too,' yelled Jess.

'That's not what I was saying—' began Milly.

'Oh, just forget it!' Jess sprang out of her chair

and stormed across to the kitchen counter where she'd left her bag and jacket. 'For your information, he's not doing a night dive – he's pissed off back to Australia to interview for a new job.'

Around the table, the reactions were of surprise. At least that was something he hadn't told her family before he'd told her.

'And Richie?' she added. 'You were right about Dan. He's leaving too.'

'Oh, Jess—' began her mother.

Jess waved her sympathy away and plastered on a fake smile. 'Thanks for dinner guys, your house is lovely. Will I see you at work in the morning, Max?'

Max blinked at the swift change from a teenage tantrum to a composed adult. 'Yes, I'll see you in the morning,' she said and kissed Jess goodbye. 'I'd hug you if I could get close enough. Drive carefully.'

Her vision swam as she kissed Richie and each of her parents goodbye but didn't meet their eyes.

CHAPTER NINETEEN

Silence filled the car on the short journey home until Milly commented on the food and how ingenious it was for Max to come up with a pasta sauce made from roast chicken juices. 'Inspired,' she said. Cam agreed and made a passing comment that Rick would never go hungry while she was around.

Milly made small talk about how she thought the baby had dropped, and she wouldn't be surprised if it had engaged. 'She's carrying very low now. It's no wonder she's running to the bathroom as much as she does.'

'Not that's she's running very much at all,' said Cam, and they both laughed harder than the weak joke deserved.

'I can't see her going full term,' said Milly.

'As long as she doesn't go into labour in the café,' said Cam. 'It's fortunate she's finishing there this week.'

Which, of course, brought them both back to the subject they'd been avoiding.

'Do you think Jess will be alright?' While Jess

had always had a quick temper, Milly hadn't seen her so overwrought since her tempestuous teenage years. 'All that carry-on about being a bastard. I thought that language went out decades ago.'

'I have to admit her reaction surprised me.'

'Hmmm, and the way she then tried to turn it onto Rick and Max …' Milly shook her head. 'Max put her in her place though – gently, the way Max does.'

They were soon turning off the road and up the long driveway to their home. Out of the car, Milly shivered and wrapped her cardigan around her shoulders.

'Lucky Tom got the grapes in on the weekend,' she said. 'There's a ring around the moon – rain is on the way.'

Cam laughed and hugged her to his side with one hand while he unlocked the wooden front door with the other. 'You and your ring around the moon. You know it's an old wives' tale?'

'Well, the old wives are very often right, and when there's a ring of clouds around the moon, this old wife knows it means rain is coming in the next twenty-four hours.' In the hall, she took her cardigan off and hung it from a hook near the door. 'Not that I'm a wife or that old.'

The tears threatened again; she left Cam standing in the hall and walked through to the kitchen, pulling down two glasses and a bottle of scotch. He followed more slowly, watching her pour measures into each glass, her hand shaking as she did.

'No, Milly, you're not old; you're in the prime of your life.' He pulled her into his arms and held her close, his chin resting on the top of her head. Milly pressed into him, his body warming her more effectively than the alcohol would. 'And even though we don't have the paperwork to prove it, you're my wife.' He pulled back enough to tip her face up to his. 'And while I mightn't have shown it over the past week, I'm grateful every day that you are,' he said before lowering his lips to meet hers.

Milly fell into his kiss with a sigh and let it envelop her. Oh, how she loved this man. She loved his quiet strength, his dependability, his loyalty, and integrity. Mostly, though, she loved how he made her feel. Not whole, because she was enough on her own, but complete. While she'd thought of Cam as a friend for so long, the first time he kissed her all those years ago, it was as though a piece that had been missing was slotted into place, and the first time they made love, they'd fitted together in a way that felt as though they'd always been making love – and that had never changed.

Cam hadn't burst into her life in the way Gary had. Gary had completely overwhelmed her and swept away everything else in his path, taking her over until she no longer knew who she was. It had been exciting. It had also been a relief. Milly was in her early twenties and alone. She was vulnerable, and Gary was, well, Gary was Gary. Gary had the charisma you couldn't ignore, and once he'd turned that on Milly, she'd fallen in a heartbeat and had been happy to be swept away.

It hadn't been like that with Cam. She'd had a feeling, a recognition really, when Gary first introduced them that this man would be important, but it was many years before she fell in love with him – and when she did, it felt very much as if she'd never *not* been in love with him. With Cam, she hadn't so much fallen in love, but the love had seeped in without her noticing until she was full of it. It wasn't brash and lusty as it had been with Gary; it was much like Cam himself – strong, quiet, and sustainable. It was comfortable – and she wouldn't swap it for any transitory excitement offered by Gary or anyone else.

Milly rested her hands on his chest and forced herself out of his embrace. 'Cam, we need to talk.'

'Yes,' he said grimly, 'we do.' He turned and picked up the glass she'd left on the kitchen counter and drained the contents in one swallow. 'But not now.' His face had taken on the determined look so familiar to her.

'But there are things I need to tell you—' It wasn't just the meeting last week – there were things Milly had been waiting for nearly thirty years to tell him.

'I know there are, love, but they can wait.'

'Gary—'

He laid his forefinger gently across her lips. 'Ssssh. I agree we need to talk about Gary, but the way I figure it, now everything is out in the open, he can't hurt us anymore. It's waited this long; it can wait another few weeks. We have other more immediate problems – a son whose partner is about to provide us with a grandchild any minute and, more pressing, a daughter whose life seems to be falling apart. What you have to tell me about Gary can wait. For now, though, know that I trust you. Completely.'

'But … I …' Milly sent Cam a quizzical stare.

His short laugh was derisive as he pulled her back into his arms. 'I know there have been times – especially recently – when I haven't demonstrated that trust, and I'm sorry for that.' He kissed the top of her head and released her to top their glasses up. 'Now, tell me, what's going on with Jess?'

'I have no idea.' Cam's expression was one of total surprise. She, who prided herself on always knowing what was happening in her children's lives, had no idea what had prompted Jess's meltdown tonight. She would, however, bet that it was only partly due to their bombshell.

She picked up her whisky and took a sip, her eyes closing briefly as the spirit warmed her from the inside. Walking across to the lounge, she sank onto it and pulled a crochet blanket over her knee. Cam sat beside her, placed his whisky on the coffee table and put his arm around her.

'What was that about Nathan being in Australia? Has Kate said anything?' he asked.

Milly shook her head. 'I haven't seen her for a few days, though. She certainly didn't mention it last weekend. I'll call her tomorrow.'

'And Dan?'

'That one I can make an educated guess on,' Milly sighed. 'I suspect he's decided it's too painful for him to work beside her any longer.'

Cam stared at her, his eyes wide. 'So that business Richie was saying about Dan being in love with Jess was real?'

Milly let out a laugh. 'Nothing gets by you, does it Cam?'

He chuckled as pink tinged his cheeks. 'What can I say?'

'Don't worry,' she soothed. 'Max had to tell Richie, and he didn't believe it either.'

'Poor bugger,' said Cam.

'Who? Richie?'

'No, Dan, of course. He's known Jess most of her life – and worked with her for the past five years. You'd think he'd know better.'

'Apparently, he doesn't. Although I suspect he didn't realise he had feelings for her until Nathan came along.'

Cam tilted his head to the side and raised his

eyebrows. 'Him leaving will be a blow to her in more ways than one, no matter what kind of spin she tried to put around it tonight.'

'We can't interfere though, Cam – especially not in the business. You know how independent she is. She's spent so long building her café to what it is; she'd hate it if she thought you needed to step in and help her out. Especially you.'

'Why especially me?'

Milly shook her head in exasperation at the obtuseness of men. Sometimes she wondered how much notice Cam took of anything. 'Because she's worked so hard to prove to you she can do it on her own. Why do you think she paid the loan back so quickly? She wanted to show you she could make a success of the café.'

'But I never—'

'You didn't need to. Richie's always been the one you turned to when you wanted to talk business. Jess was always so eager to learn, and yet all she could do was listen. She wants you to notice what's she's done, not prop her up when things go wrong.'

Cam pinched at his chin, his expression thoughtful. 'I didn't know,' he finally said. 'I didn't deliberately exclude her.'

'I know you didn't,' said Milly.

'I didn't think she wanted to talk to me about Beach Road.'

'She didn't think you wanted to hear about it.'

'Aaah Jess.' Cam shook his head sadly. 'She's all grown up, isn't she?'

Milly nodded, her lips pursed. 'She is.'

'With grown-up problems.'

Milly smiled as he grappled with the idea. Over the years, she'd watched as Jess, always closer to Cam than she had been to her, fought to be noticed. Richie and Cate were those few years older and had been close as children. Jess had tagged along whenever they allowed her to, her little chin jutting with pride, that determined ponytail swinging from side to side.

When first Cate and then Richie left home, Jess had desperately tried to fill the void they'd left. She'd tried to be the one they turned to. It was Jess who went out looking for Richie when he got stranded on a tramp last year, Jess who'd been the one they called if either she or Cam were tied up and trades needed to be organised or errands run. Jess was the one who'd stayed when the other two left. Even though she'd lived out of home for a few years now (officially anyway – she was always coming home for food), Milly thought it was probably time that Jess left the nest.

Jess managed not to cry until she closed her front door behind her, leant against it and slid to the floor – and then the floodgates opened. She cried as she did everything – enthusiastically – and the tears left her body in great noisy sobs. It wasn't until she'd stopped crying that she wondered what it was she was really crying about. So what if her parents hadn't ever married; Max was right, that didn't matter. They loved each other, and they'd stayed together and been faithful and committed and all those other things essential for a decent relationship – well, as far as she knew they had anyway. But, they'd lied about being married; who's to say the rest hadn't also been a lie?

Even as she thought it, deep in her heart, she knew her parents hadn't lied about their relationship – you couldn't fake what they had, not for that many years, and there were mitigating circumstances. When exactly would've been the right time to tell her the truth – to tell any of them the truth? Even so, she couldn't understand why Richie was taking it all so well. Apart from that momentary shock, he hadn't exploded, and surely he should have. They had lied to him as well – he had as much a right to be angry as she did.

The worst was that none of them had told her about Gary being in town. She'd gone off on track for a few days, and it was as if she was completely out of mind, forgotten. Richie had asked when they could've told her; okay, he had a little point, a teeny point, but he knew she was doing a back-to-back. He could've texted her on Friday and asked to meet. But no, it hadn't even occurred to him or to Max – who was supposed to be her friend. Even as her thoughts went in that direction,

Jess excused Max – she had baby brain, she couldn't be expected to think of everything.

There was no such excuse for Richie, who hadn't been able to wait to confide in Nathan – who, in turn, hadn't said a word. Not. A. Word. How was his form? He told her he loved her and then didn't tell her something that was important to her, something she really needed to know. What sort of boyfriend does that? Richie said it wasn't the sort of thing you put in a text, and there was a part of Jess, the logical part she didn't want to listen to, that admitted Richie might have a small point there too. Nathan hadn't even told her when they'd spoken yesterday – and given he'd already delivered her one set of bad news, what harm would it have been to give her more?

She blinked the last of her tears away and glanced at her watch. Daylight savings hadn't finished, so Cairns would be three hours behind – just after six in the evening. The stubborn in her wanted to wait for him to call, but she so desperately needed to hear his voice … right now. He'd tell her she was overreacting without casting judgement on her for doing exactly that. He'd know what to say to make her feel better.

Nathan answered on the first ring. 'Hey Jay, I was just thinking about you.'

Hearing the gravely tone in his voice made her toes curl and the tears threaten again.

When she said nothing but sat there with the

phone pressed to her ear, he said, 'Are you there? What's wrong, babe?'

'Everything,' she sputtered, no longer caring if he heard her crying.

'Oh, Jay,' he said. 'Start at the beginning.'

'That would be you pissing off to Australia,' she blurted accusingly.

He didn't even attempt to muffle his laughter. 'That's my girl. Aside from that.'

'Dan's leaving,' she said flatly. 'He's got a job in Melbourne.'

'Aaaah.'

'I know you saw it, and Max and Richie saw it, and probably everyone else in the universe knew it except me.'

'Don't beat yourself up about that,' he said gently. 'You weren't looking for it.'

'No, I wasn't – because it didn't fit my view of what should be happening. I thought we were friends; how dare he ruin that!'

'Jay—'

'I know what you're going to say – you can't tell your heart how it needs to feel.'

'No,' he said so quietly she had to strain to hear him. 'Sometimes I wish that wasn't the case.' After a short silence where Jess couldn't think of a response, he said, 'What are you going to do about that?'

'Nothing, I can't stop him from going.'

'I mean regarding the business.'

'Holl will step up, so we'll be alright.'

'But you'll miss him.' It wasn't a question.

'Yeah,' she mumbled. 'I will.'

'You're not responsible for how he feels, Jay. It doesn't have to break your friendship – but some breathing space and a change of scenery will be good for Dan. Now, what else has happened?'

'You know what's been going on,' she accused. 'Richie told you on the weekend, and you let me walk right into it!'

'Oh man!' Jess pictured him hitting his forehead. 'He did talk to me, and I wanted to text you but knew it wasn't something I could tell you in a text, and then yesterday, when we spoke, I completely forgot about it.'

'Because something more interesting was happening with you.' She squeezed her eyes shut as she spat the words out, knowing it was unfair.

'No,' he said slowly, 'because we had more important things to talk about.'

'More important than Richie's father being back?'

'More important to us, yes.'

Trust Nathan to put it into perspective.

'Mum and Dad aren't married,' she blurted. 'It came out tonight.'

'Riiiiight.' Nathan seemed to struggle to understand why this was important.

Jess sighed loudly to let him know this was a big

deal to her. 'We've always been told they were, but Mum and Gary Evans were never divorced, so Mum and Dad couldn't get married.'

'I see. Next thing, you're going to be wailing down the phone that you're a bastard or something equally dramatic.'

'What the?' How did he know that?

'I love you, Jay, but I know what you're like, and your issue isn't that your parents weren't married and didn't tell you – and before you cut in, I get that would be a shock to you, it would be to me too – but in the scheme of things, that's their business, and I feel for them if they wanted to marry and weren't able to. You can tell me the whole story another time. Tonight wasn't about that, though, was it? It was about me, and it was about Dan, and it was about you feeling as though you have no control over either of those situations.'

'I don't think—' How dare he presume to know what she was thinking?

'You know I'm right – and it's okay. This thing with Dan – you can't stop him from going, but you have a Plan B as far as the café's concerned. As for us, well, I'll be back, and we'll talk. I promise.'

'And Mum and Dad?'

'My only advice is to be gentle with them.' Jess screwed her nose as she recalled how she'd attacked them all. Nathan continued, 'This probably caused them a great deal of pain all those years ago when it was happening – and with Gary Evans in town, it has to be bringing things back up for them both.'

'I hadn't thought—' Jess sunk lower into the kitchen stool, feeling smaller than she ever thought it was possible to feel.

'I'm not saying it to make you feel bad, Jay. I'm saying it in case for a moment you forgot about that – and it would be understandable if you had.' He paused and then said, 'I'd ask you to come out here so I could hug you and tell you it's all going to be okay, but I know that with all of this happening, you won't feel as though you can leave.'

Eyes watering, she focused on the photo of her and Nathan pinned to the fridge door. 'When will you be home?'

'I'll know more tomorrow, but as soon as I can, darling. As soon as I can.'

Even though he couldn't see her, Jess nodded, squared her chin, sucked in a deep breath, and said, 'Tell me about your day.'

By the time Nathan hung up, promising to call the following day, the tears had stopped and the tightness in her chest was all but gone. She was also relieved she had a genuine excuse not to go to Australia. After all, how could she tell him she was too afraid to make that decision? She, who everyone believed was independent and fearless.

Queenstown, Beach Road, and her family formed

the boundary of her comfort zone, and within that, she was not only beautifully in control with no surprises – she arranged things so there couldn't be – she also fostered the illusion of courage. While most of her boyfriends had been into adventure sports, it hadn't mattered to her – knowing they were always going to move on; she'd never allowed herself to be close enough to worry about them. Nathan was different. He had come back and might even stay.

When he first told her about the Stewart Island project, she'd been terrified for him. She'd smiled and told him it was an exciting opportunity, and she was glad he'd be close; then she'd gone home and googled the hell out of everything that could go wrong with diving – let alone cage diving with sharks. She cringed inwardly every time he talked about it and fought against the images that crowded her head of one of those monsters tearing his gorgeous body into pieces. Whenever he was diving, her mind whirled with the idea he was somewhere down in the dark with his air running out, watching the shadowy figure of a great white approaching.

Even the tramping she loved so much had initially been a way of controlling her fear of heights and rocks and uneven ground, and she'd well and truly conquered that. Running her own business had been a way of dealing with the fear of having someone else control her success, and as for the passport she got when she first began seeing Nathan, well, she'd never used it. While on the outside, it looked as though she thrived in a whirlwind, under that chaos were just enough structures to keep her safe.

Dan was one of those structures – arguably one of the more important ones. Sure, Holly was her Plan B – and a very capable Plan B – but Dan was … Dan was more than her head chef. He was her support crew, the one she bounced ideas off, the one who kept her grounded, the one who picked her up when her heart was broken. She'd hurt him without ever meaning to, and she couldn't make that go away.

She picked up her phone to dial his number. If he was still awake, maybe they could meet for a drink and talk – like they used to in the days before Nathan. Just as quickly, she put the phone back on the counter. It wouldn't do either of them any good. Dan needed space and time, and Jess needed … she needed Nathan, and he wasn't here.

CHAPTER TWENTY

After everyone left, Richie and Max took their mugs of tea and leant against the railing surrounding the deck to enjoy the stars and the moonlight shining on the lake. Richie put his arm around Max and held her to his side.

'That didn't go according to plan,' he said, his chuckle an attempt to inject humour into a situation that wasn't funny at all. 'But your pudding certainly did the trick.'

'You could say that.' She exhaled heavily, her head resting on his arm. 'The chocolate bread and butter pudding seemed like a good idea at the time. Mum always baked it when she had news I wasn't going to be happy about. Remember when they announced they were selling up in Brookford and moving to Cornwall?'

Richie nodded, remembering it well.

'It's never been responsible for secrets like tonight's, though!' She paused, rubbing circles on her tummy. 'How do you feel about it?'

He thought for a second, took a mouthful of tea and thought some more. 'I'm fine, and that surprises me. So what if they never got married, I don't care about that, but for Dad to react in the way he did, there's more to the story than what Mum said.' He hesitated before adding, 'I can't help but wonder though … Gary hinted there'd been something between Mum and Dad before he'd left. I hadn't believed it at the time, but if they'd not told us the truth about being married, well …' He shrugged.

'Do you believe it now?'

The breeze was forming ripples on the shimmering lake. Richie watched them for a few seconds and eventually said, 'No, I don't. Nor do I know why he even said it. Maybe he wanted me to wonder – Mum didn't talk about him much, but she said he liked to play games.'

Maxi shivered slightly, and he held pulled her closer. 'Are you going to ask Milly?' she said.

He shook his head. 'No. It doesn't matter; it's all ancient history – unless he was trying to hint that I was the product of such an affair.' He snorted. 'You only need to look at Gary and me together to know we're related. Besides, I'd be honoured to have Fletch as my birth father. No,' he said again, 'I don't believe it.'

'On the bright side, Milly and Fletch seem to be talking again.'

'Yeah, they'll be alright.' He laughed suddenly. 'Hey, was I imagining it, or did Dad propose to Mum?'

Max smiled against his arm. 'No, that happened,

but then Jess got upset.'

'To be honest, I don't blame her,' he said. 'I talked to Nathan instead of her, and I could've warned her but didn't. I was so wrapped up in dealing with it myself, and I hadn't given a thought to Jess. I thought it only affected Cate and me; it hadn't occurred to me that Jess might be upset.'

'It surprised me too,' said Maxi. 'But I'm not sure whether she was more upset because your parents aren't married after all, that they hadn't told you they aren't, that no one had told her Gary was in town, or because you confided in Nathan and not her.' She tossed the dregs of her tea into the darkness. 'I'm more inclined to think, though, that it's whatever's going on with Dan and Nathan that's put her off balance. The more I get to know your sister, who, incidentally, I love dearly, the more I see she likes to control what's going on in her bubble.'

Richie frowned. 'What do you mean by that? Jess's bubble?'

'Haven't you noticed? Your family, Beach Road, Queenstown, the tramping, it's the limits of her life.'

'For that matter, it's ours too.' Richie still didn't understand what she was saying.

'Perhaps, but you've travelled, Cate travelled, I've come from Brookford, we've all had lives away from here, but Jess has stayed. You said it yourself – before Nathan, she dated guys who were here for the season only. Jess knew the outcome before it started. Has she ever used that passport she referred to tonight?'

'No, I don't think so.' Below where they stood, a possum scurried along the fence. 'You're saying that she doesn't like to push her boundaries, but Jess is fearless – look at what she's done with Beach Road. She was young when she took that on. I remember Dad had his doubts, but Mum convinced him to help her out. Now look at it – she's completely turned it around.'

Max lifted her head from his arm and reached up to stroke his jaw. 'Absolutely, she has. She's determined, hardworking, and an ideas girl, but I suspect that was the last big risk she took – and even that was on her terms. Since then, she's built the business, but now it's at the point where she needs to either expand or start something new – there's not much more she can do with Beach Road. I think she's torn between being bored and wanting to try something new but being afraid to.'

'And we all know that a bored Jess is a dangerous thing.' Richie chuckled, but his mind was ticking through what Maxi had said. She was right – every chance Jess had ever taken was on her terms. She liked to know everything that was going on – it was part of who she was – and once an idea was in her head, she wouldn't entertain any other. He remembered when she was little and always wanting to chase after him and Cate. How her little chin would jut out, and she'd stamp her feet if anyone dared suggest she couldn't do what they did. Yet, there was something in what Maxi had said.

'She's not a baby anymore, is she?' he said.

'No, my darling, she isn't. And she needs to be treated as an equal.'

Richie looked deep into Maxi's eyes and knew she was right. Despite all Jess's business success, his father still treated her as if she were still his little girl. It had to hurt, and it was no wonder she pushed herself the way she did and fought so hard to be involved in everything.

'I might see if she wants to do Queenstown Hill sometime,' he said, pressing his lips to her forehead.

'I think that's an excellent idea,' Maxi said before wincing slightly.

'Are you okay?' By the faint light of the moon, he could see her hand resting under her tummy.

She grimace-smiled quickly. 'Yes, it's just Piglet moving about, and I need to pee again.'

He chuckled in the darkness. 'Let's get you inside then.'

'Okay, Dad?' he said.

'Never better,' was the reply as Fletch made himself a coffee. Was his father whistling? And was that a glint in his eye?

'Mum okay?'

'Good as gold.'

'So, are you guys getting married then?'

A grin spread over Fletch's face. 'I reckon we could be – although it all got mixed up in the mess last night. We've got things to sort out and talk about, but that can wait. We might even beat you two down the aisle.'

Richie's grin was as wide as his father's. 'You could be right. Need a best man?'

'Yeah. You offering?'

'I sure am.' Richie walked over to Fletch and hugged him briefly, slapping his back in the way men did. 'That's great news, Dad.'

Fletch sobered suddenly. 'You heard from your sister today?'

Richie shook his head. 'No. After you guys left, Maxi told me we need to remember she's an adult and a successful businesswoman and that we should stop protecting her.'

'Have we ever protected her?' asked Fletch with a frown.

'Yeah, Dad, I reckon we do.'

Fletch nodded thoughtfully. 'Maybe you're right, Rick. Your mother said something similar.' He paused. 'It's quiet today, so why don't you see if Jess wants to go tramping?'

Richie examined his father's face and then nodded. 'Okay, sure, I'll see if she can get away. We'll do Queenstown Hill – it will only take us a few hours. Maxi's at Beach Road, and I'll be back in plenty of time to pick her up – we have a doctor's appointment this afternoon.'

'I hope she's taking it easy. If she's not careful, she'll be having that baby on the kitchen floor at Beach Road.'

Richie let out a short laugh. 'Don't get me started on that one. Today is the last day – or so she tells me.'

Although Jess protested as expected, she'd given in easily and, with what Richie assumed, was more than a little relief. It couldn't have been easy going in there this morning to face Dan – speaking of which, he needed to get to the bottom of that one.

A few hours later, he and Jess were sitting at the summit, eating the filled rolls Jess had brought.

'I needed this,' said Jess, closing her eyes and inhaling deeply. 'Thanks for asking me.'

'Didn't you only just get back from Milford and Routeburn? I think I can say I needed it more than you.' He grinned when she poked her tongue out at him. 'I only brought you along because Maxi wouldn't let me come on my own.' He reached across for another roll, opening the paper wrap to peer at the filling. 'Yes! You brought my favourite.'

Jess choked on a mouthful of her roll while trying to laugh. 'I thought your favourite was marmite and chippies.'

Richie finished chewing, a thoughtful look on his face. 'That takes me back. No, these days I'm more evolved—'

'And less hungover.'

'And less hungover,' he agreed. 'While I still can't say no to a cheese roll, this teriyaki chicken with peanut butter and avocado that Dan invented is my favourite. Maxi tried to explain what was in the dressing one time – lime and horseradish, she said, but it all sounded too much as though it shouldn't work.'

'Yeah,' nodded Jess. 'I've been lucky to have him. In the kitchen, that is,' she added, her cheeks colouring slightly. 'Nathan warned me about—' She wrinkled her nose and looked away as if even saying the words aloud was to acknowledge the truth behind them – and how blind she'd been. 'About how Dan felt about me. He's leaving because of that, you know.' She snuck a look at Richie, whose mouth was too full to answer. 'How long have you known?'

'Not long,' said Richie. 'Maxi pointed it out to me.'

'Of course she did. Not much gets past her.'

'It took her long enough to work out how I felt about her, though.' He smiled as he remembered the moment she'd finally understood. 'But then it also took me a while to realise she was feeling the same way. It's easier to see these things from the outside. Mind you,' he added, 'you'd think Dan would know better having grown up with you. Nathan's different; he has no excuse.' Richie collapsed dramatically back onto the blanket when Jess pushed at his side.

'I don't feel like that about Dan, though,' she said. 'I'm in love with Nathan.'

Richie sat bolt upright and studied her sitting cross-legged on the blanket, her eyes bleak where they'd normally be dancing. 'I know *that*. What I *don't* know is how long it took you to realise it?'

She shrugged one shoulder.

He chuckled. 'You have a great ability to see only what you want to see and know only what you want to know.' He flopped back onto the ground, lying on his side to face her. 'Did you really not think Nathan would go back? Or did you think he'd be happy diving with sharks forever and driving back and forth to see you?'

She shuddered. 'God no. The sooner he's finished with the sharks, the better.'

The last few words were forced out of her as if she hadn't wanted to admit her fear.

'It's not like you to worry about something like that. I thought you were happy he'd taken that role. He thought you were.'

'You wouldn't know what I worry about,' she snapped.

Richie's eyes widened. 'Hey, I'm sorry, but I didn't think … It's okay to admit you're concerned, you know.' When she didn't reply but sat there stone-faced, he attempted to lighten the mood. 'I'm sure I read somewhere that more people get killed each year by bees and cows than sharks.' When that didn't raise a smile, he said quietly, 'He knows what he's doing, Jess.'

'Does he?' she demanded.

'Nath's an experienced diver, and there are so many safety features in place nothing can go wrong.' Richie forced an even tone into his voice to soothe Jess, the way he'd watched Maxi do it when Jess got on her high horse about something or another.

'How do you know that? Yes, he's experienced, but he doesn't know these waters, and he said himself that sharks aren't his specialty. And plenty can go wrong. I saw a YouTube video where a photographer didn't close a door properly, and a monster of a shark almost came into the cage with them. You should've seen the size of it. Those teeth! It happened so quickly they were lucky to get out alive.' She picked up her phone and waved it in front of him. 'You can watch it for yourself. In Mexico, I think it was. And before you tell me that no one has died cage diving with sharks, there have been plenty of near misses. Anything can happen. I've googled it.'

Her voice rose as she continued to speak. For a second or so, Richie couldn't respond. He'd never seen Jess so worked up like this, scared. His sister was fearless.

'This is a research project, though,' he said, his voice calm. 'They're not baiting the sharks or encouraging aggressive behaviour, they're just observing.'

'It's a fucking shark,' she yelled. 'You don't need to

encourage aggressive behaviour. That's what they do – bite things and scare people. It's their only job in life. Would you go in one of those cages?'

'Christ no. But I'm not an experienced diver, and I'm not a marine biologist. Did you ever tell him how you felt about it?' As he watched Jess fidgeting with her phone, her sandwich discarded half-eaten on the blanket, Maxi's words about Jess and her bubble came back to him. How had he missed that about his sister? 'Have you even told him how you feel about him?'

She screwed her nose up, blinked twice, and turned away from him, pulling at the fringe on the picnic blanket. 'Sometimes I wish I'd never met him,' she finally said.

'Aaah Jessie,' he slipped in his childhood name for her. 'It's okay to be scared and to feel out of control.'

She continued to stare into the wilderness, her hands clenching and unclenching. 'Do you ever feel that way? As if you wish you'd never met Max?'

Richie smiled at the back of her head and tipped his head back, allowing the sun to warm his face. 'Yep, especially at first. I'd watch her with James or hear her talk about him, and I had to keep reminding myself that she was married, and we could never be more than friends, but I couldn't stay away from her. It was enough just to be near her. But even when it seemed so hopeless and out of my control, I never regretted meeting her.' He laid back on the blanket and watched the patterns forming in the clouds. 'I've gotta say, though, I don't think I've ever been more scared than I am now.' Jess shifted in his direction, and he tipped his head to the side to meet her eyes.

'Really? Because of the baby?'

'Uh-huh. It's terrifying. All the things that can go wrong, you know. I've googled it.' He smirked as he echoed her words. Exhaling, he resumed his examination of the clouds. 'And, like you and the sharks, there's absolutely nothing I can do about it. I don't know how I'll cope seeing Maxi in that much pain and knowing I can't take any of it off her, and I have no idea what sort of father I'll be.'

'You'll be fine.'

'How do you know that?' He used the exact words she'd said to him only minutes ago. 'What if I'm like my father?'

'How do I know? I know because I know you. You adore Max, and you'll be a great dad. After all, you had the best example.'

Of course she was talking about Fletch. He flipped onto his side, his elbow supporting him, his head resting against his hand. '*We* had the best example.'

She sighed. 'It doesn't matter, does it? Mum and Dad not being married?' He shook his head. 'And there wasn't a good time to tell us, was there?' He shook his head again. She bit at her lower lip and wrinkled her nose, rubbing at its tip as if there was something there. 'Maybe I overreacted.' When he remained silent, she added, 'Feel free to say, "you absolutely didn't overreact".'

'Is that you apologising?' he teased.

She stuck her tongue out. 'Maybe.'

'It's okay,' he said, smiling faintly. 'It will all be okay.'

'How do you know that?' Her face was so intent as if everything depended on his answer.

'I don't know it, Jessie, but I have to believe it – and so do you.'

'And Gary?'

Richie sat up and reached for his water bottle and took a long drink. 'He can't hurt us. Maybe he wants to get to know me and meet his grandchild – and then he can go home.'

'Do you really believe that?' Jess asked, watching his face closely.

He ran his hand over the back of his neck and lifted his shoulder. 'I don't know, Jess,' he said again, 'but there's nothing I can do about it, so we'll just have to wait and see.' He met her gaze. 'Mum and Dad will be fine too, you know. They're getting married, for real.'

Jess grimaced. 'I sort of ruined that moment, didn't I?'

'You sure did, but judging by Dad's mood this morning, *something* got sorted out last night.'

She screwed her face in mock disgust. 'Please,

I don't want the details, but Mum's going to need a bridesmaid.'

'She sure will.'

At that moment, Jess's phone rang. She looked at the screen and smiled. 'Nathan,' she mouthed to Richie before answering and walking off with her phone.

Richie watched her go and relaxed back down on the blanket, smiling to himself. A few minutes more and they'd start the walk back down. He'd be in plenty of time to pick up Maxi and get her to the doctor's appointment. It had been good to talk with Jess, and in admitting his fear, he hoped he'd helped her confront hers.

With the sun warming his face, Richie drifted off to sleep.

CHAPTER TWENTY-ONE

'Hey, you,' she greeted him. 'This is a pleasant surprise – I wasn't expecting to hear from you until tonight.'

'Yeah, I know. Where are you?'

'Tramping with Richie.'

'During the week? Wow, last night must have been messy for Fletch to let Richie out.'

'I'm getting the impression he was sent to talk sense into me,' she chuckled.

'Is it working?' There was a hint of a grin in his voice.

'Yeah. I'm okay. It's been good to get out with Richie – it's been too long.' There was a brief silence, and she said, 'Nathan, why have you called?'

'Can't it just have been to hear your voice?'

'No. Well, yes, but I don't think that's why you rang, is it?'

'Where's Richie now?' he asked, ignoring her question.

She looked over to the clearing where Richie was stretched out on the blanket, his eyes closed, his breathing rhythmic. 'He's asleep, I think. The poor bugger must be exhausted with everything that's been going on.' She laughed, but Nathan didn't join in.

'Do you love me?' he asked suddenly. The urgency in his voice made her tummy flip.

'Yes,' she mumbled.

'Then why haven't you said it?'

She took in a deep breath and let it out slowly. 'At first, because I haven't felt this way for anyone before, and no one has said those words to me.' It was a relief to finally say the words. 'But now I don't know whether I should love you because you still haven't told me whether you're staying.' She blinked away the hot prickle behind her eyes and was glad he was thousands of miles away.

'Aaaah,' was all he said.

'What does that mean? That aaaah?' she snapped back. Jess held her shoulders firm. The phone pressed hard against her ear. 'Does that mean aaaah mean you really love me, but there are whales or sea slugs or something you need to count and that's more important, or aaaah you've decided to torture me some more and extend the shark thing?'

'I didn't know the shark thing worried you so much,' he said after a pause that hung heavily. 'I've told you before that—'

'I know – more people get killed by bees and cows every year than get eaten by sharks, and there's a

difference between provoked and unprovoked attacks
– although seriously, if you're dead, you're dead. I also
know that by spreading malaria and god knows what
else, hundreds of thousands of people are killed by
mosquitos every year, and kangaroos and wombats
kill people by running out in front of cars. And,
according to Google, the likelihood of getting killed by
a champagne cork, a coconut or even a lawnmower is
higher than the risk of getting killed by a shark – which
is, in case you're interested, one chance in three million
or is it eleven million? I forget. Either way, someone
has to be that "one", and I don't want it to be you.'

She exhaled heavily and slumped onto a nearby
rock; the speech had exhausted her.

'You've never said.' His voice was quiet but
surprised as if it hadn't occurred to him she might
worry about him.

Jess shrugged one shoulder, raised her eyes to the
sky, and took a calming breath. 'So yes, I love you –
there, I've said it – but I don't know if there's any point
in me loving you if you're going to come back only to
leave me again. I'd hoped that because you come back
every weekend and you've helped with the harvest,
and you're such good friends with Richie, that you're
going to stay but haven't admitted it to yourself yet.'
Her voice rose on the last two words, questioning him.
'What do you have to tell me that you don't want to tell
me,' she asked. 'What's changed since last night?'

Her question hung in the air. In the valley below, Queenstown was a patchwork of houses so tiny they looked like dollhouses.

'There's no beating around the bush with you, is there Jay?'

She stood and walked around in a circle, stopping to push a stone into the ground with her heel. 'I don't see the point. Is this about the job you're interviewing for? Are you going to be away for longer than you thought?'

'Yeah. Plenty is happening here, so I might be a week or so instead of a few days. One of the cruise boats we're aligned with needs a new Master Reef Guide, and Ferg thinks I'd be good for the job. They're helping with some coral planting work and the reef census that's happening this winter. Plus, there's a new project about to start in Hervey Bay he thought I'd be keen on being involved in.'

'I see,' said Jess, struggling to find more to say than that. 'What's this reef guide thing?'

'The Master Reef Guides are trained not only in the reef but in tourism and public speaking. The boats like to have one aboard as it's about educating the tourists as well as enhancing their experience. And it's a chance for the guides to get onto the reef more often and see firsthand what's happening.'

'I see,' repeated Jess.

'I did the course a year ago – I thought it would be

useful on my resume – but no positions were available. Ferg says I can do both – come back to the research project I was on before I came here and do a few days a week out on the boat. The reef census is citizen science – we're using tourist boats, fishing boats and private vessels to conduct the biggest census on the reef that's ever been done – and he thinks it would be useful having me aligned to that. It's something I feel strongly about.'

'And the Hervey Bay thing?' Jess frowned. 'Where even is Hervey Bay?'

'It's about three and a half hours north of Brisbane and the whale watching capital of the world. It's like a rest and recreation place for the humpbacks as they head up and down the east coast each year. It's also where the females teach the calves about what it is to be a whale.'

'Surely they already know that?' Jess scoffed.

'I don't mean it like that. What I mean is it's like a kindergarten for them, so it's the best place in the world to research their behaviour. It's a great opportunity too – they're working on all sorts of research projects, but in particular looking at things like how tourism impacts whale behaviour.'

Jess's heart sank at the excitement in his voice.

'You want to stay,' she said flatly.

'Yeah,' he said finally. 'I reckon I do; both opportunities sound perfect for me.'

'What about us?'

'That's the problem. I love you, Jess, but I didn't know how you felt about me. I thought I did, but you never said, and I wondered whether me saying it had put pressure on you to feel it.'

'Oh.' His statement unsettled her. She'd been riding such a high after that night together and hadn't been able to wait to say it back to him, but now she wondered whether he'd spent the same time feeling hurt and not knowing how she felt. 'You should have said.'

'*I* should have said? I'd already told you how I felt about you. What was I supposed to do after that? Tell you how I felt about you not telling me how you felt?'

When he put it like that ...

'Why didn't *you* say anything?' he asked.

Jess raised her chin. The honesty he was asking made her feel uncomfortably vulnerable. 'I told you why.' She hesitated for half a beat. 'I thought you saying it to me meant you'd stay. Especially if I asked you to.'

God, she wished they were having this conversation face to face. Not being able to see his face was killing her.

'I really like Queenstown, but I've got to admit the travel's getting me down and, as fascinating as they are, sharks aren't my thing. When we first talked about it, you said you'd come down to Stewart Island occasionally, but you haven't visited at all. As far as I

can tell, it's been me who's made all the compromises
and to be honest, Jay, it makes me wonder whether
your heart's in this as much as you say it is.'

'Of course it is,' she exclaimed. 'I haven't been
down to see you because, in case you hadn't noticed,
there's a bit going on around here – what with Beach
Road, the guiding and the baby. And that's not to
mention Richie's father turning up out of the blue.
It's been more convenient for you to come up here.
Besides, you live in a dormitory, and we'd need to get a
hotel. Yes,' she said, 'it makes more sense for you to be
here rather than me there.'

'Except that I feel like I spend more time on the
road and on that damned ferry than I do with you. It's
the same as when I was in Cairns.'

'Except it's cheaper, you don't need a passport,
and you get to see me more often.'

He sighed and Jess got the impression he was
trying to hold on to his temper. 'The thing is, Jay, there's
nothing there for me. Sure, you're there, and I truly
love you – more than I thought it was possible to love
anyone. Mum's there too, and I've made some good
friends. I like Queenstown, but there's nothing there
for me career-wise. I'm a marine biologist – it's not just
what I do, it's who I am – and that means I need to be
near the ocean. And don't tell me that someone needs
to be researching how the eels make their way back to
Tonga or wherever it is to breed and die; it's the marine

mammals that interest me.

'I'd give it all up tomorrow if you asked me to, but I wouldn't be happy, and it would kill us.' He took a deep breath and let it out with a long sigh. 'I want what Richie and Max have – I know that now. But it can't be all your way or the highway. You need to make some compromises, too. I've had a few months in Queenstown to see how I like it, why don't you come to Cairns with me for a few months? Who knows, you might decide to open the next branch of Beach Road over there? Come snorkelling, see the reef. I'll take you to my favourite spots – the ones no one else knows about – and we'll make love on the sand under palm trees.'

'What about the crocodiles?' Jess choked on the words.

'We won't go to those places,' he said.

'And the stingers?'

'It's almost out of season for them.'

Jess imagined the scene for a second – white sand, palm trees, blue skies, crystal clear water and Nathan. 'I have a business and responsibilities,' she said with persistence. 'I'll be a godmother soon.'

'Beach Road operates fine when you're not there – even without Dan, you've got a capable team, and I'm sure Dayna would step up into a management position. As for Piglet, he (or she) will have two great parents.'

She rubbed at her temples. 'Plus, there's Mum and

Dad – they're getting married; I'm sure Mum will want me to be a bridesmaid.'

'We'll come back for the wedding.' He paused. His heavy breathing came through the phone loud and clear before he said, 'At least think about it, Jay. I truly think we have something once in a lifetime good here, and we owe it to ourselves to give it a real chance – and we can't do that if we're in different countries. If at the end of three months we decide we can't make it work, we'll both know we gave it everything we've got.'

'I love you,' she said. Her voice sounded small and scared. 'But I don't know if I can leave here.'

'I love you too, Jay,' he said. 'And I get it, I really do. Just promise me you'll think about it.'

'I'll think about it,' she murmured, wishing he was here. If only she could hold him, she'd know everything would be okay.

Out of the corner of her eye, Richie reached for his phone drowsily and then jerked up. When he looked up from the screen, his eyes were wide and panicked. He leapt to his feet and began throwing everything into their backpacks.

'Nathan, I'm sorry, I have to run. I think it's Max. I love you.'

'Jay!'

She hung up and rushed over to her brother.

CHAPTER TWENTY-TWO

'I think Cam and I might be getting married,' Milly told Kate. They'd met for lunch in a Malaysian Hawker-style restaurant they both loved in Ballarat Street.

Kate blinked twice and said, 'I'm sorry?'

'Last night,' Milly started, 'it all came out, and somehow Cam asked me to marry him – at least I think that's what happened. Jess didn't take the whole us not being married thing very well, and the proposal, such as it was, was derailed.'

'I wanted to talk to you about that,' said Kate. 'Jess, I mean. And Nathan.'

'I thought you might.' Milly smiled to let her know that whatever went on between their offspring wouldn't affect their friendship.

'But first you … You told Cam about meeting Gary?'

Milly's smile slipped. 'No. I tried to, but Cam didn't want to hear. He told me that whatever I have to tell him can wait.'

'Until when?'

'I'm guessing until when we get Jess sorted and this baby born – whichever comes first.' Milly rolled her eyes and grinned, even though both subjects had kept her awake last night. Cam might've said he trusted her, but Milly wasn't so sure he'd still be saying that after she finished saying what she needed to say. 'The Gary stuff will hang over my head until we talk about it.'

'And the wedding?'

Milly lifted an eyebrow and sighed. 'Let's just wait until after Cam knows about me meeting Gary before we start planning that.' Her laugh was short and mirthless.

Kate didn't look convinced. 'I see.'

'Don't get me wrong, Cam and I repaired a lot of bridges last night.' A secret smile came to her face in recollection of the love they'd made afterwards. 'But you know what they say—'

'You're only ever as happy as your least happy child,' finished Kate.

Milly gave a quick nod. 'Exactly. Do you have any idea what's going on there?'

Kate shook her head, not even pretending to misunderstand. 'None. Nathan called me when he was in transit at Christchurch to tell me he was on his way back to Australia.'

'What happened? I thought he and Jess were getting on well.'

'So did I – and I think they are. But Nathan's due

back at work soon, and apparently, some opportunities have come up that his boss thinks he'd want to be involved with.' She shrugged and cracked a prawn cracker in half. 'I was talking to him last night, and he said he'd asked Jess to consider joining him – even if it is just for a holiday.'

'And she's said no?'

Kate nodded. 'Apparently so. He didn't go into detail, but I know he's hurting.'

'I don't know what's going through Jess's mind,' said Milly. 'And I'm so sorry that Nathan's been hurt. I know Jess is unhappy too, but if that's the case, I don't understand why she's not going with him.'

The server returned with their shared entrees, so conversation was stalled while they arranged plates and dunked dumplings.

'We can't interfere, Milly,' warned Kate. 'Whatever happens is between them.'

'I know,' sighed Milly. 'It's just that—'

'They're so perfect for each other,' finished Kate.

'Exactly.'

'Then all we can hope for is that they work that out before it's too late.'

'Somehow, I think it's Jess who needs convincing,' said Milly. 'She's always been like this – wilfully stubborn. She'd stand and argue that black was black – until she decided it was really white, at which time she'd argue that she never thought it was black and where on earth had I got that idea from?' She chuckled and shook her head. 'Her absolute certainty has helped her make a success of her business, but it's not such a good quality to have when it comes to navigating relationships.' She reached across for another dumpling, picking it up in her chopsticks and letting it dangle in the air. 'Do you know if Nathan's considering staying here?'

Kate covered her mouth with her hand while she chewed. After she swallowed, she said, 'I don't know, but I don't think so. Nathan can be just as stubborn when it comes to standing his ground.'

'Which is why he is so perfect for Jess – he's the only person who's ever stood up to her.'

'Perhaps. And he's right to do so – he's effectively put his life on hold for the last few months. I suspect he's now asking her to do the same.'

'I might see if Cam can talk to her,' said Milly swirling the wine around in her glass.

Kate was shaking her head. 'Don't,' she warned. 'Let them work it out for themselves.' When Milly opened her mouth to argue, Kate pointed her finger and added, 'You have enough to be going on with. They can sort their issues out.'

Milly sighed and set her chopsticks down. 'I know, I just want them to be happy.'

'So do I,' said Kate.

'But, as you say, there's nothing we can do about that.' Milly drew in a breath and searched for a change of subject. 'Tell me about this knitting and nattering group you're looking to start up at Cover To Cover – or is it stitching and bitching?'

Kate slipped her purse back into her handbag and slung it over her shoulder. 'Now the shop's up and running, I feel almost guilty being out for a few hours in the middle of the day,' she said. 'Although now Sandie's doing a couple of days a week, it frees me up to work on other things.'

'Or have the occasional lunch with me,' said Milly.

'Exactly. Do you want me to give you a ride home?'

With Milly's car in for its regular service, Cam had dropped her in town that morning and had said he'd come in and get her when she was ready. 'No, but thank you. I might duck in at Beach Road and see how Max is doing.'

'Don't you mean you want to make sure Max isn't overdoing it and that Jess is okay after last night?'

Kate's smile was knowing, and Milly's cheeks grew warm. 'Yes, you got me there. Thanks for the offer, though.'

After kissing Kate goodbye, Milly took her time walking down Ballarat Street towards the lake.

Dayna looked up from clearing the outside tables and greeted her with a beaming smile. 'Hey there, Milly, it's been a while.'

'It has been. Jess and Max upstairs?'

'Max is, but Jess went tramping.'

'Oh? It's unlike Jess to leave work in the middle of the day.'

'Richie called her earlier this morning, so she packed some rolls and headed off. They were doing Queenstown Hill.'

Dayna was eyeing the queue of customers forming inside, so Milly thanked her and went upstairs to find Max.

Max was half bent, half squatting, pulling a loaf tin out of the oven. She straightened slowly, rubbing the small of her back and set the cake on a wire rack to cool. She pursed her lips as she took her oven gloves off and placed them on the bench.

'Are you okay?' Milly asked gently, not wanting to startle her. At her words, Holly, Mia and Dan all looked up from their respective benches.

Max's smile was grateful. 'Thanks, but I'm okay. I just need to sit down.'

'Have you had lunch yet?' Milly didn't like the way her face was drawn. When Max shook her head, she said, 'Why don't you take it easy and go downstairs and get some lunch. I'm sure Mia can finish up here.'

'Absolutely,' said Mia. 'I've just got some ginger biscuits to make, and I'll be done.'

'Okay,' nodded Max, her voice sounding weary. 'That sounds like a plan.'

'That *does* sound like a plan,' said Milly, stepping

forward to kiss Max's cheek. 'Hey guys,' she greeted the others, noting that Dan smiled weakly before giving the plate in front of him more concentration than the salad required. She wondered what the story was there and hoped Jess opened up to Richie today.

Max grimaced and pressed her hand to her side. 'You definitely need to sit down,' said Milly.

'I know,' she sighed heavily. 'I'm glad this is my last day; those stairs seemed double their normal height this morning.'

'That's because you come up and down them so often to pee,' said Dan, the smile on his face at odds with the concern in his eyes. 'Everything's under control, so go down, get some lunch and enjoy the last of the sun – they reckon there's a cold front coming through later this afternoon and some rain, maybe even snow.'

'As long as it doesn't come through before Richie and Jess finish their walk,' Max said wearily.

'Dayna mentioned they're doing Queenstown Hill?' said Milly.

'Yes,' said Max. 'Cam suggested they go out today. Jess was reluctant at first, but we all convinced her we could manage.' Her eyes wandered across to Dan.

Milly dipped her head slightly to let Max know she'd understood what she was trying to say – the mood must've been uncomfortable in here this morning.

'I remember one time I went up Queenstown Hill in the sunshine, and by the time I was ready to come back down, the cloud had descended, and it was snowing,' Mia said, wiping the bench down.

'Not helpful,' said Holly, her eyes on Max.

Max let out a little laugh. 'Knowing Richie's track record … Seriously though, they were walking up, having lunch, and then heading back. It's all good.' Her hands rested on the top of her tummy. 'I'm going to take you up on that offer, though, and drag myself downstairs. Let me know if you need me.'

'We won't,' said Holly.

'I'll come with you,' said Milly, keeping an eye on Max as she took the stairs gingerly, gripping the handrail tightly, ready to reach out a helping hand if needed.

'What can I get you both?' asked Dayna when they finally reached the bottom of the stairs.

'I don't have much of an appetite today,' said Max, trying to catch her breath. 'Maybe some soup? Actually, no, could I just get a cheese scone, please?'

'With plenty of butter, a scraping of marmite and a pot of tea, I assume?'

'Yes, please.' Max smiled at her predictability.

'You got it. Milly? Anything for you?'

'I haven't long had lunch,' said Milly. 'A pot of tea would be lovely, though … and I can manage a scone.'

Max waddled outside to a table by the lake and sank into a chair with a heavy sigh.

Milly smiled and said, 'That sounded heartfelt.'

'Let's just say I'm glad to be off my feet.'

'Lower back?'

Max winced and stretched her back as she sat, her hand resting low on her hip.

'Is that all it is?' Milly asked, her eyes narrowing. When Max nodded and turned her face towards the weakening sun, Milly understood she wanted to change the subject to take her mind off her discomfort. 'How was Jess this morning?'

'Subdued,' said Max. 'She mumbled a half-hearted apology—'

'Jess apologised?' Milly placed her hand dramatically on her chest.

'It was as close to an apology as I've ever heard. She didn't say anything about what was going on with Nathan – although, with Dan there, I suppose she wouldn't.'

'Is Dan really leaving?'

'Yes. He told us this morning. He's got a job in Melbourne and will head over there in a few weeks.' She paused and smiled her thanks as Nell placed pots of tea in front of them. 'It was uncomfortable, though. I don't think Mia picked up on it, but Holly knew something was going on but didn't know what. Jess was so matter of fact about it, and Dan seemed awkward.'

'He was probably hurt that she wasn't making more of a deal of it,' Milly guessed.

'I'd say so. She took Holl off to the side and told her she'd be promoted to head chef, but Jess couldn't even look at Dan this morning. She was relieved when Richie called and asked her to go tramping.' She snorted a short laugh. 'So was Dan.'

'I haven't spoken to Cam since he left for work this morning, but that was sudden, wasn't it? The tramping?'

Max's brow furrowed. 'Is everything okay, Milly?'

'Oh yes, everything's fine. We still have things to talk about, but it's okay that we haven't spoken, not that we aren't talking … if you know what I mean.'

Max's smile was relieved. 'I do know what you mean, and I'm glad to hear it. As for the hiking trip, apparently, it was Cam's idea. I suspect he's hoping Jess might talk to Richie.' Her grin was conspiratorial. 'I don't suppose you had anything to do with that?'

Milly chuckled. 'No, it's all Cam's idea – but it's a good one.'

Nell was soon back with their scones, and Milly watched with concern as Max, who usually had a healthy appetite, nibbled at the food.

'Are you sure you're fine?' she asked with a concerning glance.

'Absolutely,' said Max quickly, waving her hand to dismiss the question. 'I'm just tired. Piglet is riding low, and my back is … well, I'm sure I don't need to go into detail,' she finished with a forced smile.

Max's phone pinged with a message. She opened the text, grinned, and turned her phone around to show Milly. Richie had sent a photo of him and Jess at the Basket of Dreams sculpture near the summit. The tramp together would do them both good. Cam was full of surprises.

The two women chatted easily while they sipped and ate and had almost finished when Max moved her attention over Milly's shoulder. Milly turned to find Gary standing behind her chair.

'You must be Max,' he said. 'They told me inside that I'd find you out here.' Then, as if he'd only just noticed her presence, he said, 'Hi Melinda, I wasn't expecting to see you too.'

Milly resisted the urge to flinch when he bent to kiss her cheek.

'That's a fair guess seeing I'm the only obviously pregnant woman out here,' Max said with a grin and lifted an eyebrow. 'You must be Richie's father, Gary. Why don't you join us?' She gestured to the seat opposite her. 'Excuse me for not getting up, but that's all a little too hard today.'

He chuckled, and Milly was struck again with the resemblance to Richie.

'Only if I'm not intruding,' Gary asked, casting a loaded look at Milly and then dropping his gaze to his feet.

Well, well, Gary Evans was uncomfortable. Wonders would never cease.

Max shook her head, and a small smile played

around the corner of her mouth. 'Absolutely not. Milly and I were just chatting.'

He glanced at Milly again, who had sat back in her chair, her arms tightly crossed in front of her.

'I wanted to meet you, Max,' Gary said. 'Richie said he'd introduce us, but I confess I was getting impatient, so I thought I'd try my luck here.' A wry smile spread over his features.

Gary was, Milly noted, on the charm offensive with Max; his discomfort, it seemed, saved for her alone.

'It hasn't even been a week,' snapped Milly. 'You can't tell me you've been sitting around waiting for him to call. His life doesn't revolve around you.'

She didn't need to see the surprise on Max's face to know she'd overreacted. Nor did she know why she had. Gary couldn't hurt her now. He couldn't hurt any of them. She and Cam were going to get married, and everything would be as it was. She should, she reminded herself, be feeling sorry for Gary. He'd destroyed every relationship he'd ever had, and he'd missed out on getting to know his children.

Milly took in a deep breath and rested her hands on the table. 'Sorry,' she said. 'That wasn't necessary.'

'No,' he conceded, pulling a chair out and sitting down next to Milly, slipping his sunglasses from the top of his head to cover his eyes against the glare from the lake, 'you're absolutely right. I know he has other priorities. I'd just hoped …' He opened his hands and shrugged.

'Richie was going to call you,' said Max. 'But this is all very new to him.'

Milly raised her eyebrows. Max's tone was even, but it was firm, and as she spoke, her eyes held Gary's. Milly suppressed a smile; she hadn't seen the assertive side of Max before, but right now, she was clearly in protective mode.

Gary must've detected the intent behind her words and nodded. 'I'm not here to cause trouble for him,' he said. 'To be honest, I didn't expect that he'd be here in Queenstown – I thought I'd see Melinda, and she'd tell me all about Richie and Cate, and I'd go away again. But when I found out he was here, well …' He lifted a shoulder.

'You know it's caused problems for Milly and Fletch, don't you? You being here.'

Milly choked on her tea at Max's words.

'You don't mince your words, do you?' said Gary. He took his sunglasses off and sat them on the table. 'Richie's chosen well.' Max raised both eyebrows at his blatant attempt to charm her. 'But yes, I imagine I've caused problems for them – it's not what I intended.' He sent a look that might almost have been an apology to Milly.

'You know Milly doesn't need your permission to divorce now, don't you?'

Milly bit the inside of her mouth to control her

smile and wondered if Richie had ever seen Max like this.

His Adam's apple bobbed, and he dropped his chin to his chest. 'Yes. She hasn't needed it for years – not since the kids grew up; I don't know why she held on.' He raised his eyebrows in Milly's direction.

Max let out a short laugh and shook her head slowly. 'Now I know what Milly was talking about when she said you had a healthy ego. I hate to break it to you, but the only reason they haven't sought a divorce is that I think they both honestly forgot they weren't married.' She smiled sweetly. 'But I'm sure that's easily rectified now that it's all out in the open.'

Max reached behind to knead at her lower back and closed her eyes briefly. Milly's nerves bristled in foreboding.

'Richie said you're going to stay until the baby's born?' Max went on.

'Yes, I couldn't leave once I knew I was going to be a grandfather.'

'No, I don't suppose you could.'

He picked his sunglasses up again, and his gaze met Max's. To Milly, it felt as though an understanding had passed between them. It also felt as though they'd both forgotten she was there.

Max tensed and, squeezing her eyes shut, pushed her fist into the side of her hip. Pain flitted across her face.

Milly's tummy flipped, and she reached across the table to squeeze Max's other hand. 'Are you alright?'

'I think so,' Max said, drawing in a deep breath. 'I just need the bathroom. If you'd excuse me for a minute—'

She levered herself out of her chair, and as she did, a gush of liquid splashed onto the pavement. 'Oh,' she said in a surprised voice, her eyes on the wet concrete before bending over and holding onto the top of the chair.

Milly was beside her in a flash. 'If this is what I think it is, you need to sit back down. Let's be calm about this.'

Gary watched wide-eyed, unable to move or speak.

'Right,' said Milly. 'We need to get you to the hospital, and I don't have a car. I'll need to call Cam to get us.'

'Where's Richie?' said Gary. 'How about I phone him? Maybe we should just call the ambulance and let Richie know you're on your way to the hospital.' His voice shook as he went through the options and reached for his phone.

'No,' said Milly, forcing herself to think clearly. At the mention of Richie's name, tears had come to Max's eyes. 'Richie's up on Queenstown Hill with Jess. Even if they've already begun the walk down, it will still be over an hour before they can get back to the car and then to the hospital.' She turned to Gary. 'If you've got a car, you can drive us there – it's not far – and I'll call Cam on the way and get him to meet us. I'll phone Richie when we're on our way.' To Max, she said, 'This is your first baby, so with luck, it won't be in a hurry to come into the world. We've got plenty of time.' Milly hoped that in saying the words, she'd make them true.

'Okay,' said Gary, fumbling with his keys, panic written all over his face. 'Can you walk to the car? I'm parked down the street a little. What do I do?'

If it was any other circumstance, Milly might've laughed at the look on his face. Now she struggled to remain calm. 'You get the car, and we'll meet you at the front of the café.'

'Right.' Gary nodded and took off at a run.

Milly caught the eye of Dayna, who came straight over. 'I don't need you to panic, but—'

At her words, Dayna's eyes widened and took in the wet concrete and Max's breathing. 'Oh fuck.'

'Pretty much. I'm going to need some help to get Max out to the street.'

Dayna dumped the empty plates she'd been carrying onto the table. 'How are you getting to the hospital? Do I need to ring an ambulance? Jess isn't back. Does that mean she and Richie are still up the hill?'

'Please,' said Max, 'I just need to get to the front of the café.' She spoke slowly, but there was fear in her voice.

Milly put her arm around Max's waist for support, and they made their way slowly through the café. Milly couldn't help wondering at the picture they presented. Nell's eyes caught Dayna's as they entered the room and, taking in the situation, picked up the phone. Before they'd even reached the counter, Dan and Holly clattered down the stairs.

'Have you called Richie?' Dan asked as Max stopped to ride out another contraction. Damn, thought Milly, these were coming about every five minutes.

Max shook her head, and Dan said, 'Okay, I'll text him now, and you can call him from the car.' He raked a hand through his hair and peered through the window to the street, then brought his eyes back on Max. 'You have called an ambulance, haven't you?'

Max gritted her teeth and held onto the railing of the stairs. 'No ... ambulance,' she managed.

'Tell Richie that Gary's taking us to the hospital,' said Milly, sounding more in control than she felt.

'Who's Gary?' asked Dan.

'Richie's father,' said Milly.

Dan's mouth dropped open. 'He's here?'

'Don't just stand there,' said Holly impatiently. 'You get hold of Richie, and I'll help Dayna and Milly with Max – and get her bag too. It'll be upstairs.'

When Dan stood there, his phone in his hand, confusion all over his face, Holly snapped, 'Dan, just do it. Now!'

'Okay,' Milly crooned into Max's ear. 'Are you ready to walk again?' Max nodded. 'Off we go then.'

By the time they'd got to the street, Gary had pulled up and, leaving the engine running, ran around to open the passenger door.

'The back seat,' said Milly. 'I'll strap her in.'

Dan burst out of the front door with Max's handbag just as they got her into the car. 'I've texted Richie; he and Jess are on their way down.'

Milly mouthed "thank you" to Dan and climbed into the back seat beside Max and fixed their seatbelts.

'Do you need me to come with you?' asked Holly.

Milly shook her head. 'No, you have a café full of customers that need to be fed; we'll be fine.' *If we can ever get away from here.*

Holly slapped at the top of the car. 'Get out of here then.' To Gary, she said, 'Be careful. You have precious cargo on board.' She slammed the door shut.

Gary went to drive off but stopped suddenly, lurching Max and Milly against their seatbelts. Turning to Milly, he asked sheepishly, 'Where's the hospital?'

'It's in Frankton,' said Milly. 'About a fifteen-minute drive. I'll direct us. Now, go!'

Max braced and gripped the grab handle above the window with one hand as another wave hit. With her other hand, she squeezed Milly's so tight she thought it would break.

'Breath through it, darling.' Milly gently coaxed,

ignoring the ringing of Max's phone. It stopped, and a
second or so later, hers rang.

'Where are you? What's happening? Dan said Max
is in labour, and Gary's taking you both to the hospital!
The baby isn't due yet, and her hospital bag is at our
place still. We're on our way down; I could run—'

'Richie! Just stop. It's not far to the hospital, and
I'm sure Max doesn't intend to have this baby in the
back of Gary's car.' Milly flashed Max a reassuring
smile. 'The last thing she needs is for you to trip on
your way down and not make it in time.' There was
silence. 'Richie?'

'I'm here. Is she okay?'

'How about I hand the phone over, and you ask
her yourself?'

'I've been better,' Max said, puffing, trying to
downplay her fears before surrendering to the tears
she'd held in while they'd got her into the car. 'Oh,
Richie, I need you with me.'

Milly couldn't hear what Richie was saying to Max,
but as he talked, she grew calmer.

'Okay, but Richie—' Another contraction cut her
sentence short. She grabbed for Milly's hand again
and strained against the seatbelt. 'Oh god, here comes
another one.'

'Maxi? Darling?'

Richie's voice boomed from the phone as she took
it from Max's hand. 'We're almost at the hospital,' she

told Richie. 'Can you ask Jess if she'll call Cam please and get him to meet us here? I need to look after Max.'

'Tell Max I love her.' His voice broke. 'And keep me posted.'

'I will.' Milly hung up and closed her eyes briefly, steadying her breathing, knowing she needed to be strong for Max.

'He's on his way,' she said, wiping the tears from Max's cheeks.

When they pulled up at the hospital, Milly said, 'I know you need Richie, love, but Gary and I are going to have to do for now, so let's get you inside.'

Max smiled the briefest and bravest of smiles. 'I think I'm going to need a wheelchair.'

'Already on it,' said Gary, jumping out of the car.

'Thank you,' Milly called as he jogged toward the entrance. Laying a supportive hand on Max's shoulder, she said, 'Rick will be here as soon as he can, Max.' She just hoped he would make it in time.

CHAPTER TWENTY-THREE

'Was that Mum? What did she say?' Jess panted, trying to keep up with Richie, who was powering down the slope.

'They're at the hospital now; she needs you to call Dad. What if I don't make it, Jess?'

'Richie! Slow down! We'll make it. We'll be down the hill in no time – if you watch where you're going, that is,' she added when his toe jammed on a stone, and he stumbled. 'You're no help to her if you're stranded up here with a busted ankle or knee. Besides, no one has babies that quickly – especially not first babies.' She smiled reassuringly at his back which was a few good metres in front of her.

'Okay, okay,' he called over his shoulder.

'Right. I'll call Dad. Try not to worry,' she added. 'Mum's with her, so she'll be fine.'

'So's my father though,' he muttered, still walking but, Jess was glad to see, slowing his pace, his concentration on the path ahead.

Jess narrowed her eyes. What had Gary been doing

at Beach Road?

She dialled her father's number. He picked up at the first ring.

'I'm sorry about last night, Jess,' he started, 'I know we should've found a way to tell you, but—'

'Dad, stop, it's fine. We can talk later. Max is in labour, and Richie and I are still out on the hill.'

'O-kay,' he said slowly. 'Your mother was in town with Kate, and she doesn't have transport. I'm in Arrowtown finishing a delivery. Has she called an ambulance? I'll phone Milly and pick her up so we can meet Max at the hospital – actually, no, I'll get Milly to grab a taxi. Maybe—'

'Dad, it's okay. Mum was with her when her waters broke, and she's just arrived at the hospital – Gary took her. He's with them.' Jess briefly squeezed her eyes together as she said the last words.

He was silent for a beat. 'Gary? I won't ask what he was doing there, but as long as Max is safe. I'll head back now – I'll need to drop the truck off, though, so will be forty minutes. You guys walk carefully, and Jess?'

'Yes, Dad?'

'Look after Richie – he's going to be a nervous wreck until he's with her.'

'I've got this,' she said. Despite her concern for Max, Jess felt a smidgeon of pride that her father was not only relying on her but trusted her to maintain control of the situation.

'Of course you do.'

'And you play nicely with Gary, Dad. I know he's the last person you want to see, but however he came to be there, he's done Max a huge favour.'

'I know.' Her father's voice was gruff as he rang off.

Richie had slowed, allowing her to catch up. His face was set, his steps deliberate.

'Richie.' She reached out a hand to his arm. 'Dad's about forty minutes away, and if I know Max, there's no way that baby's coming out until you're there to hold her hand. She'll cross her legs if she has to. Besides, women have babies every day – and they've been doing it for a long time.' Her smile was encouraging, soothing.

He nodded mutely and kept his focus on the track. 'I know they have babies every day, but Maxi doesn't. I know logically she'll be okay, but knowing it here'—he tapped his temple— 'is different to knowing it here.' Richie punched his chest to illustrate his point. 'I don't know what I'd do without her, Jess.' His eyes were glistening, and he blinked a few times.

'You're not going to need to find out,' she said. 'Max will deal with this in the way she deals with everything – by being Max. If I know her, she'll be too busy playing peacemaker between our mother and your father.'

'Now there's a thought.' He looked sideways at Jess, and suddenly they were both laughing.

'Come on you big softie,' Jess said. 'Let's get you back down this hill so Max can have your baby.'

They walked in silence for a few minutes until Richie asked, 'What was Nathan calling for? Is he alright?'

Warmth spread across Jess's cheeks. 'Yes, he's fine.' She ducked her head and concentrated on the track. 'He won't be back as soon as he hoped, and I told him how I felt about the sharks.'

'There's nothing wrong with him knowing you're worried,' he said. 'It's all part of showing him you love him.'

Jess scoffed. 'A lot of good that's done me with him over there and me here.'

'So he's going back to his old job in Cairns then?'

'He said he'd give it up if I asked him to,' Jess said quietly. Richie didn't need to know that Nathan had warned that it could destroy them if he did.

'And do what?' Richie sounded surprised.

She shrugged. 'Who knows? We'll work that out, but at least he won't be swimming with sharks anymore, so I won't need to worry about that.'

Richie's chin was firm, his tone serious. 'It doesn't work that way, Jess. You don't get to assume that just because he's said he loves you that he'll give up what he does so you don't need to make any changes to your life. That's not fair. He's a marine biologist, and he's studied long and hard to do that. He loves that, and he's passionate about caring for the reef. There's nothing in Queenstown for him.'

'Other than the eels in the lake,' Jess replied, forcing a lightness to her voice that she didn't feel. 'Aren't they supposed to go back to Tonga to breed or die – or is it both? Surely someone's studying how that happens?'

'Somehow, I don't think the eels hold a great deal of interest for him – not when there are whale migrations and sea turtles waiting for his attention.'

'You forgot about me. I'm here waiting for his attention; that has to count for more.'

Jess couldn't believe Richie was even arguing with her about this – after all, hadn't he delayed his return to New Zealand for a few years because he'd fallen for Max, and she'd been married.

'Of course it counts,' he said. 'But if you're going to make a life together, it has to be about both people meeting in the middle and compromising.'

'How can you say that? Max left England for you and moved here. Who's to say that Nathan won't leave Australia for me if I ask him? He'll be happy because we'll be together – just like you guys are.'

'That was different. Max didn't have a job there, and what she wanted to do, she could do anywhere – it wasn't tied to Brookford. If it had been, we might have had a different conversation. Besides, I can do what I do from anywhere too, and if Max hadn't wanted to be here, we would've found a compromise. It's not like I'm a marine biologist specialising in reefs and my career relies on me being near the ocean and, more importantly, somewhere there is access to the animals that I study.' Richie's voice rose as he spoke. He seemed to realise this and took a breath before adding, 'When you decide to be with someone, sometimes you have to make changes for that.'

'Well,' said Jess, 'I don't know what changes he expects me to make – I own a business. There are plenty of things he can do – he likes nature, so he can be a guide during the summer like I do, or he can help you guys out at Lakeview Landscaping.' Richie hadn't thought this through as well as she had.

He stared at her for what felt like ages but was only a step or two. 'It seems like you've got it all worked out,' he said. 'I just hope he sees it the same way.'

'He will,' said Jess more confidently than she felt.

When it came to choosing to be with her or without her, how could he see it in any other way? Once he'd had time to miss her, he'd see that – wouldn't he?

'Be careful, Jessie,' he warned. 'Nathan would come back here if you asked him to, but it could destroy your relationship in the long run. You'd be fine, you'd still have your business, but he'd be left with nothing because he'd have given it all up for you. Just think about that, hey?'

As if she could think about anything else? She flashed him a tight smile. 'I will.'

Before she could say more, her phone beeped with a message. 'It's Mum. They're at the hospital and settled in. Max is as comfortable as she can be.'

Richie nodded, but his pace increased.

CHAPTER TWENTY-FOUR

'Cam's about forty minutes away,' Milly told Max, even though the only person Max wanted news about was Richie.

Gary had waited outside while Max changed into a hospital gown and was examined by a midwife but had now pulled up a chair beside the bed and was chatting away to her as if Max wasn't sitting in a hospital bed about to have a baby – or, rather, trying desperately not to have a baby before Richie arrived.

Milly, sitting on the other side of the bed, took a surreptitious glance at her watch as Max closed her eyes and balled her hands into fists, her head down and her breaths deep.

When it was over, she took another deep breath and looked at Gary, a weak smile on her face. 'Richie didn't say, what happened to the woman you fell in love with?'

Milly recognised the question as Max's attempt to distract herself from the contractions, which were too close together for Milly's liking.

'Rachel,' said Gary. Milly was surprised to see hurt flickering across his face. 'Her name was Rachel, and you're the first person who hasn't referred to her as the woman I left Melinda for.' He turned his head towards the hospital corridor, scratching at the back of his head as if he were trying to gather his thoughts. 'She died,' he whispered, the words full of pain and anguish. Milly couldn't stop the gasp that escaped her; hadn't he said …? He continued, 'Last year. Breast cancer.'

'I'm sorry to hear that,' Max said gently, reaching across to touch his hand.

Milly wanted to do the same but knew she couldn't. Instead, she said, 'You must miss her.'

The mist in his eyes and tense jaw were at odds with the casualness of his slumped shoulders. 'Thank you; I do miss her. Every day.'

He met Milly's eyes, his mouth curling into a wry smile. 'I know what I let you think,' he said. 'That I'd cheated on her too.'

Milly's nod was subtle, but enough to acknowledge the truth of what he'd said. She didn't know whether it made her feel better or worse knowing he'd stayed with Rachel all these years.

'Why didn't you say?' she asked.

'I said some other things to you too that I shouldn't have,' he went on, still directing his words to Milly. 'I don't know why – maybe it was knowing that you were completely over me.'

'Did you expect anything else after all these years?'

'No.' His laugh was short and embarrassed. 'Not really.'

Turning back to Max, he said. 'I also hinted to Richie that I thought Milly and Cam had been involved much earlier than they had been.'

'He said that.' Max shifted in her bed to ease her discomfort. 'Were you trying to make him think you weren't his father?' When Gary's eyes darted to his lap, she said, 'Anyone looking at the two of you could never mistake you for anything other than father and son.'

'I know, it was a stupid thing to say. Seeing Richie all grown up, it threw me. That and seeing Milly with Cam.'

Max tilted her head to one side and narrowed her eyes. 'Yet you say you were in love with Rachel. It sounds very much to me as if you wanted it all.'

Milly bit her bottom lip to stop a smirk. Max's tone might have been gentle, but her words were as forthright as they'd been at Beach Road.

Gary shook his head, his eyes crinkling at the sides. 'Yes, you're right. I wanted it all. I *was* selfish. I didn't want Milly, but nor did I want Cam to have her, and when she fell for him, I wondered …'

'Whether you could change her mind and break them up?'

His eyes lowered, his fingers tracing the fabric on the armrest of the chair. 'It was an ego thing.' He looked at Max and was met with raised eyebrows and turned away again. 'I tried to keep them apart – I'm not proud of that.'

'But they stayed together – the same as you stayed with Rachel.'

He nodded again. 'I'd had affairs in the past while I was with Milly, and I thought it would be the same with Rachel – it would burn out before too long.'

'In which case you wanted me in the background as a Plan B,' Milly said flatly.

Gary flinched as if he'd forgotten Milly was in the room.

'I'm sorry,' he said. 'I wouldn't blame you for not believing me, but I'm sorry. For everything.'

His eyes met Milly's, and he refused to let her look away. Finally, she accepted his apology with a small nod. Max's quickening breaths and loud cry drew her back to the task at hand, and she leapt from the chair and stood beside her, rubbing her shoulders until the contraction passed.

'Are you sure you don't want me to get someone for you? Some pain relief?'

Max shook her head, her lip quivering. 'No,' she said, her voice breaking. 'Not until Richie's here.'

With a sympathetic expression, Milly nodded. 'I understand. I'll text Jess again and check in on them.'

'Thank you.' Max dragged in a ragged breath, and Milly squeezed her hand before reaching for her phone.

'Were you faithful to Rachel?' Max asked Gary as she settled back against the pillows. Milly had to force herself not to look at him as he answered.

'Once the lust died down, I realised I was still in love with Rachel – and grew more in love with her as time went on.' He met Max's gaze. 'I was faithful to her,' he said simply.

Milly let out the breath she hadn't realised she was holding.

'But you never wanted to marry?' Max seemed to be willing herself to talk about something other than what her body was trying to do.

'Rachel's husband wouldn't agree to the divorce.'

An involuntary snort escaped Milly.

'I know,' Gary said. 'It's one of the reasons why I put roadblocks in place for you and Cam. I'm not proud of what I did.' He stood and walked across to the little window, his attention on something outside. 'Before she passed away, I made a promise to her – that I'd find Melinda and apologise and I'd get to know my children before—'

'Before it's too late,' Max finished.

'Yes.' He turned back from the window and gave Max a warm smile. 'Does everyone tell you everything?'

Max simply shrugged and returned his smile.

Milly's phone pinged with a text from Jess: *We're almost down. Tell her to cross her legs.*

Milly put as much reassurance into her smile as

it was possible to do. 'Rick's on his way, love; he'll be here soon.'

Max screwed her eyes shut and clutched at her belly, groaning with the pain.

'Is there anything I can do?' Gary asked helplessly.

Milly shook her head. 'No, but the talking is helping.'

Cam stood in the doorway, crossing his arms before uncrossing them and thrusting them into his pockets them. Milly walked across to him. 'I'm glad you're here,' she said as his arms came around her, his strength seeping into her bringing with it relief and a sense that everything would be okay.

'Rick?'

'Soon,' she said.

'And is everything okay?'

Milly didn't know whether he referred to Max or Gary, but she pulled back and gently smiled up at him. 'Yes. It's okay.'

Cam kissed the top of her head and walked across to Max, and patted her shoulder, not seeming to know what to say. Then he turned his attention to Gary.

'Thanks for driving them and being here,' he said, holding his hand out to Gary.

'No problem,' he said, taking Cam's hand and shaking it. 'I'm glad I could help.'

Milly watched the cordial exchange, glad both men had seemed to put their differences aside for the time being.

'Right, you two,' she said. 'While I'm grateful to you, Gary, now that Cam's here, how about you two find some coffee? I need to get Max up and walking through these contractions, and I can't see that she'll do that while she's worried about protecting her modesty in front of you two.'

Gary patted Max's hand. 'I'll just be down the hall,' he said.

Cam kissed her forehead. 'You're doing well. Not long to go now.'

Milly shooed them both out of the room.

'Now,' she said to Max, 'let's get you out of bed and upright. I don't know why but moving around seemed to help me and it can't hurt to try.'

'Sure. If you think it'll help,' Max said, manoeuvring her legs over the edge of the bed.

'Don't worry about that,' Milly said when Max tried to rearrange the gown. 'We're both grown women, and trust me, that's going to be the least of your worries soon enough.'

Max gripped the edge of the chair as another contraction ripped through her, swaying as she rode the wave of pain. Milly sneaked glanced at her watch – it had only been a few minutes since her last. She rubbed Max's lower back until she caught her breath.

'I'm just going to duck my head outside and see if I can't find a nurse or a doctor. These are getting very close together.'

Max nodded weakly and pinched her lips tight, but before Milly could leave, Max's doctor walked through the door. After introducing himself to Milly, he said to Max, 'I know we had an appointment this afternoon, but I didn't expect I'd be delivering your baby.'

Max's lips curled slightly upwards at his attempted joke.

'Dad's not here?' The doctor looked around the room.

'It depends which dad you mean,' said Max with a straight face, and Milly couldn't help giggling.

When the doctor looked confused, Milly said, 'Sorry, it's an in-joke. I'm surprised she can still smile.'

'Oh god, here comes another one,' groaned Max.

'Let's get you back up on this bed, and I'll take a look,' the doctor said once the wave had subsided. 'This baby seems to be in a hurry.'

Max's eyes filled with tears. 'No, not yet, not until Richie's here. I can't have it until he gets here.' Her eyes met Milly's, imploring her to understand. 'I can't have this baby without Richie. I can't.'

The door flew open, and Richie strode across the room to get to Max's side. 'I'm so sorry, darling,' he cried, holding her face between his hands and kissing her lips hard.

Max opened her mouth to speak, but the pain hit her again, and her fingernails sunk into Richie's arm.

312   JOANNE TRACEY

Richie looked across at his mother, his eyes wild with worry. 'Is this normal?'

Milly sent him a small quick smile and kissed Max's forehead gently. 'You're doing well, my dear, and now Rick's here, you can let that baby of yours make an appearance.' She walked around to where Richie sat on the edge of the bed, cradling Max as closely as he could. 'It's perfectly normal, and now you're here, I'll go back outside and check your two fathers haven't killed each other.'

She found Cam and Gary in the coffee shop. They were watching the replay of a rugby game on the television – All Blacks versus the Wallabies – and exclaiming loudly at something the referee had missed (or mistakenly seen – Milly couldn't tell which).

She rested her hands on Cam's shoulders and kissed his forehead. He reached up to grab one of her hands, kissing it before resting it briefly against his heart.

Gary watched, a half-smile on his face. 'I'll get you a coffee,' he said.

Milly sat down beside Cam and asked, 'How's he been?'

Cam tipped his head to the side and, with a tentative smile, said, 'It's actually been okay. How's it going in there?'

'She's doing well, and now Rick's here, she'll be fine. I think Piglet's in a hurry to meet the world.'

'It'll be a boy then,' said Gary, who had returned. 'Richie was the same, remember? In a hurry?'

So fast he nearly arrived in the back of the car.

'Thank you for this afternoon,' she said, offering Gary an olive branch. 'Not just for driving us but also for staying with us.'

His cheeks coloured slightly, and he handed Milly her coffee, avoiding her eyes. 'It's the least I could do. I'm sorry,' he said suddenly. 'I'm sorry for what I did and the games I played, but I'm not sorry I introduced you to Cam.' Cam's eyes widened, and he straightened in the chair. Gary continued, 'I also wanted to say thank you — for raising my kids way better than I ever would have.'

He held out his hand to Cam, who seemed unable to speak, but reached out his own to shake it.

'I didn't mean to cause trouble when I came back, but—' He coughed into his arm. 'It happened anyway. I really did just want to see how you were,' he said, his eyes meeting Milly's, 'and find out about Cate and Richie. Now I've done that ...'

He coughed again, and this time when Milly caught his glance, there was something in his face that made her tummy lurch. It wasn't so much that he was lean, but more that he was gaunt.

'You're sick, aren't you?' she guessed.

He exhaled, and with the outward breath, it seemed to Milly as though the mask he wore was slipping away.

His face sobered, and he nodded. 'I have been – it's my heart. It's why it took me so long to get over here. I'm on the mend, but it gave me perspective, I guess.'

'I'm sorry,' said Milly. 'You didn't want Richie to know?'

'Not before I met him. Don't get me wrong – it's not like I'm going to drop dead tomorrow; I simply wanted to talk to him without that hanging over us.' He paused briefly, his eyes bleak. 'I missed him and Cate, you know, growing up, and I don't expect them – or you – to forgive me; I just wanted to know they were alright.'

Milly reached for Cam's hand. 'You don't have to go home yet,' she said to Gary. 'Not if you're not ready to. Stay a while longer. Cate will come over when the baby's born, and you can't leave without meeting her.' She took a breath and added, 'Also, while you're feeling generous, there are some papers you need to finalise – Cam's finally going to make an honest woman of me.'

Gary's smile was wistful. 'I'm really pleased for you. Honestly, I am; I'm just sorry, again. It's my fault that it's taken this long to happen.'

'As long as it does happen,' said Cam, a warning in his voice.

'It will. We'll sort it out—'

Gary didn't get to finish his sentence before Jess burst into the coffee shop. 'There you are,' she said breathlessly. Noticing Gary, she pulled to a halt and demanded, 'What are you doing here? I know you brought Max to the hospital – and at some point, someone can explain to me how that happened, but don't you think you've caused enough trouble in this family?'

Her hands were on her hips, shoulders squared, and that trademark ponytail was flicking around her head, accentuating every syllable. Milly watched her daughter, her stance so full of indignation, so ready to jump in and defend, and laughed, at first catching her giggles behind her hand, and then louder. Cam joined her, while Gary looked perplexed, and Jess appeared ready to stamp her foot.

'You've already met Jess,' said Milly once she'd gotten control of herself again.

Gary grinned. 'I have, but she wasn't that scary last time.'

Cam stood and hugged his daughter briefly. 'It's okay, Jess,' he said. 'We're all okay.'

'And I'm the last one to know again?' Jess demanded, the beginning of a smile on her face.

'It would appear so,' said Cam.

'Please tell me Max hasn't already had the baby, and you all know what it is?'

'Not yet—' began Milly.

'Good.' Jess sat down. 'I would've felt cheated if I didn't get to do the waiting around part – after the rush we had to get back down the hill, that is. Oh'—she pointed to the bag at her feet— 'I dropped by the lake house and picked up Max's bag. Good thing she was so organised. Holly said her waters broke at the café and that poor Dan had no idea what was going on. Dayna said Holly had to yell at him to snap into gear.'

'Coffee?' offered Gary.

'Yes, please,' she said and then was off again, chattering in the way she did. 'While I said I wanted to do the waiting thing, I hope we don't have *too* long to wait,' she said, looking at her watch.

Milly exchanged amused glances with Cam; Jess was back to normal.

CHAPTER TWENTY-FIVE

Things moved quickly – yet at the same time, it all unfolded around Richie in slow motion. Max's contractions were coming with scarcely a break between them and lasting longer. She could no longer speak in between them; all her energy was spent riding through the pain. Not knowing what else to do, Richie wrapped his arms around her from behind and held onto her through each, mopping her forehead afterwards, massaging her back, ignoring his pain when her nails left crescent-shaped marks in his arms.

After one contraction that seemed long and especially strong, Max, who had been walking between the contractions, slumped against his chest, almost too weak to stand any longer. 'I think I'm ready for something now,' she moaned.

'I'll get the doctor,' said the midwife.

'Don't let her leave me,' Max wailed, grabbing hold of the sleeve of Richie's jacket.

'She has to darling – if she's to get the doctor,' he pointed out calmly.

'I'll only be gone a minute,' said the midwife gently.

'Oh Christ,' she groaned, 'here comes another one.'

'How are we going in here?' The doctor walked in with a bright smile, and Max glared at him. If it was in any other circumstance, Richie would've laughed at the sight of his gentle Maxi baring her teeth at anyone.

'Can you please give her something?' Richie said. His eyes implored the doctor to do something, to make the pain go away.

'Let's get you back up on this bed,' he said to Max, 'and check you out.'

Richie stayed at the head of the bed, his hands gripping hers, his eyes never leaving hers as if he could take some of her pain away – or give her some of his strength.

The doctor looked up and beamed. 'I'm sorry, my dear, but your window for pain relief has closed. This baby is well on its way. In fact, at the next contraction, I'd like you to push. Can you do that?'

Max gave a quick nod, sweat beading on her forehead, her eyes raised to Richie's in panic or exhaustion – or a combination of both.

'You can do this, darling,' he said, hoping his fear wasn't visible in his face.

Richie thought his heart would burst out of his chest watching Max feed their baby for the first time. Every time he thought he couldn't love her more than he already did, she proved him wrong. The emotion was leaking from his eyes, and he didn't care who saw.

When the midwife placed his son into his arms, the rush of protective love almost made him gasp aloud. Max was right – he had enough love in him, and he'd do whatever it took to keep their child safe.

Time passed while they tended to Max, and the baby was weighed, measured, cleaned, poked, prodded and tested. It was all a blur.

It was Max who finally said, 'Perhaps you should tell your family.'

'Hmmm.' He still couldn't take his eyes off the now sleeping baby.

'They'll still be outside waiting,' she reminded him.

He absently nodded but didn't move.

'Darling,' she prompted gently. 'We'll both still be here.'

So he wandered outside the room, still in a daze, until a passing nurse pointed him in the direction of the waiting room at the end of the ward.

'Go and put your family out of their misery,' she said.

Four heads looked up when Richie walked in.

'Well?' asked Milly tremulously.

'Almost three kilos of future All Black,' Richie said beaming. His smile was wider than it had ever been before. 'It's a boy.' He paused, tears running down his cheeks again. 'And he's perfect.'

Jess beat his mother by the finest of margins to be the first to hug him, but after that, it was much like he was at the bottom of a rugby ruck.

'What have you called him?' asked Milly.

'He's Samuel Horrie,' Richie replied. 'Sam.'

Fletch slapped him on the back. 'I think it's about time you took us to meet him … if that's okay?'

Back in the room, Richie didn't know what was more wondrous – the sight of his newborn son asleep in his crib with all fingers and toes accounted for, or Max, who was sitting propped up against pillows, a tired smile on her face. God, she was beautiful.

He bent down and kissed her lips for the millionth time in the last hour. 'You're incredible,' he whispered against her cheek. 'And I love you so damn much.'

She raised her hand to his cheek and stroked it lightly. 'I love you too.'

'Christ you're a big softie,' said Jess, punching him lightly on his arm before reaching up to hug him. 'I'm so happy for you both,' she said, her voice breaking just a little. Releasing him, she quickly turned her focus to her nephew, but not before Richie saw the glistening in her eyes.

Milly and Cam stood over the crib, their arms around each other. Cam wiped away a tear, and Milly reached up to kiss him lightly.

Gary stood a little awkwardly on one side, not sure

of his place in the room, but Richie had no space in his life at that moment for any bad feelings. Everything in his world was way too perfect for that.

Kissing Max one more time, he walked across to where his father stood. 'Thank you, Gary,' he said, 'for getting Max here and looking after her.'

Gary squeezed his shoulder. 'You're welcome. You've got yourself a pretty wonderful woman there.'

'I know.' Tears sprung to his eyes again. 'You and Dad are going to have to sort out who gets called what,' he said. 'That is if you're intending on being part of Sam's life.'

'Do you want me to be part of his life?'

Gary's words were hesitant, and he couldn't have been further from the laid-back man that Richie had met for breakfast less than a week ago. Richie was beginning to think it had all been an act and the real Gary was the stripped back version who stood before him now.

'I'd like you to be,' said Richie. 'I can't call you Dad – I already have one of those – but Sam is your grandchild, and Max and I would like him to know all of his family.'

'Is it okay with your mother and Cam?'

Milly must have been listening to their conversation. 'What happened between us was in the past, Gary. It's time we all moved on.'

Sam stirred slightly in his crib, yawning, and Jess

pounced.

Richie shook his head and laughed at her antics. 'What is it with you and Mum? Do you think that if you hover around and stare at him for long enough, he'll wake up?'

Jess's chin firmed, an annoyed look on her face. 'I can't believe he went to sleep before you called us all in. I still haven't had a cuddle!'

'Nor have I,' said Milly, 'and grandmother trumps aunt.'

'Says who?'

Richie glance back at Maxi, whose eyes were fluttering shut before snapping open again. 'You know what, guys? How about we give Maxi some space? It's been quite the day for her.'

Milly agreed. 'Yes, we'll leave and let Max get some rest.' To Jess, she said, 'Come home for dinner. We'll have a drink to wet the baby's head.' When Jess seemed reluctant to take her eyes from Sam, Milly added, 'You'll be able to have a proper cuddle tomorrow.'

Jess turned and smiled, but Richie noted the smile didn't reach her eyes. He wished there was something he could say to make her feel better, but the only person who could do that right now was in Far North Queensland.

'Are you coming, Gary?' said Fletch. 'You're welcome to.'

Richie's eyes widened, but he'd get to the bottom

of what had happened between his father and, well, his father at some other time. For now, though, it was all about Maxi.

Gary lowered his head, his hands going into his pockets. 'Thanks, Cam, but I wouldn't feel right. Not yet anyway.' He looked up, the hint of an uncomfortable smile on his face. 'Maybe next time. I'll call you tomorrow though – about that solicitor.'

'Don't be silly,' said Milly, her arm linking through Fletch's. 'You must be hungry, and you might as well eat at our place as anywhere else.'

'If you're sure?'

'We're sure,' said Fletch.

'Are you coming?' Milly asked Jess.

'Yes. I'll be right behind you.'

Milly frowned at Jess's expression and raised her brows in Richie's direction. He nodded slightly to let his mother know he'd understood.

Once the others left the room, Richie draped his arm over Jess's shoulder, and together they gazed down at the miracle of his son – surely the most beautiful baby that had ever been born.

'You said Nathan needed to be near the ocean,' she said in a small voice, not looking at him. 'You said that's who he is.'

Richie didn't pretend to misunderstand. 'It is who he is. It doesn't mean he doesn't love you; it means he's smart enough to know if he gives up what he does for you, he won't be the man you fell in love with anymore.'

'But what about me? If I give up my café, I won't be me either.'

'No one's saying you need to do that. You can keep your café. All he's asking is that you give it a go – he's met you halfway, now you need to do the same for him. The café will be fine for a few weeks – or even a few months. Dayna and Holly are perfectly capable of managing on their own, and Mum and Dad will help too. You've proven you can do it, Jessie – we all know you can do it; there's no harm in letting us help you now.'

Jess was silent for a few seconds. 'I really love him, Richie.'

'I know you do.'

'Would you do it for Max, give up everything?'

Richie didn't hesitate. 'In a heartbeat. It's why I stayed in Brookford for so long.'

'I can't go immediately,' she said, wavering.

'Yes, you can,' he said simply.

'It's worth it?' she asked. 'Even if you don't know how it will turn out?'

'You can never know how it will all turn out,' said Richie. 'You don't need to look past Mum and Dad for an example of that.'

'But it's worth it?' she asked again.

'Yeah,' he said, looking down at his son and back towards Max, her eyes closed and her breath even.

Tears came back to his eyes as he squeezed Jess's arm. 'Without a doubt.'

CHAPTER TWENTY-SIX

If anyone had told Milly that there'd be an evening where she and Cam could talk freely with Gary, she'd have laughed in their faces; yet that was what had happened.

They were all worn out from the emotion of the day, so Milly had whipped up a quick macaroni cheese. Cam poured red wine, and as they raised a toast to the new arrival, they acknowledged Sam was the cutest baby in existence, and Max and Richie would be fabulous parents. As for the grandparents, how lucky was he to have five?

Usually, Jess would've made some joke about how they were completely missing the point and not giving sufficient credit to the role of the godmother, to which Cam would've made another joke about how not everything had to be about her, but tonight, Jess was subdued. Cam had noticed, too, but as if by mutual agreement, neither of them had said anything to Jess.

It wasn't until after they'd waved Gary goodbye and Jess was getting ready to leave that she announced,

'I'm going to Australia.'

She'd said it so quietly that at first, Milly wasn't sure she'd heard correctly.

Cam, though, didn't miss a beat. 'I'm glad, Jessie. When are you going?'

She shrugged and screwed her nose up and pulled down the sleeves of her jacket. 'The day after tomorrow – if I can get a flight.' She hesitated and toed at the tiles on the front porch. 'I know it's a bit to ask Dad, but can you keep an eye on Beach Road for me?'

For the second time that day, Cam's eyes misted over as he reached for his daughter and clung to her. 'You bet. I'm so proud of the woman you've grown into, Jess,' he said. 'I know I don't say it often enough, but I am. Your mother and I both are.'

Jess pulled away and dashed at her eyes with the back of her hand. 'I have no idea whether I'm doing the right thing.'

Milly put her arm around her. *When was the last time she'd held Jess like this?* It had been different with Cate – she'd always been a hugger – but Jess? She'd been prickly and independent and adamant she didn't need anyone. If she closed her eyes, Milly could still smell that little girl smell in her hair.

'Oh Jess,' she said, tears falling down her face. 'That's what makes it so right.'

Jess submitted to the embrace. It was some seconds before she pulled away and wiped at her face again with her sleeve. She smiled a quick, forced half-smile. 'I don't know how long I'll be. I might hate it and catch the first plane home.'

'Or you might love it and stay a while,' said Cam. 'Take a break, Jessie; you haven't stopped working since you were fourteen. It's time you had a holiday. We'll all still be right here where you left us.'

Jess nodded once. 'I'll let you know what I'm doing.'

'Give our love to Nathan,' called Milly as Jess opened the car door and slid into her seat.

Cam put his arm around Milly as they waved her goodbye. 'She'll be alright, won't she?' he asked, watching the lights fade into the distance.

'She will,' said Milly, shivering and wrapping her cardigan tightly around her. 'It looks like the cold change has arrived.'

Cam tilted his head back and held his hand out. 'The first sleet of the year,' he said. 'This will probably be falling as snow higher up.'

'What did I say about the ring around the moon?' Milly said, taking his hand to lead him back inside.

'What a day.' Cam collapsed onto the lounge. 'I certainly didn't expect Max to go into labour after I sent Richie off to talk to Jess—'

'Which I thought was a stellar move, by the way,' Milly interrupted him. 'But perhaps, in hindsight, not the best day to play it.'

Cam chuckled. 'You can say that again. As for finishing the day with Gary sitting around our table and Jess about to fly the coop?' He shook his head, laughing wryly. 'We've had more predictable days.'

Milly took out two glasses from the cupboard and poured them each a whisky. 'What did you and Gary talk about while I was in with Max?'

He sat up straighter, the smile sliding off his face. 'He told me about Rachel. He behaved badly back then – and he knows it.' He stood and walked across to Milly, wrapping his arms about her. 'You know, I couldn't help but wonder—'

'If you would've done the same thing?' Milly finished softly.

'Yeah. I don't think I could've, though – not if I had a family. If someone told me I could have them or my kids, I couldn't have done it.'

Milly lifted her head from his chest and searched his face. 'No,' she said, 'I don't think you could have. Perhaps, though, Gary really thought he could have it all. Maybe he thought we wouldn't last, and custody would no longer be an issue.'

'Who knew what he was thinking,' said Cam, releasing her. 'I think, though, now we need to have that talk.'

Milly's tummy teetered at the intent in his eyes and the square set of his jaw hinting at a resolution to get this over and done with – the last piece that needed to be resolved before they could finally completely move on.

He picked up a glass of the whisky she'd poured and handed it to her before taking the other. 'I guess I'll be needing this.'

She managed a shaky laugh. 'I certainly do.'

Walking into the lounge room, he set the whisky bottle and his glass on the coffee table before taking a seat. 'Sit down, Milly,' he said. 'You're making the place look untidy.'

She smiled at his attempt at lightness and sat in the armchair opposite to his. He raised his eyebrows at the distance she'd placed between them but said nothing.

Milly raised the glass to her lips and swallowed the contents in one go, grimacing as the whisky burned its way through her.

'I met up with Gary last week,' she finally said.

'I know you did,' Cam said simply.

'How did you know?'

He shrugged, not bothering to hide the hurt in his eyes. 'I saw the text on your phone, and I saw you putting on make-up that morning and, I'm ashamed to say, I followed you out there.' He picked up his whisky and downed it before reaching for the bottle to refill their glasses. 'I know I told you this chat could wait, but the longer you didn't tell me...' He ran his hand through his hair.

'Is that why you were—?'

'Why I avoided you?' She nodded. He continued, 'Yes. I wanted you to tell me, but I was afraid of what you'd tell me. I didn't want it to be like last time.'

'Last time?' Milly frowned as she traced back through her memories.

'I know something happened between you two,' he said. 'Each of those times you met him to ask about the divorce.'

'Oh.' She reached for her glass, but this time she sipped, inhaling the rich peaty smokiness. 'You never asked.'

'I couldn't,' he said. 'Because then I'd know, and I couldn't bear to lose you – even if she wasn't mine.'

Milly looked across at him, her eyes wide, her brain racing, needing to ask but already knowing the answer. 'What do you mean?'

'Jess,' he said, holding her stare.

The blood drained from her face, and her heart skipped a beat and then fluttered around wildly. 'You think Jess isn't yours? That Gary and I ...'

He sighed, dejected. 'You were different when you came home that first time – rattled, jumpy, and snappy. Afterwards, you seemed restless and unsettled. Mostly though, when I asked you how the discussion went, you couldn't look me in the eye. And I wondered whether ...' He met her eyes, and the pain in his took Milly's breath away. 'I loved you so much and thought if I said anything, you might run back to him, and I couldn't lose either you or the kids.'

'So you said nothing?'

He nodded miserably; the memory of that night etched over his face. 'And then when you were pregnant with Jess, and you went back to talk to him again, you came back in the same state.' He gave a half-hearted shrug. 'I prepared myself then – just in case – but you said nothing, so I dared to hope your heart was still mine and that whatever had happened with you and Gary was an aberration or leftover of what you once felt for him.'

'And you could live with that?'

'Not really, no, but if I wanted to be with you, I knew I had to.' His tone was bleak as he stared into his whisky. 'And I have done.'

'Oh Cam, I'm so sorry.'

He waved away her apology. 'It's why I've been a bit, well, you know … since he's been in town. In case you still felt something for him – especially now the kids have grown and—' He paused and swallowed hard, a little pulse beating in the side of his jaw. 'But last night, when we made love and seeing you today with him—' He took another breath, a half-smile curling his lips. 'I knew you felt nothing for him anymore – other than as the father of your children, of course.'

Milly's heart had stopped thrashing about inside and now ached with the pain she'd unknowingly inflicted on him all those years ago and the pain he was still feeling now. He'd never said. She didn't know whether to be furious at him for not talking his fears through with her, but she also understood why he hadn't. Right from the start, he'd been second fiddle to Gary; he'd seen how much she'd loved Gary and knew how he'd hurt her – and he knew the hold Gary had had on her.

Milly stood and then sat down beside Cam. Holding his hands, she looked into his face, her gaze roaming across the still firm jaw, the hazel eyes glistening with a combination of love and pain, the once thick tawny hair now almost completely grey – which on Cam made him look more distinguished than old.

'Jess is absolutely yours, Cam.' She reached up for his face, turning it to her as she told him what she should've told him nearly thirty years ago. 'That day I went to meet him all those years ago, we argued. I used to think that sometimes Gary would pick an argument because afterwards, the sex would be more explosive.' Cam swallowed hard. It was difficult for him to hear what she had to say. 'He kissed me, and I let him – and I hated myself for betraying you. But that's as far as it went. He thought he had me then. I could see it in his eyes, the way he looked at me – it was the way he'd always looked at me, but this time there was something else, triumph. As if he'd been competing with you for me – and thought he'd won. That was when I knew he'd planned that we'd argue and end up in bed – that it was why he wanted to meet in a hotel bar.'

'You told me it was a coffee shop.'

She tried to swallow the lump in her throat. 'I know I did. I think I also knew what Gary had in mind when I went there. I knew, and I still went – what does that say about me?' She didn't wait for Cam to answer. 'Anyway, when he suggested we continue our conversation upstairs, I turned and walked out of there – and I kept walking. I was scared that if I went straight home, you'd see it on me – how close I'd come to betraying you and how close I'd come to losing you.' She lifted his hand and pressed kisses on his palm.

'The next time I went to him, he tried the same thing. This time I resisted. I told him I wanted the divorce; I pleaded with him even though that was playing into his hands – he wanted me to beg. As soon as he knew I was pregnant and why I wanted it so badly, he had me where he wanted me. I told him I didn't need his approval and I could get the court to agree to it, and that's when he told me he'd petition for custody. He also said he'd insist on a DNA test for Rick.'

'What the fuck?' Cam jerked away from her, his eyes wide, his face flushed. 'He said what?'

Milly nodded sadly. 'He didn't want the kids, but he didn't want you to have them either – it's the same as he didn't want me anymore, but he also didn't want you to have me.'

'And by denying you all my name, he could tell

himself that even if he hadn't won, he certainly hadn't lost.' Cam rubbed his hand down the side of his cheek, sighed heavily and reached for her. 'He always was a competitive arse. That explains his apology this afternoon.'

'I think so.' Milly laughed shortly. 'So that's why I met him the other day and why I didn't tell you I was doing so. I wanted to find out what he was here for, and I'll be honest, I wanted to look him in the eye and see whether I still hated him.'

'And?'

Milly shook her head. 'Nothing. Not a thing. I think there was still a small part of him that thought I'd meet his eyes and feel the same way I used to, that he'd be able to bring me back under his spell – and for a second or two, I wondered the same.' She pursed her lips. 'I thought him being here would cause trouble.'

'And it did.' Cam's smile was sardonic.

'Not just between us, but also for Rick – thankfully Cate was well out of the way, but I worried about what rubbish he'd feed Rick.'

'Cate would've brought him down a peg or two,' said Cam. 'Rick's sensible and wouldn't have believed any of his bullshit.'

'I know that, but it still worried me – especially given that we'd lied to him too.'

'Are you going to tell Rick what he threatened?' asked Cam.

'No.' Milly shook her head adamantly. 'No, I'm not going there. None of it matters anymore. Gary has no more influence over me, and I think he regrets what he did and the choices he made.' With a sigh, she relaxed back into his arms. 'You know Cam, I can't regret Gary. He was my choice at the time, and if it wasn't for him, I wouldn't have Cate or Richie. For that matter, I also wouldn't have you and Jess. While it was hard at the time, in hindsight, him cheating on me was the best thing that happened to me.'

Cam pulled his arms tight around her. 'And me too. It was hell watching you go through it and waiting for you to be out the other side, but even when I despaired you'd ever see me as more than a friend, I couldn't have left you.'

He pressed a kissed to her temple, and Milly raised her face so he could kiss her lips. Sensation danced across her skin as the kiss became more urgent. She pulled his head closer to deepen the kiss; her mouth opened to meet his tongue. Cam gently eased her back until she was lying on the lounge.

'I love you, Cam,' she said, gasping as his hand moved under her shirt to cup her breast, his thumb flicking against the nipple through her bra, his mouth blazing a trail down her throat. 'I always will.'

He pulled back briefly, his eyes blazing, breathing heavily, his hand still on her breast. 'I should never have doubted it.'

'No,' she said with a smile, slowly undoing the buttons on his shirt. 'You shouldn't have. Cameron Fletcher, will you please marry me?'

His kiss crushed her lips, taking what was left of her breath and removing all thoughts from her mind.

Sometime later, still on the lounge, she said, 'Well, that was a surprise. I believe that was the first time we've made love anywhere other than a bed.'

Cam lay on his back; she snuggled into him, their clothes scattered around them. 'Surely not,' he said, a satisfied smile in his voice.

Milly propped herself on her elbow and looked down at him. 'I think it was, you know.'

'Hardly surprising given we always had children running around,' he said. 'But I have to say, it made me wonder what we've been missing out on. What do you say? The kitchen counter next time? Or maybe we can lock the office door.' He waggled his eyebrows suggestively, and Milly chuckled at the wolfish expression on his face.

She poked his chest. 'You didn't answer my question.'

'What was the question again?'

'Do you need me to ask it again?'

'Yes,' he said, grinning madly at her. 'I do.'

'Okay … Cameron Fletcher, will you please marry me?'

'Didn't *I* ask *you* – thirty years ago and then again

last night?'

'You might have asked me thirty years ago, but you didn't actually ask me last night, you know.'

'Hmmm, Jess got in the way of that one, didn't she?'

'She did,' said Milly, manoeuvring herself until she was straddling him. 'So now I'm asking you. What'll it be, boy? Yes or no?'

'Let me sleep on it,' he said, and they both laughed as they realised they'd paraphrased an old Meatloaf song, "Paradise By The Dashboard Light".

She leaned forward and kissed him, pulling back when he would have deepened the kiss, to move down to nip and suckle his nipples, thrilling as his body hardened again under hers.

'So,' she said, taking him within her again. 'What'll it be? Don't you think it's about time you made an honest woman of me?'

He closed his eyes and groaned. 'There's nothing I'd rather do than marry you – although you've always been an honest woman, now you'll be my honest woman.'

'Darling Cam, I've been that for thirty years, a piece of paper won't change that, but'— she began to rock her hips—'it will be nice.'

CHAPTER TWENTY-SEVEN

Once Jess decided to act, there was, as usual, no stopping her. Before she could change her mind, she had her flight booked – for Sunday.

She'd phoned Nathan from the car on her way to her parent's house from the hospital. He'd been thrilled for Max and Ritchie and had also said he understood she wouldn't want to leave Queenstown now.

'I get it, Jay,' he said. 'You're not coming over yet.' He'd sounded disappointed but resigned. 'I understand,' he said. 'The thing is, I'm not going to be able to come back to Queenstown for a couple of weeks now. I'm helping out on one of the boats – it's just a few days a week, but it will help me decide if the gig is what I want.'

'But you're almost sure that it is,' she said, defeated.

'Yeah.'

Jess's heart sank at his answer. She almost told him then that she'd decided to come over, but before she could, he said, 'The next move's yours to make, Jay. Take a few days and let me know, eh?' There was a commotion in the background, people yelling, and he said, 'I have to go. Give my congratulations to Richie and Max, and don't forget to send me a pic of the little fella.'

'Will do,' she said. 'I love you, Nathan.'

'Love you too, Jay.'

A few hours later, sitting on the lounge with a printed boarding pass in her hand, Jess wondered whether she should call him again and tell him she was on her way. No, it could be a surprise – the best surprise. With her decision made, she opened her laptop and began making lists.

The top of the list for Saturday morning was a trip to the hospital for a cuddle with baby Sam. Jess had never been particularly interested in babies – she couldn't see what all the cooing and fuss was about. Sam, though, was different. When Richie placed him in her arms, and his wide eyes investigated her face, his little fingers on hers, Jess melted. Her eyes misted over, and her insides turned to mush. She almost changed her mind about Australia on the spot.

'We'll all still be here when you come home,' Max said gently. How had she known what Jess was thinking?

Jess sighed and then breathed in Sam's sweet baby smell one last time. How was it possible to miss someone you'd only just met? Someone who wasn't yet a day old?

When she looked up, Richie snapped a photo

of her on his phone. 'You can send it to Nathan,' he suggested.

'I'd better be going,' she said, tightly, handing Sam back to his father. 'I've got a lot to do. Packing, planning, all of it.'

She used her hands to illustrate the size of the undertaking and plastered on a brave smile so neither Richie nor Max would see how desperately she wanted what they had. Maybe not motherhood yet, but the security of being in a committed relationship. She wanted someone to look at her in the way Richie was gazing at Max.

No, she corrected herself, she wanted Nathan to look at her in the way Richie gazed at Max. In his look was everything they'd been through to get to where they were. In his face was wonder at having arrived at that place where they could go forward together, that they'd deal with whatever was thrown at them together.

At Beach Road, Jess sat around the kitchen bench with Dayna, Holly and Dan and told them what was happening.

'I'm not sure how long I'll be gone for,' she said. 'And with Dan leaving in a few weeks too—' Jess shrugged, her eyes flitting away from Dan's.

Dayna looked at Holly and said, 'We'll be fine. We manage when you're on track, and you don't even have phone reception out there.'

Holly added, 'We'll do a video call once a week. It'll be fine. How lucky are you, though? Escaping the cold in Far North Queensland.'

'Very lucky,' Jess agreed. 'Anyone want to see some photos of the baby?'

Jess left her phone with Dayna and Holly, and as they were scrolling through the photos of Sam, she rested a hand on Dan's shoulder and tilted her head toward the stairs. She'd spent the drive back from the hospital that morning practising what she'd say to him, but when the moment came, all she managed was, 'We ... uh ... need to talk.'

'Yeah,' he muttered, 'I reckon we do.'

'Beers after work?'

He nodded. 'Sounds good.'

With the last afternoon customers settling their account, Jess flipped the sign on the door to Closed, flicked the deadlock over, pulled the door shut and joined Dan on the footpath.

The cold front had, as predicted, brought with it the first of the season's snow to the peaks. The sky might've been blue, but the temperature had plummeted into single figures.

As they wandered to the lake and through the park, the Saturday market stalls were closing, but many people were still milling around. By unspoken agreement, they chose a bar down at the Steamer Wharf, selecting outside seats despite the weather. Jess pulled her scarf high around her neck and grabbed a blanket, wrapping it around her body, as much for warmth as for the comfort it gave her to hold something.

'Richie's asked me to be godfather to Sam,' said Dan once they were settled with beers.

'He told me,' said Jess. 'You're a great choice – even if you're buggering off to Melbourne,' she added with a grin.

'I won't be there forever,' he said. 'Besides, he needs someone who'll be a good influence on him. With you as godmother, he'll need all the help he can get.'

He returned her grin, cheeky and smug. Jess breathed a sigh of relief … They would be okay.

'Do you even have godparents if you don't get christened?' she asked. Richie had told her they were planning a naming ceremony in a month or so when Max's parents were in town.

'Who knows? I'm happy to go with the flow, though.'

'Yeah, me too. Will you come back for the naming day?'

'I'll certainly try,' Dan said.

'Me too.'

Dan's head jerked up at her words. 'Is this more than a couple of weeks on holiday?'

She picked at the soggy cardboard coaster under her beer glass. 'Maybe.'

He let out a low whistle. 'Good,' he said. When Jess met his eyes, she saw he meant it. 'If I can't have you, I'm glad you've chosen someone like him.'

'I'm sorry, Dan,' she said, squeezing his hand.

'I know you are, and so am I. But'—he smiled wryly—'I'm sure I'll get over you quickly enough.'

'Oh, you ...' Jess flipped a coaster at him and laughed as he plucked it from the air.

'Seriously though, Jess, it'll be good for you. The change will be good, and Beach Road will be fine.'

She briefly closed her eyes. 'I know.' She said with more confidence than she felt. Then added, 'Will you be okay?'

'Yeah,' he finally said after swallowing a mouthful of beer. 'I'll be fine. A change is what I need too. What did Nathan say when you told him you were coming over?'

When Jess finished her beer and turned to watch the *Earnslaw* steam out across the lake, he said, 'You have told him, haven't you?'

She hunched her shoulders up to her ears and screwed her nose up. 'Not exactly.'

He raised his eyebrows. 'It's a pretty simple question, Jess.'

'Well, I have spoken to him. I told him about the baby – and he said he could understand why I didn't want to come over immediately but said he was helping on one of the boats and wouldn't be able to get back here for another couple of weeks to see me.'

'Which is when you said you'd come to him?' Dan prompted.

She tipped her head to one side and grinned at him. 'I thought I might surprise him.'

Dan closed his eyes and rubbed at the furrow on his forehead. 'Do you think that's a good idea?'

Why was everyone so worried about this? When she'd called in at C2C to ask Kate for his address, she'd had the same reaction; from Milly too, who was there showing off the photos of her new grandson.

Kate hadn't been able to hide her smile. 'I'm so glad you're going,' she said. 'I know Nathan will be thrilled.'

'I want it to be a surprise,' Jess had continued. 'So please don't tell him I'm coming.'

While Kate looked concerned, Milly said, 'Do you think that's a good idea?'

'Absolutely. Nathan loves surprises, and I'll be the best surprise of all.'

Jess had decided to ignore the fact that neither Kate nor Milly were convinced. And Dan was now wearing the same look.

'Nathan loves surprises,' she said again, with a confidence that was wavering by the minute.

'I'm sure he'll be glad to see you,' said Dan. 'Once he's over the surprise, that is …' He grinned to let her know he was joking – at least, she hoped he was joking.

'When do you go?'

'Tomorrow afternoon. Via Brisbane.'

He let out a short laugh and shook his head. 'I gotta say, Jess, once you make up your mind, there's no messing about!'

'I love him,' she said simply.

Jess stayed the night at her parents' house, sleeping in her childhood bed. Milly cooked her favourite lamb roast and potato bake, with chocolate pavlova for dessert.

When they dropped her at the airport the following day, Fletch and Milly assured her she'd be involved with all the planning for their wedding and would miss nothing despite being in Australia.

'I can't make decisions without my bridesmaid,' said Milly.

'Be happy, Jessie,' said Fletch.

Jess's throat closed over at the catch in her father's voice, but she didn't dwell on that in case it brought her undone too.

It was only when she was on the plane with her seatbelt fastened that she stopped to wonder whether she was doing the right thing – not just in going to Nathan, but in going to him *this* way, surprising him.

It was, she decided, too late for that, and she settled back in her seat, determined to enjoy the journey.

After spending the night in Brisbane, Jess finally

arrived in Cairns late the following morning. It was no wonder Nathan had relocated temporarily to Queenstown rather than make the return trip too often.

Despite being officially autumn, the sky was clear and blue and the temperature so warm that Jess divested herself of at least two layers of clothing before she'd even left the airport terminal. She checked into her hotel, grabbed a quick lunch, and explored the city centre, keeping a close eye on her watch as she counted down the hours until Nathan's cruise would dock back at Marlin Wharf.

Just before five pm, she wandered down to the waterfront and secured a table outside a bar overlooking the marina. After ordering a glass of white wine, she settled in to wait.

It wasn't long before his boat docked, and the passengers disembarked, all smiling, chattering and slightly sunburned after a day out on the reef. It was another twenty (long) minutes before she caught sight of Nathan – and just a glimpse was enough to make her heartbeat scatter. She couldn't wait to see his face when he knew she was here.

Picking up her phone, she dialled his number and watched as he took the phone from his pocket, looked at the caller ID, frowned, and answered.

'Jay,' he said hesitantly. 'How are you?'

'I'm great,' she said. 'In fact, I'm—'

A tall, slim blonde woman came up to Nathan,

linked her arm in his and gave him a big, white-teethed smile. With surfer-girl hair and long, brown legs, she was the sort of woman who belonged in Queensland on a boat. She'd know all about the things Nathan knew. She'd know what a nudibranch was without having to google it (for the record, it's sort of a sea slug but also not quite a sea slug). She'd be an accomplished diver, and Jess imagined her below the surface with Nathan, pointing out turtles and brightly coloured fish and discussing issues such as coral bleaching and the impact of sunscreen. Her skin would taste faintly of salt, and they'd shower it off together. The images all crowded together in Jess's mind and exploded out of her mouth.

'Who. The. Fuck. Is. That?' Jess was out of her chair and yelling the last couple of words.

'What the? Jess?' Nathan looked wildly around, and as his eyes met Jess's, she picked up her bag and ran.

She had to get out of there, back to the hotel, repack her bags and book the first flight home. This had been such a mistake; it was always going to be a mistake. She should never have listened to everyone telling her to come over here. She certainly should never have allowed herself to be convinced that surprising Nathan was a good idea. He hated surprises – she knew that!

So, she ran. Past diners in waterfront restaurants

enjoying a late afternoon drink and bar snack, past the anglers on the jetty, down the path through the palm trees that only an hour ago had reminded her of a paradise found.

'Jay! Slow down!'

While she was used to climbing mountains, running required another set of lungs and Jess's soon began to burn. She was slowing down but knew she had to keep going. Through the park, past the research vessel moored at the cruise terminal, across the street, that was all. She'd be at the hotel, and she'd be safe.

She risked a glance over her shoulder; he was only a few metres behind. Then, she was face down on the footpath, her palms stinging, her bag landing on the lawn, its contents spilling out.

As she scrambled to her feet, cursing the root of the giant fig tree bulging across the path, Nathan was there, holding her elbow. Jess batted his hand away, scooped everything back into her bag, and planted her hands on her hips to suck in the air. He did the same before linking his fingers behind his head and looking toward the sky.

While his attention was elsewhere and her lungs had reinflated, she made a move to run again, but he caught her wrist.

'No, Jay. No more running. What the fuck was that about anyway?' He sounded more perplexed than angry.

Jess pulled her arm free and turned to face him, and in a controlled tone, asked, 'Who is she, Nathan? You didn't waste any time replacing me, did you? Or was she waiting for you to come back?'

'What are you talking about?' His eyes narrowed.

'I saw her put her arm through yours, and I'm sure she would've kissed you, but I was there.' Jess sucked in another deep breath.

Nathan's face slowly broke in into a smile, and he burst out laughing.

'It's. Not. Funny,' she said through gritted teeth.

'Actually, it is from where I'm standing.' He took a step to close the gap between them. 'That was Kristy; she's the senior dive guide on the boat—'

'Of course she is.'

Nathan ignored her interruption. 'And she was checking in on me – we had a bit of a heart-to-heart last night about you.'

'It looked very cosy from where I was standing,' said Jess, her breath finally settling; if only her heart would do the same.

'Trust me, Jay, even if I was into her – which I'm not – I'm absolutely not her type.'

'Really?' Jess crossed her arms.

'Really. You're more her type.'

'Oh? Oh,' Jess said as she suddenly understood.

'Are you going to run again?' he asked.

Jess shook her head.

'Good.' Finally, a grin spread across his face. If he wasn't wearing wrap-around sunglasses, she'd see the smile in his eyes, in the crinkly bits beside his eyes. He let out a huge breath. 'God, it's good to see you.'

'It's good to see you too,' she said. 'And sorry about the running thing before,' she added, finding it strangely awkward – the two of them standing in this park, staring at each other, grinning stupidly (in the case of Nathan) yet neither making a move to close the gap.

'It's alright,' he said, maddeningly still.

'So,' said Jess, 'what's a girl got to do to get a hug around here? I've come a long way for one, you know.'

'You've come all this way just for a hug?' He pushed his sunglasses on top of his head; his eyes were dancing just as she'd imagined.

'Okay, you got me. Maybe I want more than a hug,' she said, taking one step towards him, holding his gaze.

'It's a long way to come otherwise,' he said, taking a step towards her.

'I've missed you so much.' Jess's shoulders slumped, and she no longer cared whether he saw how much it had hurt when he left.

'I've missed you too, Jay,' he said, running a knuckle down her cheek.

With all the breath she had left, and with all the love in her heart, she slid her arms around his waist and pulled his body to hers and kissed him deeply, passionately.

'How long are you here for?' he asked when he finally came up for air, resting his forehead on hers, cupping her face in his hand.

'I need to be back in September for the wedding. I told you Mum and Dad were getting married, didn't I?' He nodded. 'But let's see how it goes – after all, I'm only here for the secluded crocodile-free beach and the love-making.' She wished he'd lower his mouth and kiss her again already.

'Just that, hey?' He raised his eyebrows, but his mischievous grin told her he didn't believe her.

'Okay, you too. I'm here for you.' She bit her lip and tried not to smile. 'I love you, Nathan.'

'I love you too, Jay – and I was beginning to lose hope, you know, of you coming to see me.'

'How long would you have waited?' She stroked her finger over his lower lip. He nipped at it, sending sensations scooting right to her core.

'I don't know – does it sound sappy if I say forever?'

'Yeah,' she said, grinning, 'It sounds sappy, but luckily I'm so happy to see you I'm prepared to forgive a little sappy.'

Unable to wait any longer, Jess pulled his face back to hers.

'Please tell me you have a hotel room,' he said, forcing himself away from her when a group of girls giggled as they passed.

'I do. I didn't know whether you lived with anyone, and I didn't want to assume ...' Her cheeks grew warm.

'You'll be moving in with me,' he said, 'but I hope this room of yours is close by because I don't think I can wait too much longer to show you just how much I love you.'

His words curled around all the parts of her that had missed him over the last few weeks.

'And how sappy you can be,' she teased.

'That too.' His grin was wicked, and Jess decided she needed him – all of him – right now.

'See that hotel over there – right across the road?' she said.

'Ah-ha.'

'How fast can you run?'

CHAPTER TWENTY-EIGHT

Six months later ...

'Oh, Mum, you look beautiful!' Cate air-kissed Milly's cheeks as she handed her a flute of champagne.

'It's not too much?' asked Milly, smoothing down the skirt of her wedding dress. Despite Jess urging her to replicate the look from their commitment ceremony so many years ago and Cate telling her repeatedly that she wasn't too old to have a long white dress, Milly had opted for a compromise. The result was a cream tea-length A-line dress, with an organza overlay appliquéd with long-stemmed wildflowers. She wore nothing in her hair but would carry a simple posy of lupins in purple, pink and lavender.

'It's perfect, Milly,' said Max.

'Yeah, Mum,' chimed in Jess. 'It's very you.'

'But for a wedding in the backyard?' Milly asked, looking in the mirror and combing her hair with her fingers. Just how waterproof was her mascara?

'Especially for a wedding in the backyard,' said Jess.

'Do you think Holly has everything under control?' Holly and Kate were plating the canapes and had ordered Milly out of her kitchen.

'She's fine, Mum,' said Jess. 'She's an old hand at this now. Dayna and Nell arrived a few minutes ago, so they'll help finish and will be there to pass around the food once the ceremony is finished.'

'It's such a pity Dan couldn't make it back,' said Cate, zipping up the back of Max's dress. While Milly had encouraged them to choose for themselves, Cate, Max, and Jess were all wearing floral dresses too.

Milly exchanged a glance with Jess, whose cheeks coloured slightly before she looked away. 'Yes, it's a shame, but he sent his congratulations.' Neither Jess nor Richie had told her the entire story about what happened with Dan, but Milly knew enough to guess the rest.

'Him leaving was so unexpected – especially so soon after you went away too,' said Cate, oblivious to Jess's discomfort. 'Have you heard from him?'

'Richie was talking to him only last week,' said Max, who was sitting cross-legged on the floor. 'He's been house-sitting for our friends, Brad and Abby, while they were in Bali for a couple of months. Now they're back, he said he needs to get serious about finding a rental. The job's going well, though. I don't think we're supposed to tell anyone – so keep it quiet – but he's been asked to take part in a team challenge for *MasterChef* next season with the crew from the restaurant.'

'Wow,' said Cate. 'At that rate, he'll never come home. Next time Harry and I are down there, we'll need to look him up.'

There was a knock on the door, and Richie said, 'Is everyone decent?'

'Yes,' called Jess. 'You can come in.'

Milly stood from the dressing table and twirled. 'You look great, Mum,' he said, grabbing her hands and lightly kissing her cheek. 'Dad's ready to go, and everyone's arrived,' he said and turned to Max, adding with a grin, 'You are planning on wearing shoes, aren't you?'

Max rose to her feet in one fluid movement, the filmy layers of her dress flowing around her, not a drop of her champagne spilling. 'I thought I might,' she said, reaching up on her toes to kiss Richie's mouth. 'Seeing as how it's a special occasion.'

'You look beautiful,' he whispered. 'Are you sure we can't double up and get married today as well?'

Milly's heart was about to burst with the love she had for her son and Max, and she prayed her mascara would hold up.

'I'd love to, but today is your parent's day. We'll have our turn soon enough,' Max replied, sending Milly a wink over Richie's shoulder.

'Not soon enough for me,' he mock-growled and

pulled her towards him.

'Ahem,' said Jess loudly, unable to hide her grin. 'Did you come in here for a reason?'

'What?' He dragged his eyes away from Max's. 'Yes, we're ready to go.'

'Is Harry back from …?' Cate asked, her eyes swivelling to her mother's.

'That's an excellent question,' said Milly. 'Where did Harry disappear to with our overnight bags?'

Her children had been displaying some shifty behaviour over the last couple of days. They had something planned for her and Cam's wedding night, but she had no idea what that might be.

Richie glanced at Cate and then Jess. 'Should we tell her?'

Jess nodded eagerly. 'We might as well.'

Cate spoke up. 'You said you didn't want a wedding present, so the three of us have put in to buy you a couple of nights at Blanket Bay Lodge.'

Milly's hand flew to the base of her throat, her eyes wide. 'You didn't! That's too much!' It had always been a secret dream of hers to stay at Blanket Bay, a luxury lodge on the shores of Lake Wakatipu near Glenorchy, but neither she nor Cam would ever have been able to justify the expense.

Cate stood from the bed and walked over to Milly, wrapping her arms around her, their cheeks touching. 'It's not nearly enough, Mum. You and Dad have waited so long for this day; it's the least we can do.'

A rush of emotion prevented Milly from saying more, and she worried again about the staying power of her mascara.

'It's time Mum. Time for me to give you away.' Richie held out his hand for his mother to take; Cate handed around the bouquets of wildflowers, Max slid her feet into ballet flats, and they were ready to go.

'Is Sam still asleep?' Max asked Richie as they walked down the hall.

'Yes, he's in his pram. Gary's keeping an eye on him.'

Milly pressed a finger to the side of her eye to stop a tear from escaping. How was it possible that not only were she and Cam finally having the wedding day they'd dreamt of, but that Gary – who was utterly besotted with his grandson – was here as well.

As the little party walked through the kitchen, Holly, Dayna and Nell stopped what they were doing and clapped. Holly rushed over and planted a quick kiss on Milly's cheek and whispered, 'That dress is perfect. Fletch is a very lucky man.'

Milly squeezed her hand briefly and smiled gratefully. She hadn't expected to feel this overcome by emotion. They had been together for so long that surely today was just a formality? She shouldn't be having this much trouble holding it together.

They paused at the entrance to the deck, the glass

doors having been slid wide open. Across the lawn, someone had set white chairs in neat rows on either side of a grassy "aisle". Since when had they owned chairs like that? She raised a questioning brow at Richie.

'Flynn Murphy lent them to us for the day,' he said. 'Along with the wine glasses.'

Richie had completed the terrace at Flynn's Folly earlier in the month, and it had been a roaring success. They were already open for business and kept the team at Beach Road busy with weekend picnic hampers. Holly had been booked to cater for her first wedding there at the end of October. The job at Flynn's had led to commissions with two other wineries in the region, with the possibility of more in the pipeline.

Fletch had admitted to Milly only the other day how wrong he'd been to try and hold Richie back.

'You weren't wrong, love,' she'd said. 'He needed to slow down and get the timing right, and that's exactly what's happened.'

At the end of the aisle, a triangular timber frame had been erected. Tied haphazardly to it were more bunches of lupins and other wildflowers. Through the structure, the creamy heads of flax swayed softly in the light breeze and beyond, the lake with the mountains rising against the bluest of late spring skies. And beside it stood Cam and Tom.

At Milly's entrance, everyone had stood and turned in her direction, but she only had eyes for her Cam.

Her tummy flip-flopped at the beaming smile he wore, and the wave of love that washed through her took her breath away.

'Okay, Mum?' asked Richie.

Jess, Cate and Max stood on the deck waiting for their signal to begin their walk.

Milly closed her eyes and took a deep breath. Then she turned to Richie and smiled. 'Let's go get me hitched.'

Jess took a profiterole from the tray Nell was walking around with and popped it into her mouth in one piece. Holly had done a fantastic job with the canapes. Later they'd fire up the barbecue, but for now, these morsels were perfect.

As she took another sip of her bubbly, Nathan slipped his arms around her waist, drawing her back into him. She tilted her head so he could nuzzle into the side of her neck.

'You look beautiful,' he said. His voice was all gravelly and sexy. 'I've never seen you all dressed up before, and no ponytail!'

Turning in his arms, she planted a quick kiss on his lips. 'Don't go getting too used to it.'

He kissed her back, sucking on her bottom lip. 'I've learnt not to get used to anything where you're concerned – and that suits me just fine.'

'I've missed you,' she said, leaning her head against

his chest. While Jess had arrived home a week ago to help her mother finalise the wedding arrangements, Nathan had flown in only yesterday.

'Me too.' He put his finger under her chin to lift her head. 'Have you told them yet?'

She tried to look away, but he placed his hands on her cheeks and held her eyes firm. 'No. The time never seemed to be quite right.'

Since landing in Queenstown, Jess had thrown herself into the wedding planning and catching up on everything happening at Beach Road. Although between Holly looking after the kitchen and Dayna in charge of service, the café was humming along. While Max hadn't yet come back to work – officially, anyway – she was still taking care of the café's social media and had recommenced baking a few bits and pieces for Cover To Cover. Mia had settled in beautifully and, thanks only partly to Max's photography, her cakes and slices were listed as some of the most Instagrammable treats in Queenstown.

Holly's canapés were also getting the same reputation, and the catering side of the business had grown to the extent where Holly was now spending more time overseeing that and the seasonal menu changes at Beach Road and less time on the pans. She'd even sourced a new artisan baker who had set up business down the road at Glenorchy and provided the café with bread and savoury pastries.

Everything was under control, and Jess had to admit there was a small part of her that was disappointed they hadn't missed her as much as she might've hoped – although Nathan assured her that was because she'd built such a competent team. The truth was she could've made time to tell them her news; she just hadn't wanted to – not until Nathan was beside her.

'They'll all be happy for you, Jay,' Nathan now said. He cocked his head, his eyes narrowed. 'Unless you're having second thoughts?'

'No, it's just—'

'Good. Let's tell them.'

Nathan held her hand and led her across the lawn to where Milly and Fletch were chatting with Kate and Tom.

With Dayna and Nell passing around the food, Holly was free to relax and stopped Jess as they passed by. 'Jess, I don't think you've met Cody,' she said, grasping the arm of a tall blonde man.

'No, we haven't met,' said Jess, holding her hand out. 'But I've heard a lot about you.' She grinned when Holly's cheeks turned bright pink.

'And I, you,' said Cody.

'Have you managed to get Holly into the jet boat yet?' Nathan asked. Cody was a jet boat pilot on the Shotover River.

He smiled down at Holly and kissed the top of her head. 'She's an old hand now, aren't you?'

Holly giggled and stuck her forefinger in the air, twirling it around in a circle in the signal for what was known as a Hamilton Turn – when the jet boat would complete a three hundred and sixty degree turn at speed. 'I sure am.'

'It's been good to meet you, Cody,' said Jess. 'We'll chat later, Holl, but Nathan and I need to have a quick chat with our parents while they're still all together.'

'Ooooh,' teased Holly. 'That sounds ominous. A big announcement?'

Jess smirked as her face grew warm. 'Perhaps, but not the one you're thinking,' she chuckled. 'Great food by the way,' she called as they walked away.

Richie passed by carrying Sam.

'Oh Sammy,' Jess cooed, holding her arms out for the baby. 'We haven't had a cuddle all day!'

Richie placed his son in her arms. Jess wrinkled her nose and almost gagged as she smelt his nappy-clad butt before handing him straight back. Richie and Nathan burst out laughing.

'I was on my way inside and to change him,' said Richie. 'But you can do it if you like.' His voice ended on a hopeful note.

'Yeah … nah,' said Jess. 'I'll leave that with you.'

'Thanks for that.'

As he left them, Jess looked up to see Max watching the exchange with a gentle smile on her face. She was standing with Harry, Cate and Gary, and once Richie headed into the house with their son, she resumed her conversation.

'How unexpected is that?' commented Nathan. 'Gary, I mean.'

Jess shook her head gently. 'I still find it difficult to believe, but this is the third time he's been over since Sam was born. He only stays a few days, but Mum said he really wants to be involved in Sam's life. He's still treading carefully with Max and Richie, and, of course, Mum and Dad, but this is the first time Max has convinced him to stay with them at the lake house. Cate and Harry have met up with him in Sydney as well.'

'And your parents are fine about it?'

'Surprisingly, yes. It helps that he doesn't wear out his welcome, and Mum said he's a different man to how he was when he was younger.'

Nathan shrugged and pressed a kiss to Jess's forehead. 'As I said, who would've believed it?'

'We were just talking about you two,' said Kate as they approached.

'Your glass is empty,' Fletch said to Jess. 'I'll get you another drink. Are you right for a beer, Nathan?'

'I'm fine, thanks, Fletch.'

'Having a good day, Mum?' asked Jess.

Her mother's smile was answer enough. It was as wide as the lake.

'So what were you saying about us?' Nathan asked Kate.

'Milly just wondered how long you were staying, and I said I didn't know.' Kate turned her palms up in a "nobody ever tells me anything" way.

'You trying to get rid of me already, Mum?' asked Nathan, putting his arm around his mother in a loose hug.

'Of course not. It's just—' Kate shook her head in amusement.

'It is a good question, though,' said Milly. 'Are you home to stay or …?'

Fletch was back with a fresh wine for Jess. He'd heard Milly's question and raised his eyebrows as he waited for the answer.

'Well,' said Jess, looking to Nathan for support. 'We did have something we wanted to talk to you about …'

Milly clapped her hands in excitement.

'Is this *that* sort of announcement?' Kate asked, her eyes twinkling and her smile wide.

Jess looked at everyone in their circle. 'What? No! Why does everyone keep saying that?'

She glanced at Nathan, who gave a one-shoulder shrug. 'What Jay is trying to say is we've decided we'll be moving south at the end of this season.'

Milly's face showed surprise before she frowned, and Fletch scratched at the side of his head.

'I don't understand,' said Milly. 'I thought you loved Cairns.'

'I do,' said Jess, 'we both do – although I have no idea how I'd deal with the summer up there – and it isn't going to work for me from a business viewpoint. We thought about splitting our time – the whale season in Far North Queensland and the summer here, but that's not going to work either.'

'I've been offered a position on the research team in Hervey Bay, and we've been down for a look and ...'

'There's a little café down there that would be perfect as the next iteration for Beach Road, so ...' Jess looked again at Nathan and grabbed his hand.

'So we've compromised,' he said, pulling her towards him. 'I'll have downtime in the off-season to catch up on some of the academic work I've been putting off, and Jess can weave her magic on Beach Road The Sequel – have you decided what you're going to call it yet?'

'Not yet; it might end up being Beach Road Too.'

Milly chuckled. 'Nothing wrong with that.'

'Dad,' Jess asked, suddenly uncertain. 'What do you think?'

'We'll miss you here, but I'm very proud of you, Jessie; we both are.' He shook his head and laughed wryly. 'Our little girl has somehow turned into a very astute businesswoman. When did that happen?'

Milly laid a hand on Fletch's arm. 'When we weren't looking, love.'

Jess pulled in a deep breath. She was filled with

so much pride she couldn't speak for at least a few seconds – something Nathan couldn't help passing comment on.

'I don't believe it – Jay lost for words. Wonders will never cease.'

She aimed a light punch at his arm, but he caught it easily and used it to draw her in for a hug.

'See,' he said, kissing her lightly on the lips, 'I told you they'd be pleased.'

'You did,' she agreed, her lips skimming across his.

Nathan excused them and steered her to the edge of the lawn where the ceremony had taken place. 'You didn't tell them you're considering offering Holly a partnership.'

'I'm still not sure about that,' she said. 'Let's see how things go.' She smiled to herself. 'How funny was it that both our mothers thought we'd be making a different type of announcement?'

'Holly did too,' he pointed out. 'Do you think we should talk about that?'

'About what?' Jess frowned as she attempted to follow the line of conversation. Nathan had a weird look on his face.

'*That* sort of announcement,' he said with a meaningful glance over at her parents.

Jess's heart momentarily stopped. 'Seriously?'

He lifted one shoulder. 'Everyone else seems to be doing it. Your parents have, and Richie and Max will be next. God only knows what stage Mum and Tom are up to. Besides, we love each other.'

'And we want to be together,' she added, trying to ignore the skipping her heart was now doing. 'But we're just starting out. Let's give it a few months, eh?'

He lifted her hand to his mouth and kissed her palm, his eyes crinkling wickedly behind his sunglasses. 'Is that a promise?'

'Yeah, it's a promise.' Jess grabbed a handful of his shirt to pull him closer.

'A few months, eh?' He lowered his head and kissed her deeply.

'Maybe less.' Jess said when she came up for air.

RECIPES

Are your taste buds eager to try some of the food from the novel? Here are the recipes, with plenty more available on my website: Brookford Kitchen Diaries – BKD for short.

Unless otherwise noted, oven temperatures are in Celsius for a static oven. If you're using a fan-forced oven, reduce the temperature by twenty degrees. All eggs are large (and free-range), butter is unsalted, and tablespoons are 20ml.

Lemon Drizzle Cake

This is my go-to lemon drizzle cake, the one I make so often I could make it blindfolded. I usually make two at a time – one to give away and one to keep. It's perfect as a dessert or pudding cake – slice and serve with some vanilla ice cream or a dollop of cream. If you're feeling extra fancy, lighten the cream with some Greek yoghurt and grate over a little extra lemon zest.

Ingredients:
For the cake:
140g plain flour
¾ tsp baking powder
¼ tsp bicarb soda
pinch salt
60g unsalted butter, softened
135g caster sugar
1 egg
5 ½ tbsp buttermilk
1 tbsp grated lemon zest
For the syrup:
100g sugar
5 ½ tbsp lemon juice

Method

Preheat the oven to 180°C and do the usual buttering/lining of your tin. I use a small loaf tin, but you could also use a 20cm round tin.

Sift together the flour, baking powder, bicarb and salt and set aside.

In a stand mixer, cream together the butter and sugar until light and fluffy. Add the egg and beat it into the mix enthusiastically.

Fold in a third of the flour, followed by a third of the buttermilk, the next third of the flour and so on. Stir in the lemon zest and spoon the mix into your prepared tin.

Bake for 30-35 minutes or until a skewer inserted into the centre of the cake comes out clean.

When the cake has about 10 minutes left to cook, prepare your syrup by combining the sugar and lemon juice in a small saucepan over low heat.

As the cake comes out of the oven, spoon the syrup evenly over the top, tipping and rotating the tin gently to make sure that it's all covered.

Cool in the tin on a wire rack and dust with icing sugar before serving.

Ginger Crunch Slice

This oaty ginger slice appeared in *Wish You Were Here* and is a quintessential Kiwi classic. You'll find it in bakeries all around the country – usually sold as Ginger Slice. To simply call it ginger slice, though, is to miss acknowledging the oats – which adds the texture this fudgily sweet slice needs.

Ingredients:
For the base:
150g plain flour
1 ½ tsp baking powder
1 ½ tsp ground ginger
75g desiccated coconut
165g rolled oats – not the instant variety
150g light brown sugar
150g butter
70g golden syrup

Method:

Before you start – preheat the oven to 180°C. Lightly grease and line the sides of a slice tin – about 11cm x 34cm.

Sift the flour, baking powder and ginger into a medium bowl. Add the coconut, rolled oats and brown sugar.

Melt the butter and golden syrup in a small saucepan over low heat. Pour into the dry ingredients, mix until combined and press the mixture into the prepared tin.

Bake for 25-30 minutes or until golden brown.

For the Icing:

290g icing sugar

1 tbsp ground ginger

120g butter

115g golden syrup

Method:

Sift together the ginger and icing sugar into a small bowl. Melt the butter and golden syrup in a small saucepan over low heat and mix it all together until smooth.

Spread evenly over the cooked base and leave to set in the tin before cutting into small pieces.

Lemon Curd Shortbread Slice

Two of my favourite ingredients are lemon and butter, so it won't come as a surprise that my resolve *not* to eat my baking is overturned when lemon curd or shortbread is involved. If lemon curd is great and shortbread is great, imagine what they're like together. Imagine no longer.

This slice is a beauty and one that will always be in the sweet's cabinet at Beach Road.

It's not difficult to make but requires a little palaver in waiting and grating time, but trust me, it's worth it.

A note on the lemon curd – you can make your own if you like (I use Nigella's recipe) but you don't need to as there are plenty of lovely curds available in the supermarket. I used a 450g jar and found that was plenty to go across the slice. If your lemon curd is thicker, you might need up to 600g to cover the surface. You only need a thin layer, but it needs to go all the way into the corners. Besides, if you have any leftovers, it's fabulous on toast or scones.

Ingredients:
500g plain flour
1 tsp salt
280g butter, at room temperature
220g caster sugar
1 tsp vanilla extract
1 bottle of lemon curd – about 450g, but you may need

up to 600g (see the note above)

Method:

Preheat the oven to 180°C. Lightly grease and line the base of a slice tin (20cm x 30cm or thereabouts. My tin is 23cm x 33cm). If you line it so the baking paper overhangs the long side of the tin, you can use it to pull the slice out in one go *#handyhint*.

Sift the flour and salt into a bowl and set aside.

Using your stand mixer with the paddle attachment, beat the butter, sugar and vanilla together until it's pale and creamy.

Add the flour (and salt) and mix until it comes together into a dough.

Take one-third of the dough and flatten it a tad. Wrap it in cling film and pop it in the fridge for now.

Press the rest of the dough into the base of your tin and bake for 25 minutes, or until golden brown. Once cooked, you want to allow it to cool completely in the tin.

Once the base is cool, spread the lemon curd across it. Retrieve the remaining third of the dough from the fridge and grate (use the coarse grater you'd use for cheddar cheese) it across the top of the lemon curd. It looks like a coarse crumble, and I dare you not to pick off pieces.

Pop it back into the oven and cook for another 30 minutes, or until the nubbly bits are golden brown. It will need to cool completely in the tin before you can even think about removing it to slice.

Chocolate Bread and Butter Pudding

Let's not beat about the bush – this is a proper pudding and bears absolutely no resemblance to anything remotely healthy. This is a mid-winter pudding for when you need deep, deep comfort; pudding for when nothing but squidgy chocolate custard-soaked bread pudding will do.

I first saw this pudding in Delia Smith's "Winter Collection", published in 1995. I've been making it ever since, tweaking it here and there. I've used torn up croissants, added a touch of orange zest, and once I even used leftover panettone, which gave the whole thing a chocolatey rum and raisin taste.

The biggest problem with this pudding is that Delia instructs it should be prepared (at least) a day ahead to let all the chocolate custard soak into the bread – and let's be honest, who thinks that far ahead? When you need this pudding, you need it now and not in two days' time. I tend to put it together on a Saturday morning for baking on Saturday evening and, with apologies to Saint Delia, I've had no complaints, although on the odd occasion when I have done the in advance thing, it has been even better.

Ingredients:
10 slices, about half a loaf, of white bread. Cut off the crusts and quarter the slices
200g block of dark chocolate – the good stuff – cut

into small pieces. I take the rolling pin to it while it's still in its packet. Don't worry if a few pieces disappear for the purposes of taste testing

3 whole eggs

½ cup caster sugar

300ml double or thick cream

3-4 tbsp rum

A good shake of cinnamon

75g butter cut into small pieces

Method:

Lightly butter an ovenproof dish about 18cm x 23cm. I use either an enamel baking dish or my glass Pyrex bowl.

Deal with the bread by cutting off the crusts and then cutting each slice into quarters.

Into a large bowl, combine the cream, chocolate, rum, butter, sugar and cinnamon and pop it over a saucepan of barely simmering water. Make sure the bottom of the bowl isn't touching the water. Stir from time to time until it's all lusciously melted together.

In a separate bowl, whisk the eggs and then, still whisking, pour the chocolate mix into the eggs. Tip: To ensure you don't scramble the eggs, allow the chocolate mix to cool slightly before mixing a small amount into the eggs before adding the rest.

Spoon a thin layer of chocolate custard onto the bottom

of your dish and arrange half the bread triangles in overlapping rows. Now add more chocolate, another layer of bread, and the last of the chocolate.

Press the bread down with the back of a spoon until it's all covered with chocolate. Don't worry too much if some of the bread pokes up – it adds an extra texture once it's been cooked.

Pop some cling film over it, let it sit at room temperature for an hour or so (if you don't live in Queensland and it's not a hot day) and then place it into the fridge for as many hours as you can. This is the part you're supposed to do the day before.

When you're ready to bake it, bring the pudding back to room temperature, preheat the oven to 180°C, and cook for 30-35mins. The top should be crunchy and the middle squidgy.

All it needs now is ten (or so) minutes to sit and some pouring cream, ice cream, or custard to serve.

Tan Slice

A shortbread slice topped with soft caramel and a buttery shortbread crumble top. Sounds good, eh?

Super simple to make, I do mine in a square tin – 23cm x 23cm – but a normal slice tin would be fine. I also use dark chocolate chips in the topping as they seem to work better against the sweetness of the caramel filling. I tried a recipe that substituted some of the flour in the shortbread base with oats – while it gave the base a lovely ANZAC biscuit flavour and texture, I didn't think it worked quite so well on the topping, so I stuck to the original shortbread. Some things don't need messing with.

Ingredients:
For the shortbread:
180g unsalted butter, at room temperature
90g caster sugar
½ tsp vanilla
200g plain flour
1 tsp baking powder
½ cup dark chocolate chips
For the caramel:
100g butter
1 x 400g tin condensed milk
2 tbsp golden syrup

Method:

Preheat the oven to 180°C and line a 23cm square tin with baking paper. Letting the paper overhang the sides a tad will help you lift the slice out.

Cream the butter and sugar together, then add the vanilla and mix some more. I do this in a stand mixer with the paddle attachment. Tip in the flour and baking powder, lower the speed and mix until combined and coming together in a soft crumbly dough. Press ⅔ of the mixture evenly into the tin and set the rest aside.

To make the caramel, combine all the ingredients in a small saucepan and heat over low-medium heat, stirring all the while, until everything has melted together and it's thickened slightly. Take care it doesn't catch on the base of the pan and burn.

Pour the caramel over the base. Mix the remaining base mixture with the chocolate chips and crumble over the caramel.

Bake slice for 20-25 minutes or until lightly golden. Allow to cool in the tin before slicing.

Cheese Scones

These scones are at their absolute best soon after they come out of the oven. All they need is good butter – and more of it than is probably good for you. After all, these are a treat.

Okay, the recipe – which, depending on the size of your cutter, will make about 12 scones. At Beach Road, they're served in massive wedges.

Ingredients:
450g self-raising flour
½ tsp baking powder
1 tsp salt
1 tbsp mustard powder
100g cold butter
250 grated cheese
120ml cold milk
120ml cold water
1 egg, beaten with a splash of milk

Method:

Heat the oven to 220°C.

Stir together the flour, baking powder, salt and mustard powder into a large bowl.

Grate in the butter, then rub it in with the tips of your fingers until it looks like sandy breadcrumbs. Work as quickly as you can with this to avoid melting or softening your butter too much. Pop it in the fridge for about 10 minutes.

Add the cheese, leaving a handful to scatter across the top (if you're doing the scattering over the top thing), and stir to combine. Mix in the milk and water with a knife until the dough just comes away from the edge of the bowl – remember, don't handle it any more than is necessary.

Tip on to a very lightly floured surface and use your hands to flatten into an approximation of a rectangle about an inch high. Cut out with whatever you use to cut your scones – I like my cheese scones to be a bit bigger than I make my usual scones. Reshape your dough as necessary while handling it as little as possible.

Put on a baking tray, brush over the eggy milk and scatter the remaining cheese over the top. Bake for about 12 minutes until golden.

Allow your scones to cool slightly before splitting open.

Roast Chicken Pasta

This is more of a collection of ingredients rather than a recipe, but I'll do my best. It's based on Nigella's Tagliatelle From The Venetian Grotto, but at its simplest, it's roast chook torn into pasta with the roasting juices acting as the sauce.

Texture is added by some toasted pine nuts and (wait for it) crispy chicken skin. Getting that skin crispy takes a little more effort, but it's worth it. You might like to try leaving the chicken uncovered to dry out in the fridge overnight. I've also been known to dry the skin out with a hairdryer ...

As for the chicken itself, I heat the oven to high (220°C), usually stuff it with a lemon, some herbs (tarragon is good), and a few unpeeled garlic cloves. This will help to flavour the juices. I then rub oil over it, season it with salt and pepper and whack it into the hot oven (breast-side down) before immediately reducing the temperature to moderate. Feel free to roast your chicken however you'd normally roast it.

The important part of this dish is the chicken fat (schmaltz) and pan juices. Once your chicken is cooked, take it out of the tray to rest for about fifteen minutes and carefully pour the pan juices into a jug.

Put your pasta water onto boil and while that's happening, dice a few banana shallots (the ones that are a cross between an onion and an eschalot or spring onion) and sauté them slowly in some plain olive oil in a large frying pan. When soft and pale golden, mince a couple of garlic cloves into it, add a tablespoon of chopped rosemary, a big handful of toasted pine nuts, and the roasting juices.

By now, your pasta water should be boiling, so add your pasta of choice – spaghetti, penne, tagliatelle, fusilli – cook it according to the instructions on the packet and get to work on your chicken. Don't be too precious about how you tear this up – and don't forget to keep some of the crunchy skin for scattering across the top. As a rough idea, you'll need about a handful of shredded meat per portion. Toss it into the sauce and stir it about.

If things aren't saucy enough at this stage, you can add some of the cooking water from the pasta once it's done.

Once your pasta is cooked, scoop out a cup of the cooking water, drain the pasta and toss it straight into your chicken pan. If it needs extra moisture, tip in some of the pasta water. Add a few tablespoons of chopped parsley and a few tablespoons of grated parmesan or the equivalent. I should say at this point that Nigella and I don't agree on the cheese thing, but then she also uses sultanas in her version, and I don't agree with that.

Mix it together again. Serve with more chopped parsley, grated parmesan, that crispy skin you saved and a drizzle of olive oil. And a side salad if you must.

BEFORE YOU GO

If you enjoyed *The Little Café By The Lake* I'd love it if you left a review in the usual places. If you'd like to stay up to date with my next happy ending, you can sign up for my newsletter at my website: https://joannetracey. com.

You can also drop by and see me – virtually speaking, of course – at any of these places:

My blog: https://andanyways.com
Facebook: https://facebook.com/joannetraceywriter
Instagram: https://instagram/jotracey

ACKNOWLEDGEMENTS

I was always going to write Jess's story, but a trip to Cairns last June – and a snorkelling tour of the reef and a random chat with the Master Reef Guide on that tour – gave me the inspiration I needed.

That's the thing about inspiration – very often, it's the random connections that provide it.

The most important thing about indie publishing is the team you build around you. The usual thanks to the usual people –and, as always, apologies if I've missed anyone.

To my family – Grant, Sarah, and Kali, aka Adventure Spaniel – I couldn't do what I do without your love and support. Thanks for suffering through my baking as I test out recipes.

To my early readers – Pieta, Heather, Donna, Deb and Sue. Thanks for your feedback – and your friendship. You guys really are my cheerleaders. Thanks also to Deb Cook for being part of my "tribe" and always being ready and willing for a catch-up bubbly whenever I'm in Hervey Bay. I'm so looking forward to collaborating on our top-secret project. (I could say more about that, but then it wouldn't be top secret anymore).

To my structural editor, Nicola O'Shea, I'm so grateful you took me on back in 2014 for *Baby, It's You,* and I can't believe we've been working together for seven years. You really do inspire me to continually improve, and when I'm stuck in a story hole, you help me see where I need to go.

To Jo Speirs, my copyeditor, thanks for polishing my words and helping me make this story one I'm proud of. Man, I'm hopeless with detail!

To Louisa West, thanks for another fabulous cover and for working through my delays and rambling descriptions.

To Keith Stevenson, my thanks for turning the manuscript into a book. It's magic! Thanks also to Mike O'Shea for sharing some of your cage diving experiences with sharks (shudder).

I'm fortunate to be surrounded by people who inspire me not only through their work but their work ethic. One of these is Jodi Gibson – I'm not sure I know anyone more supportive of Australian authors and independent authors.

Last but absolutely not least, thank *you* for picking up this book when there are millions of others for you to choose from. If you enjoyed it, I'd love for you to pop a review up in the usual places.

ABOUT THE AUTHOR

Joanne Tracey lives on the Sunshine Coast in Queensland Australia with her husband, daughter and a cocker spaniel who takes her role as guardian of Jo's office very seriously. She has, however, been known to sleep a tad too much on the job – the dog, that is, not Jo.

An unapologetic daydreamer, eternal optimist, and confirmed morning person, Jo writes contemporary romance, romantic comedy, women's fiction and what she likes to call foodie-lit – which is the perfect excuse to indulge her baking habit in the name of research.

When she isn't writing or day jobbing, Jo loves baking, reading, long walks along the beach, posting way too many photos of sunrises on Instagram and dreaming of the next destination and the next story.

Jo's life goals (apart from being a world-famous author) are to be an extra on *Midsomer Murders* (perhaps a dog walker in Badger's Drift), to appear on *Desert Island Discs*, and to cook her way through Nigella's cookbooks – yes, all of them.

CPSIA information can be obtained
at www.ICGtesting.com
Printed in the USA
LVHW031920070222
710327LV00010B/208

9 780645 073539